HE
SAVED
EVERYONE
BUT
ME

D0861278

novel by **CARL KORN**

COVER PHOTOGRAPHS BY Paul Thayer, used with permission.
BOOK DESIGN BY The Troy Book Makers

Printed in the United States of America
The Troy Book Makers • Troy, New York • thetroybookmakers.com

To order additional copies of this title, contact your favorite local bookstore or visit www.shoptbmbooks.com

ISBN: 978-1-61468-772-6

AUTHOR'S NOTE

Our childhood memories sculpt us on our way to adult-hood. They shape how we see ourselves and others, and perceive the world around us. And because we are human and fallible, it follows that our recall is subjective and un-reliable. Over time, we come to believe the memories of our memories! The arbitrary nature of what we remem-ber — and, of course, what we suppress or forget — also means that we often rely on hazy and faulty memories to form opinions and make decisions that alter the course of our lives.

This novel, a fictional memoir, is about the power and limitations of our childhood memories. Despite my use of the first-person narrative form, this work is no au-tobiographical striptease in which I bare myself naked to an audience of readers. Those who know me will imme-diately recognize that the family created on these pages is invented. Most events and anecdotes have been man-ufactured for dramatic effect or embellished from scraps of truth to advance the narrative. A few tales, I admit, are close to my own life and are recollected here to the best of my own imperfect memory.

This book is dedicated to Edward and Gladys. My parents offered generous helpings of love, encouragement, support and quirky humor, but mostly love. While family dysfunction and the life-long grip of memory inspired this book and are central themes, this work is most assuredly not about them.

Carl Korn
Indian Lake, N.Y.
October 2022

For Cara, Haley and Joshua,
'One word frees us of all the weight
and pain of life: That word is love.'

– Sophocles

ONE

'I have to get my head on straight.'

MONDAY, JULY 17, 2013
West Palm Beach, Florida

It's too goddamn hot for a round of golf. I might as well go bury my father.

In a split-second, that churlish non-sequitur surged wildly like a cataract past my stress-weakened defenses.

It took another instant for me to regret my words.

Remorse and forgiveness would come much, much later.

It's been nearly one full year since my father died. Almost four complete seasons and a full rotation of the earth around the sun. Still, I remember the alien sound of my own anguished voice that day like I remember my morning breakfast.

Bloody fuck! I snarled, my savagery stirring fright.

I slapped the steering wheel in anger. A middle finger to the dead.

Ah, the memories. Writing on a crystalline night in a bygone year, I understand everything better now. I am not the same man I was. As it turns out, my rage that sweltering afternoon marked a turning point. A watershed in my personal growth.

My next memory from that day: I exhaled deeply, my hot breath huffing into the rental car. Shame and guilt — twin companions from my youth — materialized to place their heavy knees on my chest and slap me from cheek to cheek until I sagged visibly embarrassed behind the wheel.

What am I doing here? What the hell was I thinking? I cried out in exasperation, my voice rising again as my self-control skidded sideways to the gravel shoulder of panic. A rhetorical question, it was. My outburst had already made it abundantly clear.

I had not been thinking at all.

To begin with, I don't know the first damn thing about golf.

I have to get my head on straight, I muttered next.

My pent-up anger, which I had unleashed with the explosiveness of a supernova, had violated a solemn promise. Less than 48 hours earlier, I had sworn an oath to Lauren, my sweetheart and soul mate, that I would remain composed. Even-keeled. Already my promise had been broken. Smashed to bits, actually.

I winced in embarrassment.

Not exactly an apology.

Unsure of what to do next, I sheepishly checked the side mirrors on my rented Chevy Impala. I lifted my foot from the gas to open more distance from the car ahead. That afternoon, I coasted along at exactly 70 mph, scanning the chaos of traffic in the surrounding lanes. I pride myself on my careful driving. Not a single traffic ticket or fender-bender in all my years of motoring about in hair-raising weather where I live full-time in the rugged Adirondacks of upstate New York. I've never even hit a deer — or a big, dopey moose trundling across Route 28 at dusk.

Go ahead, laugh. It's a minor accomplishment, I know. As a lifetime achievement, it falls considerably short of winning an Olympic gold medal or curing cancer. You won't see me strutting around like Michael Jackson in the *Thriller* video or building a magnificent glass trophy case in tribute to my superior driving. Still, safely navigating twisting mountain roads on a daily basis requires considerable skill. Or so my insurance agent reminds me.

Truthfully, my attentiveness in the heavy I-95 traffic outside West Palm Beach offered me a sense of control and a few extra seconds to think. I ignored the gas-guzzling pick-ups charging like chrome-and-metal rhinos and used those precious seconds to corral the tornado of emotions that threatened to demolish me like a Mississippi trailer park. Or to at least make a valiant attempt to do so, for my emotions bucked wildly to escape. My tone, I recognized, had been too harsh and my voice too loud by several turns of a knob. After my unseemly outburst, I needed to buy time to concoct a passable defense.

I looked to Lauren sitting across from me in the passenger seat and worried about what might come next. Very slowly, hoping to avoid detection, I took in the full of Lauren's profile glowing in the sunlight as if her natural beauty and perfect figure were gifts from the gods.

Lauren has creamy white skin — smooth and sweet like a soft-serve vanilla cone — tightly drawn over a delicate hourglass frame. Her cheeks and chin appear like fine marble, with a dappling of pink freckles spaced across her perfectly sculpted nose. Her hair, which cascades to just below her shoulders, is the color of ripened strawberries.

Drinking in her radiance rolled a spasm of queasiness inside me.

I shouldn't be such a dick, I remember thinking.

As a first stab at penitence, I offered a silent prayer, hoping to assuage my swelling guilt:

Please God, I know I am better than this. Guide me to the right path. Forgive my vile words and unacceptable disrespect for the dead. Let my sudden burst of anger at my father go unnoticed or, at least, uncommented upon. Amen.

I desperately wished to be spared further shame and a complicated explanation. I suspected — or perhaps just hoped — that Lauren had been daydreaming and my emotionally charged missile had whizzed past her ears, unheard.

From my periphery, I noticed Lauren nodding omnisciently. She remained silent and appeared serene, almost as if she had been meditating. Her big, bright eyes, blue as a gas flame, peered straight through the front windshield. Behind a sphinx-like stare, she appeared to be trying to calibrate a response to my spasm of anger. The whole time, she maintained a laser focus on the rumbling

18-wheeler just ahead in the next lane, its shipment of goods hidden behind layers of grime and a skin of steel.

Maybe this won't be too bad.

I close my eyes, as if squeezing my eyelids shut can easily convey the past to the present. I can smell the sweet of just-fallen rain and the damp steeped in the old shag carpet in my apartment's little study. As my fingers rattle across the laptop's keyboard, my memory spits back an image of Lauren bobbing her head and wetting her lips with her tongue. I can visualize her thoughtfully placing a pink-painted nail between her pillowy lips like a baby nursing at a nipple.

Alas, she had been fully in the present all along. Lauren had, indeed, heard me desecrate my father's memory with profanity and disrespect and she did not approve. Not one single bit.

To my relief, however, Lauren opted not to pass judgement.

Calm down, Harry Loev. Breathe, darling. It won't be that bad, she said finally, as calmly as a mother cooing to her infant.

Yes, it will. You wait. You haven't met my family, I answered.

Lauren's encouragement, although well-meaning, did nothing to calm my buzzing nerves. Despite her soothing tone, I remained all torqued inside. My fury and fear rumbled under the surface like magma. The blood in my neck felt hot and my face burned with embarrassment. I flushed with shame that the contempt I reserved for my father — a bitterness that I normally concealed deep within — had been revealed, and so coarsely.

The life of my father, Lt. Natan 'Nathan' Loev, would be remembered at 10 the next morning. As I drove on the highway to the hotel, his approaching funeral filled me with dread. My apprehension displayed itself conspicuously, like Beyoncé shopping at a rural Wal-Mart. With each tick of the second hand, my stomach ratcheted tighter into what seemed a permanently fixed knot, impossible for even the most grizzled mariner to unravel. My mouth felt dry of saliva and my left leg shook involuntarily against the car's plastic door panel, bumping to the beat of my pounding heart.

Can't this be over already? How long until I'm back on the plane, away from all this bullshit?

My fucking father's funeral, I instead spit into the silence, challenging Lauren's vast reserve of patience once more.

As those words escaped my lips, I wondered whether my alliterative jujitsu could serve as a balm.

Perhaps my string of juvenile swear words, if recited like a mantra, could have a therapeutic effect on my rattled psyche. Maybe I could retreat in time and walk back my seething indictment of our shattered relationship. Walk it back decades to when I revered my father and he treated me like his son. Foolish thoughts. Every single one of my recent and, admittedly, shameful outbursts had only re-enforced the conclusion that traveling to South Florida meant inviting a disaster of historical dimensions.

In my mind, the timing of my father's death could not have been worse. After two decades of near-total estrangement — let's call it a Loev family Cold War — I was about to come face-to-face with my blood-line while still concealing from Lauren an industrial-sized dumpster of secrets.

All this Lauren didn't know, or at least not yet:

At the funeral home the next morning, I, Harry Truman Loev, feared that my painful childhood memories — demons appearing as angry words, slammed doors, silent treatments, accusations of crimes, bitter memories, sweat-inducing nightmares, war-time footing and rampaging mental illness — would be ingloriously visited on me all over again.

Old grudges would be pulled out and dusted off. Shown off like a magician's trick. Emotions would be dialed too high. Nerves would tightrope a thin wire. A puff of impatience; an undiplomatically uttered remark; repressed pain rising from the deep like a sea monster would be all it would take. One cross word or ill-considered slip of snark would be the detonator.

Fucking kaboom.

A splintered family mourning its patriarch would metamorphose into savage combatants.

They would have to call the police. Maybe even deploy the National Guard.

As my rental car chewed up distance in the center lane, white lines whizzing by as a blur, I continued to summon monster-movie imagery. Soon, the whole damaged Loev family would be together, faking bonhomie.

What could go wrong? I suspected I knew the answer and the sour taste of acid and bile rising in my throat confirmed it. A bad omen for when the clock struck 10 the next morning.

At that point, I remember, Lauren had turned to gaze at the colorful billboards and the palm trees dotting the roadside, fronds spread like fingers shimmying to the beat of a tropical breeze. She dialed up the air conditioner as a defense against the merciless heat and fiddled once more with the dashboard radio.

This was Lauren's first-ever visit to Florida. Heck, it had been my true love's first time on an airplane! During the three-hour flight from Albany, Lauren had expressed hope that we would have time to experience the ocean for the first time. She wished to dip her toes in the sand and feel the power of the surf crashing against her knees. Lauren already knew, I surmised, that the pull of the Atlantic aside, she could never spend more than a few days in Florida. Just maneuvering the short distance from the terminal to the rental car had left her drenched in sweat, her hair frizzed and porcelain skin flushed as a rash. She fanned herself with a now-limp boarding pass and settled on an Oldies station, leaving me to mumble and stew as she watched the exotic scenery flash by.

That memory from the trip is a fleeting one. It evaporates like a mist because, yes, I wasn't paying full attention to Lauren. Instead, I had mentally moved on — to furiously question whether she could ever truly understand why, at 40 years and seven months old on that July day,

I still smoldered with resentment at the old man whose seed had gifted me life.

Oh, if she only fucking knew.

Honestly, I had pondered ways to tell Lauren my whole sad story countless times back inside the Blue Line — the great Adirondack Park in far upstate New York — where we now live together as a couple. Home for us is among roving bears, ever-changing weather, ridiculously unreliable internet and the call of loons breaking the stillness in remote Hamilton County, an area nearly the size of Delaware and not a single goddamn traffic light.

During the just-past spring months we call mud season, when black flies swarm and draw blood like tiny, ravenous Draculas, I thought hard about confiding to Lauren the source of all my rage. Back when my father was still alive, I debated opening up to Lauren, musing whether — *No, when!* — I would share with her the ugly secrets that dominated my childhood memories. This act of emotionally cleansing honesty would be curative medicine, I told myself. It would bestow on me inner peace and newfound strength. My rebirth would cement our relationship and serve as the precursor to the Big Question and her joyous answer — the exuberant, tearful Yes — that, when I rose from bended knee, would allow me to live in her warmth forever.

That I did not know and could not yet see the safe path forward to emotional honesty haunted me. Each time I readied myself to finally confess aloud to Lauren the past that I had buried deep — to lance my infected childhood memories and finally share my whole life story — I could not bear to open up about the injuries and scars that a lifetime of humiliations had marked on me. Instead, I made excuses and procrastinated.

I climbed a rickety aluminum ladder and cleaned the gutters of wet leaves. I mindlessly vacuumed crumbs from the cupholders of my car. I binge-watched a cooking show on Netflix and alphabetized my collection of vinyl records. Anything would be better than admitting my past and revealing my shame and weakness.

One time, I pulled out a pad of notebook paper and scratched out a list, a thick black line dividing the page north to south. Columns of pros and cons.

Sadly for me, my labors added up to pencil marks of lame excuses.

More days passed. Days turned to weeks. The mountainous snowbanks of winter diminished to crusty, bone-colored bumps lining the sides of the road like bowling alley bumpers. I still lacked conviction. Or maybe it was courage that disappeared somewhere in the dark woods. Perhaps, I knew the path to honest communication but was too afraid to take the first steps.

A little more than a week prior, Lauren and I had shared a picnic blanket and a bottle of red watching the July 4th fireworks on the sloped banks of Adirondack Lake. On that warm Independence Day, eternity would not be long enough for us to be together.

I drew a deep breath and opened up, Honey, there's

something on my mind. Something that I to want to tell …

A hiss and a thundering boom from an exploding rocket echoed across the lake. Screaming roman candles streaked across the sky. Bursting blooms of colored light reflected on the perfect, stilled waters as the crowd exclaimed oooh and ahh and even a Fuck yeah from a burly townie wrapped in a Confederate flag. He held aloft a can of cheap beer, posing like a racist Statue of Liberty, and then sunk back — spent by the effort —into a camp chair in the bed of his pickup. Then he belched mightily, expelling the scent of hops and halitosis.

Silenced and defeated, I lost myself in the pandemonium of exploding fireworks while the smell of gunpowder lingered in my nose. The next morning, I started with the self-doubt and questioning all over again.

Why do I still harbor such anger and resentment toward my father?

How do I help Lauren understand why I am the way I am?
How much of my darkness can she stand?

What if I share my incredibly shitty life story and she leaves me?

Inaction trounced action. Excuses dressed up as reasons. Indecisiveness spun around and around like a needle on a scratched record, the same string of uncertain notes playing, bump, bump, bump, over and over.

I'm such a goddamn wuss.

When the regular work-week resumed, I retreated again to the decision I had long resisted making. Alone in the house, I paced back and forth, wearing out the scuffed oak floorboards examining my repressed and unsettled feelings once more.

I should really listen to my therapist. I should trust Lauren's love for me. Trust myself.

Shit, Harry. It's time to finally be honest. To share your life. Open up and confide in Lauren why you declared yourself an orphan and told your entire family to go fuck themselves.

All my truths. Told clean and pure like a gurgling stream.

How will she respond?

Again.

I blew out, emptying my lungs of depressing air.

It will be fine, I remember telling myself. This time, the timing is perfect. Lauren loves me.

■ ■ ■ ■ ■

When word of my father's death came in a phone call, I found myself in the muddled grip of middle age. Past 40 and still unsure of too much. Yet, I glowed positive about this: The instant attraction I felt for Lauren had bloomed into something stronger and more permanent, the way molten iron is forged into steel. Just seven months into our romance, we had discovered true love and believed it would last forever.

From the morning we met — when the bare tree branches of early winter had only tried on their coats of ice — our romance accelerated at break-neck speed, like a bobsled racing a perfect line.

In January, we traced the Hudson River as it snaked

through the mountains. We followed the Northway past Glens Falls, Saratoga Springs and Clifton Park. We survived the chaos around the Twin Bridges and reached Albany at noon. I remember we gawked at the grand but corrupt Capitol and later spent hours aimlessly wandering the soulless malls.

By February, then dating just two months, we already reveled in waking up on mornings when our world had been dipped in a coating of white. Instead of shivering outside like a washer on its spin cycle, we would stay under the covers, post-coital, cuddling for warmth, our breathing in perfect rhythm and our souls content.

In March, we drank until we were stupid during a St. Patrick's Day game of Irish Road Bowling near the old town dump. In mid-April, when the morning sun appeared hungover and the spring rains fell in gray, unrelenting sheets, we once spent the entire day lounging, legs intertwined, on the worn but serviceable couch I had picked up at a second-hand store. Lauren devoured a steamy romance novel, flicking the pages with her long, thin fingers, while I streamed an early season Yankees game on the television.

For as long as I live, I won't ever forget the moment when Lauren looked up from her book and scanned the manicured ball-field before her on the TV screen. Her eyes lit up — an Aha! moment — and she cleared her throat to get my attention. Then, she asked one of her adorably clueless baseball questions.

Honey, why do they call it the warming track? she

wondered in the voice of an angel.

At the time, I was feeding a log into the mouth of the wood stove. Before I could explain, Lauren answered her own question.

The warming track, she repeated aloud.

I know, she added with misplaced confidence. It's because that's where the Yankees players warm up before the game.

I sighed and shook my head ruefully. Secretly, I thought, Do you see why I love her so?

In the indecisiveness of early June, we planned a rugged hike to the High Peaks. We made peanut butter and jelly sandwiches the night before and filled our backpacks with extra water and snacks. We packed our hiking boots and trekking poles in the car and set the alarm on my phone for 4 a.m. — an hour when the ever-wise sun still slumbered.

Lauren had begged me to let us sleep in.

We have to be out super early if we wish to park near the trailhead, I reminded her.

The ringing alarm shattered our sleep, but we moved that morning with purpose. Sure enough, we approached Lake Placid in time to watch a tangerine sun rise over the ski jumps. We signed the trail register with a nubby green pencil and warmed our muscles on the flat stretch to Marcy Dam, where our climb to Algonquin's summit began in earnest. Our hamstrings and calves groaned as we made it through Misery Mile. Beads of sweat ran down our faces and we muttered creative epithets as we scrambled over boulders emerald with moss. Finally, our boots touched the bare rock roof of New York's second-highest peak. After lunch and selfies for Facebook and Instagram, we started back down, reversing our steps. Our quads cramped, pain stabbing like daggers, as we gave back the elevation we, just hours earlier, worked so hard to gain. As we sank into black mud that swallowed us to our ankles, I half-joked to Lauren that she had been right: We should have stayed in bed.

We played mini-golf at a cheesy tourist trap in Lake George; necked at the drive-in outside Glens Falls to an action hero movie and cooked elaborate meals together. Afterwards, we jostled at my little sink and alternated turns scouring aluminum pots of baked-on food, dislodging burnt chunks of blackened rice and despairing over our cluelessness in the kitchen.

I think you're trying to poison me, I recall saying, and she laughed with mirth in response.

By then, we practically lived together as husband and wife — absent gold rings and our vows. Spare clothing, but also toothbrushes, deodorant, medicines and a collection of shoes, migrated from my place to hers, and from hers to mine, gradually finding new closets and drawers to nest and resettle.

Joyfulness surrounded every minute, unbound and unrestrained. How could it not? Lauren's sunniness was contagious. She detected good omens in the ordinary and enthusiastically told me about it. Each sunset lowered a curtain of serenity. Not a single drop of unpleasantness fell upon us.

To the outside world, we appeared as characters in a day-time pharmaceutical commercial. Lauren and Harry. Harry and Lauren. Look at them — the adorably happy couple on screen holding hands, smiling rapturously, madly in love. They play backgammon by the fireplace and paddle their kayaks across a glassy pond while a narrator promises relief from disease, before warning of unpleasant but rare side effects.

Like explosive diarrhea or dark family secrets smoldering beneath my skin.

Around the summer solstice while playing pool at The Fox's Den, a shot-and-a-beer joint frequented by Indian Lake's townies, Lauren sipped a Coors Light from a sweaty can and lined up a shot. Our good friend Martha stacked her quarters into a neat pile and, although it was pretty obvious, asked Lauren about the seriousness of our courtship. Martha hinted good-naturedly at an Adirondack wedding, maybe on the broad, flat summit of Castle Rock overlooking pristine Blue Mountain Lake.

Seriously, what's next for you two lovebirds? Martha queried hopefully. You've been going out seven months now. You're perfect together and, well, let's be honest, you're not kids any longer. I mean, just how close are you … ?

Oh, our love is real, Lauren had answered, sending the cue ball ricocheting off the felt bumper and into the orange ball, which dropped into a corner pocket.

In love and inseparable. Like those famous Siamese

twins Chang and Eng Bunker, I echoed, as Martha's husband, Woody, readied his own shot.

Joined at the hip and stuck with each other forever, I joked.

Everyone laughed. Woody hoisted his beer in a Viking toast.

Chang and Eng became our pet names for each other — our own private joke about the impenetrable bond of our relationship. Sometimes, Lauren would deliberately mix up our made-up identities for comic effect.

Hey, Chang, what's up?

I'm not Chang. You're Chang, you dummy. I'm Eng, I would answer, as from a script.

We would giggle uncontrollably at our silliness and hold each other impossibly close, like we were, indeed, conjoined.

Like we were one.

By mid-July, I reveled in newfound certainty. I would finally cast away my slag of lame excuses and reveal to Lauren my personal story of struggle and shame. She deserved to hear my past in its entirety. Every ghastly detail about the torment I had faced as a boy.

Instead of autobiographical scraps scattered randomly when I let down my guard, this time Lauren would hear everything about my formative years. She would learn the whole history of the tumultuous relationship I had with my father; why it deteriorated and, ultimately, how it all snapped violently like a bone.

My ghosts, like snakes writhing in a paper bag, would

be freed and exposed to the light, where they could be fully examined.

Hope and light suddenly descended on me. Lauren's loving magic would be an asset. Yes, an asset! Radiant Lauren would be my portal to a lifetime of happiness. Her deep reservoir of goodness would help me to transcend the emotional wall I had erected so that I might fulfill my potential as a husband and man.

Perhaps it was fate. Meant to be. While I planned, God laughed in my face. My careful timing would be bum-rushed. The phone rang and my Big Plan crumbled into dust. My father lay cold and stiff in a wooden box, awaiting my arrival as I sped through heavy traffic on a Florida highway.

Memories.

I shook my head slowly and sadly. I remember a deep sigh as I sucked in my breath, tapped the left turn signal and smoothly maneuvered into the next lane— very carefully, turning my head, looking twice — in order to pass an under-powered Honda barely maintaining a safe highway speed.

The contrails of a passing jet billowed white overhead, crossing under a lone puffy cloud. Its shape seemed to form an abstract question mark against the pale blue sky.

This time, I mercifully remained silent.

TWO

*'Every heart sings a song, incomplete,
until another heart whispers back.'*
— PLATO

DECEMBER 26, 2012
Rachel's Restaurant
North Creek, N.Y.

Lauren and I met on December 26 — the morning of my 40th birthday.

My first memory from that day is looking in the mirror. Through the dust spots and streaks, it revealed a man who felt unmoored, drifting and rudderless. Forty years on this earth and still not settled. Anxious and tentative most of the time. Indeed, my stunted emotional growth and tendency to indulge in self-pity had left me feeling down, empty and lonely on the inside — a despondency that I mostly hid from others. Not clinically depressed, I'm sure, but my melancholy sometimes seemed to leave me dangerously close to the edge.

Despite my inner sadness on this morning after Christmas, I presented a starkly different picture to the outside world and hurray for that.

When I stepped back from the bedroom mirror, I admired a vibrant, fit and athletic 40-year-old man. Sure, my joints crackled and popped like Rice Krispies when I climbed out of bed and my back took a few minutes to loosen up — as did my prostate as I stood bow-legged over the bowl first thing in the morning — but, overall, I could rightly proclaim to be in great shape. No one would argue that I was remarkably fit for a man at the dawn of a fifth decade of life.

To be clear, I'm not equating fitness with handsomeness. I don't claim to be the best-looking guy in any room. I'm quite aware that I'm no GQ model or anyone's idea of a leading man. Still, no one beat me over the head with an ugly stick, either. Despite being somewhat of a loner and aloof, I've had my share of girlfriends and one-night stands. Most of them were even attractive. And I know that people say that I appear considerably younger than my 40 years — except for my hairline, which began to betray me long, long ago.

Today, my once jet-black hair is speckled with a distinguished dusting of gray at the temples. Nothing alarming about that. On the gloomy December morning when I first met Lauren, however, it was my ever-expanding scalp that worried me and kept me standing at the mirror longer than necessary.

Indeed, my bare patch had been gaining territory, advancing like a Navy SEAL on a Taliban outpost. Until a few years ago, I had combed my ring of hair to creatively camouflage my folic inadequacies. That vain arranging and patting of stray strands eventually struck me as a ridiculous, self-defeating endeavor. One morning, I surrendered to the inevitable and asked my barber, an ex-Marine named Steve, to buzz my hair almost to the scalp. No more silly comb-overs. I proclaimed to the world, Let baldness be. Hallelujah!

To compensate, I worked out even more vigorously at home and at the gym. In my second-floor apartment, I religiously committed to my sit-up and push-up regimen and deep stretches in the hot shower. I twisted myself Gumby-like into yoga poses and worked the steel dumbbells by the side of the bed. Small weights were my armaments against the tub of ice cream and box of glazed donuts that beckoned me like a cheap stripper from my tiny kitchen.

At the time of my 40th birthday, my morning gym routine rarely varied. When my work schedule allowed, I would wake up at 6:15 a.m. and catch a little of the *Today* show, fantasizing what it would be like to date Savannah Guthrie or squire the weather girl with the cool haircut, Dylan Dreyer, around on my arm. Then, three or four times a week, I would head to the little gym 20 minutes down the road. Before breakfast, I would complete a full circuit of heavy weights, drink a little water, then set the treadmill program for four miles of intervals and hills at a pace quick enough to get my heart pounding and thick sweat darkening my shirt.

The entire time I ran on the treadmill, my legs churning and the mileage clicking off like a metronome, I tried to ignore *Fox News* playing on all four TVs. Instead, I kept my eyes peeled for a pink yoga mat and hot pink gym bag — and the enticing red head who toted them jauntily over her shoulder.

For several months, I had been watching this alluring young woman closely. I knew enough about her to spend lonely nights visualizing her laying provocatively on a weight bench, or arching her back sensuously, chest pushed out proudly, while she repped on the shoulder press.

Yet, I studiously avoided eye contact and did not dare introduce myself. Nor did I seek her out on Instagram or Facebook. I was too cautious. Too afraid to look her up — and unsure what I'd do if I actually found her. I admit it. I was petrified of rejection. And I remember taking great care not to let my gaze linger too long at the gym. North Creek is a zero stoplight town. Everybody knows everybody else's business. Better not invite any whispering that I am some kind of voyeur, a stalker or, worse — a pervert and a creep. Yet, virtually every minute I spent working out at the gym in her presence, I can now freely admit that I was consumed by my infatuation. Calculating how best to introduce myself to this ginger-haired beauty provided ample distraction as the treadmill belt whirred under me and Tucker Carlson bleated his usual nonsense.

Funny how fate works. As Christmastime rolled around, I had no calculated plan. None of Gen. Norman Schwarzkopf's strategic brilliance to help me in my fantasy-filled romantic pursuit. If I did one day happen to meet this woman, I had no idea how I would twist open the top and let my own personal brand of smooth flow out.

Kismet intervened, I guess you could say.

Good fortune blew me a kiss.

The 26th of December was a Sunday morning. Grey like an oft-washed undershirt. The wintry air smelled sharp and stinging, like the remnants of a battle. It had snowed an inch, maybe three. After a vigorous workout, I stopped for coffee at Rachel's, a cozy breakfast shop on Main Street just a stone's throw from the state-owned ski area where, the night before, I had worked the snow guns and groomers for exactly $14.50 an hour — plus a holiday bonus.

When I stepped through the door of Rachel's, stamping the snow off my feet onto the tile floor, I found myself behind this bewitching redhead in line. I silently admired her tight jeans and fashionable boots. My eyes followed the spread of freckles across her shoulders where the neckline of her wool sweater did not cover. On her jacket, petals of crystallized snow sparkled in the light. Her face was delectable; her eyes emitted an other-worldly blue glow and she smelled great. I wanted to lean in and deeply inhale, like I would a perfectly formed rose.

I silently observed this woman, slender as a reed, as she ordered her breakfast in a voice that practically sang — perky, confident and strong. I can also recall my next thought clearly: This woman is straight out of central casting. She could be a model. In her high school, she would be captain of the cheerleaders. Maybe female lead in the spring musical. Probably voted most popular in her class, too.

She's way out of my league.

I'll have two egg whites on a hard roll. No bacon or cheese, I heard this ravishing woman tell the counter girl, a goth teen with a safety pin pushed through her eyebrow at an awkward angle. And a regular coffee, black please, she added.

In a hard roll, I blurted from behind.

Not *on* a hard roll. The eggs go *inside.*

Not *on*, I added stupidly.

Goddamn me. Like it really fucking matters.

In a nano-second, I became a kite hijacked by the winds. My thoughts careened like a shopping cart with a spastic wheel. I kicked the floor in panic and considered fleeing the cafe. In the moment, however, I could not quickly summon a plausible — or graceful — excuse. I remained in line, cemented to the floor in embarrassment.

Wait! A wonderful surprise awaited me. My secret crush turned to me and smiled brightly. Her cheeks bloomed into a blush. She was gorgeous — *is* gorgeous — and she stood before me like she absolutely knew it. She cocked her head to the side, like an unseen but appreciative Broadway audience had burst into a wave of applause that crescendoed into a standing ovation.

Do you always edit strangers like that? she chided me with smiling eyes. She glowed like a force-field, and it nearly stopped my heart. Before I could open my mouth to apologize for my inane comment, this heavenly woman spoke to me again.

Technically, you're right you know. The eggs *do* go inside, I remember her saying. I really never thought of it that way.

She examined me more closely, giving me the once over with squinting eyes.

You look familiar. I've seen you before.

A spark of recognition followed.

Never mind. I know. You and I work out at the same gym. That's where I know you from, she said.

I nodded confidently. Cool on the comeback.

I'm very sorry. I apologize. I was out of line, I said.

I usually don't interrupt strangers and say dumb things like that, I also recall telling her.

I couldn't resist the urge to explain myself.

I've always had this thing for words. For language. I pay attention to words and usage and, ah, never mind. You look familiar to me, too, I said. Yes. From the gym. You usually take yoga around the time I'm there, right?

I concentrated hard to avoid speaking directly to her tits.

My name is Harry — Harry Truman Loev. Some of my friends call me H.T, but I like Harry the best. That's the name that I go by.

She did not notice my inappropriate stare.

So when you fly, Loev is in the air, she teased instead.

We both smiled at her wordplay. Wow, she's got a flirting game, too, I thought.

Something like that, I said. And your name is …

Lauren. Lauren Kelleher.

I answered, Very nice to meet you Lauren. I quickly debated whether it would be too forward — or just too weird — to shake her hand in greeting.

As long as I don't correct her grammar again.

I stepped to the counter to address the cashier with the painfully pierced brow.

I'm treating my new friend here. Put her breakfast order on my bill, I said with courage and conviction.

I pulled my debit card from my wallet and ordered breakfast for myself, too: A toasted sesame bagel with butter and a large coffee with cream, sugar and a double helping of Holy Shit, I Can't Believe My Luck.

Lauren thanked me for breakfast. I cleared a table and we sat down together in the back. Once we slipstreamed past a few awkward moments, Lauren and I fell into a groove. We shared easy conversation for what, to my amazement, turned into a breakfast that lasted nearly two hours. Animated by caffeine and excitement, we alternated talking about our lives to that moment. We linked our autobiographies effortlessly, unencumbered by self-consciousness. Neither of us slacked off or ran out of new topics to explore.

Although I've lived in the North Country for more than 20 years, I am a transplant from downstate, specifically the New York City suburbs, I explained to Lauren and which my accent readily revealed. Loev is from my Jewish, Eastern European roots and spelled unusually.

It's pronounced like that deep, aching feeling of undying affection, I said with a flirtatious grin, venturing outside my comfort zone as if guided by an alien force.

Lauren countered that she's mostly Irish, although French-Canadian loggers also dominate the thick trunk of her family tree, which had been planted in the rocky soil of the Central Adirondacks for more than a century. Her ancestors, she said, had settled in an area known as Little Canada near Indian Lake in the late-1800s, until a diphtheria epidemic broke up their settlement near Chimney Mountain and scattered families like blowing seeds. Generations of her family still populated these parts.

Look in the phone book, she said as if it were a challenge. Kellehers fill half a column and all of them are my aunts, uncles and cousins.

Hunched over my laptop, fingernails clicking on the keyboard, I can readily summon only a few additional snippets from that initial meeting. We bemoaned having to work over the Christmas holiday but agreed the extra money came in handy. At one point, I also remember, we reviewed the cafe's music selection — a playlist piped in via bookshelf speakers resting on a dusty side table. Cautiously, I expressed that I didn't care for country music and its sad caterwauling about dogs, pickup trucks and unrequited love.

I like Johnny Cash and Emmylou Harris, maybe even a little Garth Brooks. That's about it, Lauren parried in a neutral tone.

To my delight, Lauren preferred classic rock. She favored the Lumineers, Coldplay and U2. To my shock, she'd seen none of them perform live — not a single concert at the outdoor amphitheater in well-heeled Saratoga Springs.

And, I recollect, we also shared our experiences of the Thanksgiving just past — me, alone, in the quiet of my little apartment with a turkey sub and chips from the Tops supermarket on Main Street; she with her rambunctious extended family gobbling a 25-pound turkey and polishing off two cases of domestic beer.

I only eat the white meat, Lauren pronounced, planting a stake firmly in the ground.

I prefer the dark, I countered.

Duly noted. I guess there's nothing for us to fight over next Thanksgiving, she flirted, and this time I noted her eyes adoring me.

Lauren didn't care that I had a classic case of male pattern baldness. Nor did our six-year age difference ruffle her. She had nodded in knowing assent when I explained how, after my college years, I had cobbled together seasonal jobs that required physical strength and stamina but little in the way of critical thinking. She appeared unconcerned that I drove a battered, 14-year-old Toyota with 195,000 miles and squeaky brakes. Or that I rented a shabby top-floor apartment with peeling paint on the walls and a bicycle propped up against the kitchen table.

Lauren leaned in keenly when I revealed to her with some trepidation that I had earned a bachelors' degree in the Classics with a minor in Literature from SUNY Plattsburgh.

I know what you're talking about. We're not all hayseeds up here, she said with a hint of defensiveness. But, truthfully Harry, I haven't read any of the so-called Great Books. Nobody I know has, either. The classics? This is the North Country. I've never met a single person who has read any Plato or Homer. You're the first one.

They are important books, even today, I responded. Studying writers and philosophers like Homer, Plato and Socrates can lead to a better, more rounded understanding of today's world.

Lauren thought about that for a moment.

I always wanted to read *The Odyssey* — or try to read it anyway, she said. Maybe you can lend me a copy, she added, flirting some more.

I wondered whether her interest was genuine. Lauren read my uncertainty. Or my nerves. She reached out and touched my hand gently. A light pat, nothing more. I smiled and changed the subject. I wanted to explain that I had discovered too late in my scholarly pursuits that, in my view, there existed two career paths for those with proficiency in classic literature and ancient texts.

You see, I could get a prestigious job at an elite liberal arts school. Become one of those tenured professors who write books and wear corduroy jackets with elbow patches and try to impress pretty co-eds. Or, I could work my ass off in the freezing cold for little pay in a small upstate ski town.

I upturned my palms like they were scales.

I'm guessing you wonder if you chose the wrong path, Lauren said.

Her smile exposed teeth so white, she lit up the room. I nodded.

If she only knew the truth.

In actuality, my crippling fear of rejection and failure blocked me from applying for fellowships and seeking a masters' degree at a big-name university. If I had been braver, or even a tad more ambitious after graduation, one day I could have earned a tenure-track appointment, published a book or two and changed the course of my life. If I had only possessed a mote of self-confidence and drive.

My two seasonal jobs — snow gun operator and groomer at Gore Mountain in the winter and crewman on the Saratoga-North Creek tourist railroad in summer — did not reflect the brainpower or work ethic of a four-year college graduate. I know I have only myself to blame.

I'm not unhappy with how it all turned out, I mused to Lauren. Sometimes I ask myself, what if? Mostly, though, I'm okay with my life. I'm not rich by any stretch but I get by. I have what I need.

Lauren commiserated. She, too, had suffered the sting of regret. She, too, had learned that big dreams and lofty aspirations can collide with reality on life's bumpy road with unforeseeable results.

Growing up, Lauren didn't burn with ambition to waitress and clean motel rooms, dusting furniture, bleaching toilets and changing linens soiled by horny tourists, drunk tourists, unwashed tourists — sometimes all three checking out of the same small, tacky rooms. She found that both her jobs bombarded her with annoyances, which jabbed at her like nap-deprived pre-schoolers.

Lauren had, indeed, once dreamed big. She wished for a career acting on Broadway or in television sit-coms. Maybe, with a lucky break or two, she would land a part in a movie.

I knew it. I was right.

Growing up, I had big plans, Lauren told me over breakfast. I wanted to be rich and famous. A celebrity who didn't have to worry about money or any anything else. My whole childhood, I plotted how to get out of here. To leave this crappy little town. Set myself up in New York City or California. Study singing and dancing. Audition for parts. Maybe I would land something off-Broadway or on television and go on from there.

To fulfill her dream, Lauren told me that she initially pursued a degree in drama and won minor roles in summer stock in Lake George and Glens Falls.

Life intervened, she sighed. Her face revealed ache and disappointment when she said it.

Instead, Lauren explained that she earned a two-year degree in marketing from the community college in Queensbury, which has proven to be practically useless. The population inside the Blue Line is rapidly shrinking and, other than the Adirondack Experience in Blue Mountain Lake — or whatever name they call that museum these days, she said sarcastically — there are too few thriving businesses in the Adirondacks to effectively market.

About then, I confess that I stole a second glance at her cleavage. I pretended that I noticed the silver cross dangling from her neck like a climber rappelling down a rock face. Late in the second hour of our first meeting, I grew bolder. This time, I slid my hand toward hers. I extended my middle and index fingers and caressed the fine hairs on the delicate bone of her wrist. I slipped my hand atop of hers and closed it gently, holding it like I already knew that I never wanted to let her go.

She did not push it away.

By the time we had our last sips of cold coffee, I badly wished to lean in for a memorable first kiss to leave no doubt about how I felt. I was aware I had not showered and, honestly, froze as I was about to make a first move. We parted with a warm, thin hug, instead. More importantly, we exchanged phone numbers — and firm plans to meet that Friday night for dinner and an early New Year's celebration at the homey Adirondack-style grill across from the train depot where the summertime tourists stepped off to shop North Creek's antique shops and woods-themed boutiques.

When I stepped back into the cold outside Rachel's, I felt positively ebullient. Lauren and I had been drawn to each other like metal shavings to a powerful magnet. From far-flung points, we had each reached the same waypoint on our life journeys. The two of us, from opposite ends of the state and from dissimilar upbringings, had defied clichés to meet in a quaint Adirondack ski town all lit up for the holidays. We had each muddled through too many days that were decent enough, but which, in sum, added up to lives that had fallen short of our dreams and ambitions. We both wished for something more.

Plato wrote, Every heart sings a song, incomplete, until another heart whispers back.

Looking back on that momentous Sunday, two hearts, indeed, sang that gray morning at a little cafe in North Creek. In the days and weeks that followed, Lauren and I heeded our hearts' song. Our hearts spoke to each other, so just the other one could hear. It sounded like a joyous symphony blanketing a winter's worth of loneliness and despair. We had both interpreted that first overture in exactly the same way.

It sounded like hope.

■　■　■　■　■

December 26. My birthday, enmeshed with Christmastime on the calendar.

Exactly 40 years earlier, as the Watergate investigation simmered on the nation's news pages, my father stood firm and issued a non-negotiable demand to my mother.

Natan 'Nathan' Loev insisted that I be named after President Harry Truman.

From the family's collective memory bank:

My mother's water broke in mid-afternoon as the city recovered from its holiday hangover. After hurriedly scrambling through the narrow rooms in their Bronx flat to pack a small suitcase — a nightgown, toothbrush and a change of clothes — my parents arranged for dinner and a babysitter for my older siblings, then climbed into the car for the ride to the hospital.

As my father's big, brown Plymouth Fury rumbled

down the Major Deegan Expressway, the expectant couple rode in silence listening to CBS Radio News. Before
they had parked and checked in at the maternity floor
desk, the announcer had interrupted the station's regular
programming with a special news bulletin: Former President Harry S. Truman had died at the age of 88.

In between contractions as nurses scurried and I prepared for my grand entrance, my parents watched tributes
pour in from foreign capitals around the globe on a small
black-and-white television. When I finally entered this
world at 11:42 p.m. on December 26, 1972 crying, squawk-
ing and flailing my arms just hours after President Truman's
soul broke his earthly bonds, it seemed to the new parents
that I, too, deeply mourned the president's passing.

I don't remember any of this. Growing up, however,
that's the story my father told me about my birth and my
namesake. I had no reason to question him or to doubt
my own personal origin story. Why would I? Other babies had been named after the famous, like Mickey Man-
tle and Marilyn Monroe. Who could forget the serial
killer John Wayne Gacy? My parents never offered me
any explanatory context and I never sought any. I was the
youngest of three. Everyone seemed to have better things
to do.

While in Florida to attend my father's funeral, I
learned the true reason why he had adamantly insisted —
demanding, to the point of argument — that I be named
after the newly deceased 33rd president of the United
States of America.

The real story behind my very identity is another one of my father's crimes.

Alas, it's a story for another chapter.

Let's not get too far ahead of ourselves.

THREE

'You see, it's complicated.'

Early Evening
SUNDAY, JULY 16, 2013
North Creek, N.Y

Lauren and I had been watching a re-run of *Cops* when I learned of my father's death. The ring tone from my cell phone suddenly filled the room like a fanfare. I had planned to ignore this unwelcome interruption and let the caller roll to voicemail. Better to keep my attention on the overweight sheriff's deputy handcuffing a suspected meth dealer somewhere in West Texas. After four or five rings, however, curiosity won out. I looked down, repositioning my glasses so I could read the numbers on the screen.

My brother? Why is Jonathan calling now ... ?

We had not spoken since Thanksgiving. He did not yet know about Lauren.

Jonathan said hello. In a warm tone, he first asked about my job, the weather and, finally, my health. In that order. My antenna, finely tuned to recognize bullshit, twitched at his rote pleasantries. I asked after his family. He did not seem to hear me.

How bad are the bugs? he murmured, distracted.

While Jonathan tap-danced, I restlessly waited for the true reason for his call. He must have sensed my impatience.

Let me get to the point. I don't know how to say this, but you need to know. Dad died a few hours ago, he said.

His tone was flat and unemotional. Like he was checking off boxes on a to-do list.

Mail a letter. Take out the trash. Empty the dishwater. Inform your wayward baby brother that their father had died.

After a shallow pause, Jonathan continued.

My father had passed away peacefully that afternoon. His life ended with one final, shallow breath — in his own bed, in his own home, with a hospice nurse administering a morphine drip to keep him comfortable and ease his final hours. His last breaths marked a kind of coda to a hero's life, although Jonathan shared that the last month had been trying on everyone.

Not that you would know, of course, he jabbed.

Jonathan sighed into the phone, his breath in my ear. From 1,500 miles away he must have sensed me stiffen and he quickly retreated. He didn't intend to antagonize me with a gratuitous dig.

I'm sorry, I didn't mean that, Jonathan apologized. He was simply exhausted and emotionally drained from watching our father shrivel and crumple like a dried autumn leaf.

Jonathan provided spare details, but invited me to Florida for the funeral in two days. I surprised myself by spontaneously accepting, unable to think of a plausible reason to refuse.

I'd like that very much, he said after I had agreed. We can talk more when you get here.

Yeah, we can talk some more later, I said, and scrawled the details into a notebook in a shaking hand.

I'm not saying it's going to be fun. But this all has to end sometime, Jonathan said.

I knew he was right. Still, I swallowed hard at the thought.

He added with a bit more enthusiasm, Your sister Helen and I would like to see you again. We'd all like to see you.

Jonathan's gesture felt genuine. Sincere, even. It again stirred something inside me — a renewed desire to finally end my bitter estrangement, confront my demons and come home.

To be part of the family again.

. . . . .

I have asked myself a million times: How did our family splinter into such jagged scraps strewn all over? Once, we had been a real family. Connected like the electric cables strung atop the utility poles along the road. Then, a fierce storm raged. The poles toppled like dominos, pulling the electric lines — and their indispensable connections— to the ground with them.

39

How did we get to this wretched point? Why did I command it? Perpetuate it?

My recollection about exactly *when* I began to feel so alienated that I drew a blade and severed myself floats before me in sepia tones. When it comes to my family, there's no black X to scrawl in a calendar or memorial dirge to play to commemorate the moment it all blew up into a steaming pile of shit.

The *why* behind my decision to liberate myself and start my life largely apart from them has more certain roots. It springs not from a single exchange of harsh words; nor a slip of manners; nor a bruising joke gone awry. Rather, I finally weighed years of mistreatment — a massing of malevolence that piled up like a freeway crash — and decided that I had had enough. A stack of straws broke the camel's back.

I remember, too, that my decision resounded like the smashing of crystal, sending shards flying and inflicting deep and painful cuts.

My parents, I remember, flatly denied their culpability in the fracturing of our family.

They declared my memory to be faulty and worse, a bald lie. Mother, especially, tried to gaslight me into believing it was all my fault.

Harry, you are imagining things.

No, I was not. I assure you of that.

Not long after that, my bond with my brother and sister splintered like old barn wood, dry and brittle from the sun.

In my remembrance, Jonathan and Helen gripped cotton candy reminiscences about our childhood, sticky with sugar and even more ruinous. Their childhood memories seemed to be shaped by selective amnesia and an inexplicable desire to appease, rather than a moral obligation to honor the truth, however uncomfortable.

From my vantage point, the three of us lived the same dysfunctional childhood. Jonathan and Helen witnessed what I witnessed and endured what I endured. Yet, while our childhood experiences nuzzled tightly, the memories we processed — and the trauma imprinted on us by our experiences — diverged in ways that I could not understand or accept.

They chose long ago to forgive my parents. To acquit and absolve. To move on.

Helen suffered at their hands, just as I did. Yet, she could not summon even an ounce of the hostility which had consumed me like a fast-spreading cancer. In my mind, Helen was just too sweet. Too ready to forgive. She let my parents off scot-free. No questions asked.

I just don't feel like you feel, she firmly stated in one of our last meaningful conversations.

They did some things. Sure, they did, she mushed on. But I don't want to hate them. I want them to be a part of my life, especially now that I have children of my own. My kids should know their grandparents. To be part of their lives as they grow old. It's more important for me to have a relationship with Mom and Dad.

And that was that.

Jonathan, too, developed a too-convenient amnesia. When I sought him as a listener and an ally, he accused me of being overly sensitive. He nodded politely as I listed my grievances. Then, he, too, dismissed my feelings, brushing me off like I was a crumb on his table. He, too, had decided to grant mother and father a full and complete pardon.

Jonathan countered that he had weighed the real-life pressures our parents faced — demanding jobs, three active children and a pile of bills to pay. He claimed to understand stress in ways I could not. He wouldn't take sides. He would be Switzerland. Neutral. Jonathan had determined in his oldest-child wisdom that a little un-orthodox parenting should be understood and, ultimate-ly, fully forgiven.

Look, they weren't perfect by any stretch, he excused them, echoing Helen's reasoning. I recall Jonathan pa-tronizing me, lecturing that parenting didn't come with a step-by-step instruction manual.

Look, there's no how-to book to study. No roadmap. Mom and Dad did their best. They provided for us the best they could. They just didn't live up to your expectations.

He added, Don't be such a jerk about it. Be a little more grateful.

I found my siblings' reasoning flawed and infuriat-ing. I told them so, too. The way they dismissed my feel-ings and attempted to justify my parents' cruel behav-ior stabbed like a dagger. I screamed, my voice making unnatural sounds. I made horrible accusations, which, truthfully, I have regretted for a long time.

Jonathan and Helen became defensive. They backed away from me, like I was some sort of monster.

Jonathan and Helen looked at me as if *I* was the one who had committed terrible crimes. That it was me who had taken an axe to the nucleus and drove the blade in deep between the shoulders.

I wasn't having it.

You're sacrificing your sense of right and wrong, I self-righteously lectured them.

You're twisting yourself in knots to justify what they did, just so you can have a little inner peace, I threw in for good measure.

I pointed an angry finger at them, too.

I'm not going to sell out like you're doing, I accused.

In the end, it was how my siblings reacted to my feelings of isolation, sadness and desperation which over-watered the roots of our discord. Our relationship reached a terminus, like a city bus sputtering into a deserted station at the end of a long run.

We each made a choice. We fended off our demons in our own ways.

Ahh, memories.

■ ■ ■ ■ ■

The unexpected Sunday evening phone call ended with me extending a quiet, resigned goodbye to my older brother. I touched the red circle on my iPhone to end the call. I set the device on the side table, spinning and reeling in that surreal space between disbelief and sadness.

I walked slowly back to the couch and to Lauren as if I were under water.

My father's gone, I said softly in her direction, still processing.

Lauren held me tightly for several minutes, whispering reassurances.

Next, I phoned Bill, my supervisor at the railroad. I told him, My father passed. I asked for the next few days off. He promised to re-arrange shifts. Others would be put on the schedule to cover for me. He offered his condolences and wished me a safe flight.

Don't worry, Harry, he said. We got you. Go be with your family.

Bill's voice resonated with sincerity.

Thanks, buddy. I owe you one, I said.

The moments after that are a fog. I knew, however, the cap on the bottle had twisted open. No longer could I debate when to share my past with Lauren. Rather, now I weighed how much I should share — and in what order — once I began my telling.

I envisioned measuring volatile chemicals in a beaker or tweezing out milligrams of a scarce, life-saving drug. I would proceed slowly, in measured steps. My hidden secrets would be released to Lauren in wafer thin layers, bit by bit, so I could carefully gauge the effects. And call a stop if necessary.

In the living room, I mumbled to Lauren that I had something important to say. I turned down the music and poured myself a whiskey. Neat, for courage. Lauren accepted a glass of white wine, waiting for me to wipe away a water stain with the front of my shirt.

Make yourself comfortable. This is going to be tough, I said.

Lauren curled her hands around a globe of chardonnay and folded her legs underneath her.

I want to talk to you about my father. Some family history that I had planned on telling you about a while ago. Bad things happened to me when I was young, and which have weighed heavily on me, but I never got around to sharing with you, I began.

I moved the magazines and old mail scattered on the coffee table into a neat pile to signal that the ensuing conversation would be consequential.

I need you to listen. Really hear me out, I said.

I had, at last, summoned the courage to speak. I was finally ready to unbosom memories that I had kept concealed for two decades — secrets that, for all my adult life, I had found too scary to speak aloud.

My memory and history, well, they don't always waltz in step, I prefaced, the news about my father's death still settling. It's not an excuse, really, I told Lauren. Sometimes, my childhood appears to me like an out-of-focus photograph — a little fuzzy around the edges but clear enough that I can still make out the big picture.

I underscored to Lauren, This is my life story. My early memories. My truths. It's my past to interpret, even as others may hold differing impressions of what happened in the Loev household all those years ago.

I elaborated, You need to understand that I had a dysfunctional childhood. The things that happened to me are right out of a horror film. Because of that, I'm damaged goods — permanently damaged, probably. You need to know that about me. If we're going to be together as a couple, you need to make peace with it because I don't expect to ever be able to escape my past. Not entirely. There's no cure for what I went through. No aspirin I can pop. No magic lotion to apply that will make my trauma fade and eventually go away. The scars that I bear are very real — factual and indisputable, like a fire burns or a river flows with a current.

I took a deep breathe and said, Lauren, if you want to leave, to find someone else without all this baggage, I'll understand. You're terrific. You deserve a great life, Lauren. No hard feelings if you packed up and got out. Really, I wouldn't blame you if you left me and found someone else.

Sheepishly, I caught myself. I was already spinning out of control. Too quickly I had retreated to my youth, when I survived by living in a protective crouch. A childhood that drained my energies and canceled my soul.

I closed my eyes. I lowered my head in apology, as if to say:

I know. Calm the fuck down, Harry.

I looked to Lauren for her initial reaction. I waited to see if her face twitched nervously or if she looked away in revulsion or, even worse, pity.

I didn't want her pity.

Lauren's face remained open. Her eyes radiated compassion. She leaned in earnestly and waited for me to go on.

Even now, when grace and common decency toward my father is the right thing, I can't forget. I said. Or make allowances. Or readily forgive everything that happened to me. I trusted my father completely. And he shattered my trust. He hurt me deeply.

There, I said it.

Because of that and a lot, lot more, I'm very bitter towards him. I resent him. Here's the thing: Now he's dead, and I feel this intense guilt and shame for being so bitter, for being so angry at him. His funeral is in two days. I can't fix it now. I blew my chance. I ran out of time.

Why couldn't I have forgiven him while he was alive?

Yes, I know that's royally fucked up, but that's where I'm at right now, Lauren. Feeling guilty and angry at the same time. Honey, maybe you would be better off cutting your losses now and finding someone else. Someone who isn't so screwed up inside.

Lauren chuckled softly and shook her head side to side. No. No. No.

He's not going to chase me away.

Lauren would listen to me with all her heart. She would be my passport out of the abyss. She knew it even if I did not.

■ ■ ■ ■ ■

Long before I delivered my feverish speech, Lauren had me figured out.

Lauren recognized my emotional detachment as a North Country trait. She had seen this aloofness bred in other men, the way I existed as remotely as the rocky peaks outside our window, hiding my innermost thoughts and feelings.

Lauren could not guess the source of my anguish or why I looked at my life through a prism of internal combat. But, she knew that, as surely as a woodsman knows how to build a shelter from pine boughs or start a fire using flint, I had become adept at walling myself off. Cloaking my true emotions was a survival skill that I had, indeed, fully mastered.

My emotional distance bothered Lauren more than she let on. It allowed doubt to sow in the tiny space where her love for me was not yet complete and unconquerable. Lauren wished for me to be emotionally intimate with her, to help erase the ache she felt for the man she loved but feared she did not fully know.

To her credit, Lauren did not nag. She understood that I had to *want* to change. I had to be *ready* to share my past and my secrets. Still, she believed that our happiness as a couple hinged on my willingness to allow myself to be vulnerable with her.

Back in March, when the white and cold of winter gave way to blustery winds and brown, she had begun to gently press me to reveal some of the darkness that dwelled inside my heart.

Something's bothering you, she had gently poked at me. You don't have to keep it all bottled up inside. You can tell me. I'm here for you if you want to talk about it.

When she attended church on Sundays, Lauren prayed that I would develop a complete faith and trust in her. Her blue eyes shut in focus, Lauren prayed that she could be a worthy partner on my difficult journey. And she quietly beseeched her God to guide me with a loving hand as I learned to communicate my feelings.

She also vowed that she would stand alongside me without judgement, in strength, for eternity — or for as long as it took.

A little selfishly, she also wanted me to hurry along.

At 34, Lauren saw herself a flower in bloom whose time was passing quickly. How long, she worried, before her petals browned around the edges and dropped by her feet? How many years until she bent and wilted, her fragrance and her beauty gone? What if I never learned to trust?

Nothing happened. I remained emotionally distant, mildly depressed and resentful.

Closed off to her.

If my father hadn't died, who knows what, if anything, would have changed?

■ ■ ■ ■ ■

Seated in my small living room, a small fan whirring in the background, Lauren urged me to release my feelings to her. In the moments after my brother's phone call, she again encouraged me to be honest with her, but to myself above all.

Go on. I'm listening, she had said, sweetly and supportively. I want you to trust me. Share your life with me. Tell me about your father. About your whole family. Don't worry, Harry. You're not getting rid of me so easily.

She tacked on, I'm not one to judge. I have a past, too. We all have a past. There's some darkness and skeletons in my own closet. Dark things from my past that embarrass me and I don't like to talk about, she said, foreshadowing.

Lauren slowly sipped her wine. She fiddled with a napkin on the coffee table, tearing off little strips and rolling them back and forth between her fingers. She shifted her petite frame on the worn couch. Somewhere, a dog barked. She used the passing seconds to frame her words with care.

I know that you can't change what happened to you. Your past is your past. And maybe you can't ever forget it, she said.

I also know that in every person's life, there is a before, an after and a now. There's a time long ago that is the past. It's gone. Poof. The time now is today. Right now. This moment. And there's time in the future. We exist in the present, Harry. I'm here. I am the now. Today and all the future are ours to dictate. It can be whatever we want it to be. As great as we want to make it, as long as we are together. We just have to grab it.

We have to grab it together.

■ ■ ■ ■ ■

You see, it's complicated, I began.

With those simple words, the first chapter of my life story reached hesitantly for the air. My voice trembled.

A mutiny of nerves. I recovered and began to unfurl for Lauren the prologue of my childhood.

My father didn't get angry in the traditional sense, I said. I can't remember him ever striking me. He never slapped me or roughed me up, either. Not even a hard shake. He rarely raised his voice or yelled at me either, in case you're wondering.

It's true, I reminded myself. My father never thundered at me with God-like wrath.

Lauren must know that my father had never crossed those lines.

I can't think of anything that my father did that would have qualified as child abuse. At least, not in the legal sense, I expanded. Nothing my father did would have concerned Social Services or the police — or made a tempting story for the tabloids, even though he was sort of famous. Kind of a celebrity.

Well, that's good, Lauren responded.

I suppose, I admitted.

Lauren dipped down to her most comforting voice.

What is it then? It doesn't seem to be in your nature to hate anything.

I did not respond, so Lauren filled the silence.

Get it off your chest. You'll feel better when you do, she soothed.

I now have the benefit of time. I can assess the previous 12 months from the point of view of a bird peering and gliding down through the blue. In between the spread branches and green leaves, I see myself, a tiny, insignificant speck below, beginning to confide my life story.

From the sky high above, I see that Lauren had bookmarked my use of that loaded word: Celebrity.

A single noun plucked from all my college-level vocabulary.

Not an incidental use of the word in my emotionally charged rant.

Not an accidental slip of a mourning tongue.

Celebrity.

From the Latin *celebritas,* meaning honored. The state of being well-known.

Lauren easily could have missed it before it evaporated into the air like steam.

Instead, like a veteran angler she hooked my use of that word. Reeled it in and landed it with the aplomb of a guide netting a fighting trout, without letting on that she had felt a nibble.

… Kind of a celebrity.

Lauren filed this piece of new information in the storeroom of her own memory. She understood the value of patience and restraint as I reached within to finally touch the long ago. Lauren had made an instantaneous calculation. She would wait before asking me to explain my use of that word. She silently prayed that her careful listening and attentiveness would be rewarded.

Lauren sat straighter on the couch. Her thin eyebrows arched. She blinked twice, and committed my surprising description of my father to her own memory.

Sort of famous. Kind of a celebrity.
There would be a time for that, too.

■ ■ ■ ■ ■

Lauren's blue eyes drilled into me and she closed a soft hand over mine. Looking back, I can not recall any other moment like it. No one had ever wrapped me in that kind of love, understanding and acceptance before. I could practically feel Lauren's reassuring love pass from her body to mine. It inspired a newfound confidence to release more — to reveal secrets so intimate, the realization initially caused me to recoil, like my bare leg had brushed against a snake.

It was abandonment that I suffered as a child, I finally admitted.

In many ways, it was much worse than any physical beating my father could have laid on me, I confessed.

It's because of what my father *failed* to do all those years ago that I don't trust anyone. I don't rely on anyone but myself for anything. I am suspicious of everyone's motives. It's my biggest failing. I know it. Even with you, in our relationship. I don't want it to be like this but it is.

In my earliest childhood memories, I told Lauren, my father metaphorically perched himself at the edge of the surf where mighty ocean waves gasped their final, dying breaths.

I said, My father looked out from the edge of the sand and saw a drowning boy flailing for help just a few yards offshore. The little boy's face was under water. He was drowning.

I envisioned myself struggling to breath.

Struggling for life.

Yet, never once did my father enter the waters or out-stretch a hand, or even offer words of encouragement, to save this boy, I said. He looked away. He ignored the panic and the terror. He never left the sand.

Lauren, her eyes now downcast, hugged herself tight. The depth of bitterness contained in my metaphor stunned her.

I swallowed hard and plunged my face into my palms. The flotsam of secret shame, humiliation and despair that indelibly stamped my childhood surfaced anew. I again tasted fear.

It should be obvious. The drowning boy was me, I said in surrender.

At least, it always felt like I was sinking into the blackness, going under with no one to help me.

You poor thing, Lauren finally responded. I had no idea. No inkling this is why you have all this sadness and anger bottled up inside. It's awful. I don't know what else to say.

Lauren moved closer to me on the couch. I rested my head against hers. Over the swell of my emotions, I could faintly detect the scent of perfume when she soothed back my hair. Again, I swallowed hard, my self-control scrambling to gain a footing.

It's all true. I continued. I spent my entire childhood afraid. Tip-toeing around on egg shells. I lived in constant fear, feeling lost and hurt. Rejected. Like I had no value. Unworthy of my father's love.

Lauren's eyes welled up to match mine. I did not want her to be sad or to cry tears for me so I looked away. My gaze settled on the picture window across the room. Outside, I could see the interlocking arms of towering trees. Despite the summer evening, dark grey clouds threatened a reptilian chill.

I groped for a better way to help Lauren to understand what it was like.

My childhood home was like a spider's web, I finally said. It was a home and yet, at the same time, a deadly trap.

Yes, that's right, I thought. The spider stalked the vulnerable insect until it became trapped. Unable to escape the web.

I was the insect in the trap, I told Lauren.

I yearned for my father's love. I was his son. His flesh and blood. I called to him to protect me. Yet, he never moved a muscle to help. He watched the spider stalk me and devour me and he did nothing to stop it.

All these years later, I still don't completely understand it. The celebrity was indifferent. He could not be roused to protect his own son.

Shifting my body to face Lauren directly, I said, It's why I am so angry and resentful. And why his funeral is going to be so, so hard for me.

I summoned something more. I opened the bays and, from deep within, dropped a payload of verbal napalm.

So, fuck him, I said too loudly. The emphasis was on the fuck.

So deep-set was my trauma from a childhood beset

by turmoil — and my father's cowardly indifference to it — that I stooped to violating a societal taboo. I sullied my father's memory before they could lower his coffin into the ground. I sought to destroy my father's legacy with the full understanding that this exorcism of sorts was like vandalizing a masterpiece, an impetuous act that risked my own personal self-destruction.

Because my conscience sang out to me, *De mortuis nil nisi bonum dicendum est.*

Of the dead, speak nothing but good.

Right there existed my internal conflict, the lion eating my soul.

Lauren, I said. It wasn't always this way.

■ ■ ■ ■ ■

Fury and resentment had not always consumed me like a flame. To be fair, I also possessed a storeroom of happier memories that, over the years, I had pushed to the corners.

Indeed, I had once idolized my father in the way that wide-eyed, smooth-faced little boys revere the alpha male figures who pitch them baseballs under-hand and tuck them in snugly at night. Once, I believed my father could tear apart an entire hit squad with just a garden rake; win a Triple Crown while playing centerfield for the Yankees, or run for president and win in a landslide.

I could easily summon pleasant, early memories of spontaneous trips to the Dairy Queen on Main Street; joining him on fishing trips from charters on the Long Island Sound; joy-filled birthday parties with friends gathered around; raucous family visits to stuffy apartments in Queens, and nights of riotous comedy around the family dinner table.

Yet, in the autumn of my disappointing adolescence, still too timid to coherently express my own sinking doubts, I also began to realize that I loved a naive, idealized version of what my father *should be* more than the flesh-and-blood man himself.

All the while, I wrestled with another truth: Undeniably, my old man cast a special aura about him.

His celebrity status just confused everything even more, I said aloud, with a shake of my head.

Lauren nodded sympathetically.

That word again. Used several times in a span of minutes.

Lauren again squeezed my hand tight, hard enough that I could feel the bones of her fingers and I could not forget that she was with me.

I understand, or at least I think I do, Lauren had answered.

. . . . .

Many months later, I learned that Lauren had lay in bed that night next to me, unable to sleep. The fan whirred on high, in sync with her spinning thoughts.

The power of her imagination took flight.

Lauren grasped that I had been victimized by something terrible. She believed me — that, as a child, I felt abandoned by my own father. I had faced mental anguish and some kind of emotional harm. In her insomnia, Lauren questioned, too, why my father had failed to protect me as any other father would.

Mostly, Lauren had tossed in bed, tortured into sleeplessness by an unanswered question:

Who was this face of evil? Who was this poisonous spider who built and set a deadly trap?

It is not yet time, friends. There are more memories to reveal.

More secrets sealed in the amber of my youth that must be unlocked and set free.

FOUR

'A hero of the highest order.'
— CITATION FOR BRAVERY

I resolved that, once I had begun my telling, Lauren must know more about my father. It would be unfair for her to be singed by my anger or to suffer my despondency any longer without knowing why. Lauren would need additional context and detail to understand the complicated place that my father occupied in my world.

How else will Lauren deliver me from despair?

Talking it through will be good for you, she encouraged me.

It will be good for both of us, actually, she also said.

We'll see, I responded, to rein in her expectations.

Secretly, I wondered how far I would actually go and worried how she would react.

■ ■ ■ ■ ■

Lt. Natan 'Nathan' Loev, the eldest son of immigrants, did not speak often of his own childhood or the experiences and memories that shaped him. Thus, I grew up knowing very little about his upbringing in The Bronx in the 1930s and 40s.

Whether my father's aloofness was lingering embarrassment about his own childhood; or a peculiar trait of his generation or something else entirely, I am left to wonder about forever.

Truthfully, Lauren, my father shared very little, I said.

Indeed, my father had me late in life, when he was already in his 40s. Maybe, he surveyed his own world, judged it sufficient — good enough — and decided to soldier on, unruffled by the privation and indignities he suffered as a young boy in the fallow years after the Great Depression. Maybe filling the role of breadwinner, husband and father occupied him completely, leaving no space — or energy — for anything of a personal nature. Or, perhaps, my father didn't know that we were interested and that we cared.

Honestly, he was a cypher. Impossible to read, I explained to Lauren. What I know about his past comes from a few stories that I heard and my own interpretations. My father concealed a lot from us.

Lauren shot me an incredulous look as if to say, The apple didn't fall far from the tree.

I let out a little more string, conceding Lauren's point.

On occasion, I acknowledged, an invisible switch seemed to flip. A spigot would open and my father would share anecdotes from his youth. When these rare moods struck, my father would pour out stories in vibrant bursts of color. Memories of growing up in the '30s and '40s would rise to the surface suddenly and then disappear into the deep — quietly, like a submarine — until the next time he surrendered to a whim.

Over the years, I had built a scaffolding of my father's life from stray reminisces, which he scattered about as if from a draft.

I explained to Lauren that, in my storeroom of recollection, my father drank up all the air in the room until he loomed larger than life. In our suburban town within commuting range of New York City, my father was well-known — in some circles, yes, even famous — for exhibiting uncommon bravery and a steely resilience forged by fire.

Just about everyone in our bedroom community seemed to know Nathan — rarely Natan and never Nate — personally. Or, because my hometown was just small enough, they had heard captivating stories about my father's exploits, or had caught on gossip's wind the details of his latest close call.

I bit my lip. I wished to choose my words diplomatically.

They just didn't see the dirt hiding in the crevices, I told Lauren. It was hidden. Obscured from view.

Thus, I had great difficulty reconciling my father's life, burnished as it was with its patina of courage and heroism, with my own reality.

My childhood was like watching a magic act from behind a thick velvet curtain, knowing the secret of the performer's trick and being amazed that the audience could still be so easily fooled. Early on, I had resigned myself to stewing quietly whenever I observed my father in social settings, watching sullenly from a distance as a crowd circled him like seagulls at the beach to listen spellbound as he reluctantly owned up to one wild tale or another.

And just like the goddamn seagulls, I spat, he dropped loads of crap everywhere.

Lauren eyes registered disappointment. I swallowed and stared at my shoes for a minute.

Honey, let me try it this way, instead.

■ ■ ■ ■ ■

My father wasn't as well known or worshipped with the reverence reserved for football stars, matinee idols and historical giants. Nevertheless, my father still enjoyed the prestige of a decorated warrior, celebrated as an honest-to-goodness, swear-to-God, hey-look-at-him local hero known in our hometown as simply The Lieutenant.

While technically correct, Lt. Nathan Loev's military-sounding title did not originate on the blood-soaked beaches of Normandy, or at the Battle of Midway, or Inchon or Heartbreak Ridge. He didn't fight at the citadel surrounding the imperial city of Hue as some mistakenly believed.

Vietnam had ended. Our soldiers had come home. We were at peace. Still, the war remained fresh in everyone's minds, I explained.

Understandable, answered Lauren.

Besides, my father was a Navy man. But he didn't serve in war-time like many assumed. And he wasn't an officer, either. He was an enlisted man. A sailor. He signed his papers and joined up just as World War II was ending. He actually earned his lieutenant's bars on what he always called The Job.

The Job? Lauren queried, as if I had slipped into a foreign tongue.

My father was as a career fireman, I explained. A smoke-eater. A first responder. He was one of New York's Bravest. FDNY steeped in the marrow of his bones. A decorated medal-winner. A rescuer of cats and dogs and more than his quota of desperate humans, who clutched him as the breath of life itself.

Lt. Nathan Loev of Engine 43 was a pyromancer, as skilled at divining the pace and direction of fire as a snake charmer playing a cobra from a basket.

He was a firefighting superstar.

A celebrity warrior in helmet, boots and turnout coat.

Lt. Nathan Loev earned his cherished sobriquet battling toxic black smoke and billowing orange flames. He flirted with danger and death like a shapely model sashaying before hardened street toughs. He ignored imminent peril to rescue careless smokers passed out cold in their beds; lonely housewives from grease fires licking from their stoves; and filth-covered squatters who sought refuge in abandoned brownstones, only to be trapped by arsonists seeking the few bucks they needed to score their next fix.

Despite my lingering resentment about my father's personal failings and my life-long grappling with the detritus of our complicated relationship, I would always be an energetic defender on one, larger point.

If you tilted my father's life story into the light, I conceded, it would be fair to conclude he served as a respected combat leader of brave men who, as brothers, faced mortal peril on every shift.

Crouched low to the floor to stay below the acrid black smoke, my father — The Lieutenant — led Engine 43's men through four hazardous tours a week for nearly 35 years against the red devil himself. Together, he and his macho brethren pushed back fire and took wild-eyed joy in it. As a team, they stared down super-heated gases and backdrafts; random sniper fire; metal garbage cans hurled in racial fury from tenement rooftops; and the menacing hoodlums who ruled the projects. All were as deadly as any guerrilla ambush or German pillbox bunker.

In the South Bronx through much of the 1970s and 80s, in the underbrush of the most crime-ridden neighborhoods in the poorest congressional district in Jimmy Carter's and Ronald Reagan's America, they all could kill you just as dead. Of this truth, my father would remind our neighborhood's white-collared attorneys, architects and bank vice presidents with their crisp business cards, neatly trimmed fingernails and biceps slack from under-use.

Thus, Lt. Nathan Loev's war was a civilian war, fought over race and poverty and frustration and despair. And, sub-standard housing; out-of-control crime; and humid nights where air-conditioning was just a fever dream. To be very clear, *that* was how my father came to be publicly lionized for his courage. He was an iconic firefighter in the days when the South Bronx more resembled war-torn Iraq than an outer borough of New York City.

Naturally taciturn, my father would occasionally rouse from his non-communicative state to paint vivid pictures of fighting fires and saving lives. Like a comet arriving after years in earth's dark orbit, he would suddenly become animated. He would rush to describe what it was like — the smells and sounds firing an adrenaline rush as he charged as part of a balletic team into a burning building, as everyone else fled in panic and fear.

Once, the local Kiwanis Club invited my father to address its monthly meeting about his firefighting career. That my father agreed to speak in public was so far outside his comfort zone and our understanding of him, we thought it was an error — a humorous communications mix-up. Against his wishes, the entire Loev family dressed up and attended the event. We nibbled on cheese and crackers and sipped apple juice before the club president jingled a bell to call everyone to their seats. I recall sitting mesmerized and proud throughout my father's entire presentation, in which he read off a few hand-scribbled notes on looseleaf paper and never made eye contact with anyone.

Indeed, for his entire life, I explained, my father remained closed off and humble about his displays of heroism.

One time, for example, he saved a young black boy he found semi-conscious, hiding from the smoke and flames. The boy was just seconds from death when my father reached under a bed and touched his leg. My father rushed to the fire escape to give the boy mouth-to-mouth resuscitation on the fourth-floor landing. Seconds later, the boy miraculously coughed back to life. It all happened in front of a television crew, which heard The Lieutenant's urgent calls on the scanner and pointed a camera to a sky lit orange by flames just in time to capture the miracle of life — one of the heroic resuscitations that helped shape my father's legend.

I heard whimpering and I thought it was a dog, my father matter-of-factly told the street reporter from NBC. He sounded surprised when he added, I had no idea it was a kid.

Another time, a fellow firefighter had the misfortune of accidentally stepping in wet paint — a bright yellow used to mark the parking area for the hook-and-ladder, which shared quarters with Engine 43. As a lark, the firefighter smeared left-over paint over the bottom half of his rubber boots. He even decorated part of it with a smiley face for laughs.

A few days later, the firefighter joined his company in battling a three-alarm blaze. He entered the building through an upper story window and crawled along the floor to stay below the billowing smoke. Suddenly, the fire-weakened floor gave way, sending the firefighter collapsing down with the floor boards, plaster and fixtures to the floor below. My father, on the nozzle in another room, raced to the jaws of the collapse, which belched newly ignited flames like the mouth of a dragon. He shined his flashlight down into the hole as smoke and dust swallowed him, a mushroom cloud cloaking the approaching specter of death.

My father swept the void in light until his beam caught the firefighter, who lay 15 feet below, upside-down and injured in the rubble. The yellow paint smeared on his boots saved his life.

The official citation for valor read:

'At great personal peril, Lt. Natan Loev of Engine 43, 5th Battalion, bravely rappelled down a rope into the smoking debris, unburied the injured firefighter with his bare hands, and carried him to safety through the smoke and flames on his back, before additional personnel could arrive at the scene to help effectuate further rescue and evacuate the injured firefighter for treatment. In demonstrating bravery in the line of duty above and beyond even the highest standards of this Department, Lt. Natan Loev is a hero of the highest order.'

My father initially failed to mention it. When he called home, it was only to tell us that that he would be late.

I caught a job, he phrased it and left it at that.

Later that year at the Fire Department's annual ceremonies honoring the city's bravest, the mayor pinned another medal to my father's chest — this one, the second-highest honor a city firefighter could attain. Only dying in the line of duty could earn a medal more prestigious, the official program said. With the firefighter's paint-splattered boots at center stage, I learned the details of my father's heroics for the first time and joined almost everyone else in questioning his sanity.

You know, Nathan, you don't have to be the hero all the time. You can share the danger, let others go first, I recall my mother saying, imploring him to be more careful.

You have a wife and kids at home, she said.

I know, he answered, and it was all he had to say about that.

For his entire life, The Lieutenant remained mostly allergic to notoriety and fame. He didn't consider himself a celebrity. Only when the news media caught wind of one of his super-hero feats did anyone outside the NYFD learn about his daring. His reluctance to say anything, much less take any credit, only enhanced his reputation.

Lauren, from a hometown more populated by deer and bears than people, listened bug-eyed. She struggled to absorb this colorful nugget of family history and the large, puzzling shadow that my father had obviously cast on me.

I lowered my voice to a whisper.

I absolutely hated it, too, I said. I resented it. I resented him.

At one point in my life, gripped by rampaging adolescent hormones, I wanted to grab those so-easily-impressed tightly by the collar. They deserved a rough shaking. A nose-to-nose wake-up call.

Couldn't they see? How could they not see? I sputtered in exasperation. It was all a deception — a stupid fun-house illusion.

I inhaled deeply and looked at Lauren. The room felt stuffy, so I opened a window and turned on the oscillating fan in the corner. It sucked in the fresh smell of outdoors, which overpowered the clinging scent of dirty laundry from the basket tucked in the corner. I shifted my body again. I released decades of stored resentment and anger at my father with the speed of a viper's strike.

At 16 and full of acne and murderous hate, I often dreamed of plastering what I believed to be the stark naked truth about my father on colorful highway billboards and on the waxy cardboard sides of milk cartons, next to the sad pictures of abducted children.

Looking back, oh, how I schemed some imaginative schemes, I continued on. You wouldn't believe what I thought of doing.

In one especially elaborate fantasy hatched the summer I got my learner's permit, I had imagined commandeering the tinny loudspeaker at the community swimming pool, where families gathered on weekends to slump sloth-like on beach chairs, cooking themselves painfully red in the sun's rays between handfuls of potato chips and long sips of powdered tea.

In my fantasy, I had hijacked the office microphone, ripping it away from the protesting recreation supervisor. I would then freely and loudly broadcast the damning facts across the sun-splashed pool apron.

Attention please! May I have your attention! I visualized myself shouting at the top of my lungs so that my urgent words would not be snatched away by the breeze.

I imagined transmitting my scandalous exposé about my father across the broiling concrete; over the crumpled wet towels and reclining chaise lounges; past the snaking line at the snack bar all the way to the pool's three-meter high dive. If only my father's contemporaries — lithe figures of their youth rearranged by time and gravity — could experience their own Eureka moment.

I'm the more honest witness, I envisioned myself shouting for the record.

I would righteously trumpet to our suddenly startled neighbors, By virtue of blood and DNA, I bear the burden of the most important truth of them all.

My father a hero? Please ... I would shock them, marinating deeper into my own bizarro fantasy world. You've been duped all along. My father abandoned me. He's no man of action. He's a fraud. A real man is more than a collection of firefighting heroics.

I breathlessly carried on, eyes closed, picturing myself an artist signing a masterpiece. I felt like an eagle soaring across an infinite blue sky.

Get a grip, honey, Lauren suddenly interrupted. She saw my face tensing and sensed I was losing it. Lauren wondered where this was all going and feared how it would end. She stroked my leg as if to caress away my dangerous mood. She hoped that it would help but wasn't sure, and it kindled in her a nervous tingling. When it came to my father and the rest of my family, Lauren was beginning to see that I was lost in the roiling waters of a troubled sea and badly in need of a rescue — one she suddenly was not sure if she had the strength to pull off.

Don't you understand, Lauren? I knew what the others didn't, I said.

Like the warrior Achilles in Homer's *Iliad*, my fearless and valorous father also possessed a mortal weakness. When my grandmother playfully dipped him in the ocean as an infant, this dunking — a rare story once shared at a family gathering — did not confer upon him the invulnerability of the gods.

Great? Heroic? Hah!

The canon of my father's life story must also contain the barest, most painful truth of all truths.

It's our family's dirty little secret, I said. My hero father radiated courage everywhere but at home.

In his helmet, facing down a raging inferno with his men, my father exhibited the strength and bravery of a Marvel action figure. When charging up a back staircase to save an elderly man and his wife from certain death — an act of courage that catapulted him to Gotham fame and yet another medal for exceptional bravery — testosterone and raw courage poured like sweat on a hot summer day.

Yet, behind the floral curtains in our tidy suburban home, my father was a coward; a chicken; a gutless weakling; a frightened sissy; a plain fraud; a wussy who abandoned his paternal duty to faithfully defend his children from harm. Strip away the heavy brass nozzle, soot-stained turnout coat and defiance in the face of choking smoke, my father laid himself bare as a spineless namby-pamby; a Superman denuded of his cape cradling Kryptonite on his lap.

On the home front, he was a coward.

Damn everyone else.

Nathan Loev once saved a mongrel dog by giving it CPR under a streetlight. He saved frightened black and brown children, coaxing them from hiding in the blackness under beds and inside dark closets to light — and life. He saved chain-smoking housewives; fat unemployed homosexuals; emaciated addicts with dirty needles stuck in their sore-pocked arms. He saved shaking elderly widows in cotton house dresses, their skin — thin like parchment — reflecting amber as their meager possessions burned to ash around them.

He saved everyone, I cried to Lauren, my spirit bleached of hope.

He saved everyone but me. I needed a protector, too. I screamed for his help but he never came. Why wasn't he my savior? When I needed rescue, he was no hero. He was a phantom. Invisible as a ghost.

Yes, he was.

He didn't try to write a new chapter until it was far too late.

Now cresting the apex of middle age, I had abruptly come face to face with this life-altering moment, compelled by my brother's unexpected phone call bearing the news of his death.

Should I continue to be consumed by a tortured past I cannot change?

Or, although I am no god but merely a fragile vessel forged from clay and fire, should I summon the simple courage to face my past demons, in whatever form they take, and seek the healing salve of forgiveness and grace?

I suddenly felt exhausted by the effort it took to hate my father.

With newfound resolve, I realized there was no actual decision to make.

The ship is about to set sail, I said, fully aware I was about to mix my metaphors.

Elvis is going to leave the building, I added with a wry smile.

I finally understood that I could not erase the past. To be truly free, I had to see my father's funeral as my last opportunity for a rebirth.

I looked toward Lauren and I very clearly remember my next words to her: This is my cathartic moment. My chance to heal what has been rotting my soul. I know what you are thinking, Lauren. The final accounting of my father's life should lead me to love and acceptance, and not to more bitterness and resentment.

Our eyes met and locked. I wondered whether Lauren could see clear inside me.

I know that I must find a path to forgiveness, I said with conviction. I must clear the wreckage and start anew, with my whole entire family.

I vowed to begin my quest with a newly open heart. I yearned for the seeds of redemption to break through the dry soil of the past and grow strong and tall — for all of us.

FIVE

'Tell me more about him.'

You're not getting off so easy. I want to hear more, Lauren challenged me.

My breathing had slowed and I calmed. My fury deflated. A pin stuck in a balloon. When a hush crowded the room, Lauren spoke to me from her heart. She coached me about the wonders of discovery and transformation, and the difficult terrain I must cover in order to find the inner peace that I proclaimed to desire.

I'm not going to judge you, Harry. I'm here to listen to you, Lauren said. Why don't you just start? Tell me more about your father. I don't care where you begin. Whatever comes to mind.

I stared into Lauren's eyes. The tiny blue dots of her iris's dazzled like a constellation of far-off stars.

Nothing's coming to mind. I'm a blank. Everything's just a big, jumbled mess right now, I responded.

Look, Lauren reassured me. Just start. You'll find the right words. Why don't you describe him to me? That's a safe place to begin. What did he look like? Do you have his features?

Just a little bit, was my truthful response.

Well, do you have a picture you can show me?

I crossed to my desk and rifled through old papers in a middle drawer. I pulled a white-bordered photo creased in one corner from a manilla folder that rested under some menus and long-expired supermarket coupons.

The photo pulled me into the past like a powerful undertow to stare into my father's eyes once more. Those eyes, black like onyx, sat inside hooded lids that appeared drawn from charcoal. His untamed eyebrows appeared in the photo like two furry animals peering from a dark hole. My eyes immediately tracked to father's most distinguishing facial feature — his grotesquely misshapen and scarred left nostril.

Lauren gently took the photo from me without a word and scanned it.

A muscular Nathan Loev, a man of about 50, sat confidently in a straight-back chair. The backdrop appeared to be the patio of a busy restaurant, perhaps at a beach resort on a warm island. A blurred hint of sand and aqua blue sea stretched out broadly in the background. My father wore his hair stylishly long and parted from the side. His skin had been browned by the sun. He looked relaxed, smiling for the photographer. In the picture, he exuded a dash of nobility.

Lauren tilted the photograph to the light.

I can see a resemblance. You look a lot like him, actually, she said.

The photo obscured most of my father's torso from view. In my memory, he had a chest like a whiskey barrel that tapered to a trim waist, with just the hint of middle-age well after he began collecting Social Security. His thick neck and bulky upper body, built through a life of manual labor, connected to spindly legs as if a manufacturing error had resulted in his top half being mistakenly fitted onto the wrong bottom half at the factory. He had olive skin, like a vintner from the mountains of Spain. And, despite a physique that, as a whole, resembled a squat fire hydrant, none of this drew any particular attention.

Look closely, I implored Lauren, drawing her eyes to my father's portrait and moving it nearer to the glow of the lamplight.

He had this deformity, this really bad scar, I pointed out for her benefit. You can see it in the picture. His nose is what a lot of people noticed about him first.

Lauren drew the photograph closer. She could see that the bridge and angle of my father's nose appeared normal. Almost distinguished. His left nostril, however, flared out drunkenly, twice as large as the right one, like an old, worn catcher's mitt.

Mostly, people were too polite to mention it. They thought maybe it was boxer's nose, but no … it wasn't that, I said. My father loved to tell the story of how it got that way. It was one of the only stories from his childhood that he readily shared. He was proud of it. He wore his scarred nose like a badge of honor.

I want to hear the whole thing. From the beginning, Lauren said.

■ ■ ■ ■ ■

In my father's regaling, a small jagged stone hurled by another boy in a wild street brawl took flight in exactly the right trajectory as if commanded by Mission Control. The rock defied all mathematical probability, swirling winds and angles of flight to score a direct hit — straight up my father's nose.

The other neighborhood boys squealed in laughter and back-slapped the rock-thrower on pinpoint accuracy that didn't seem humanly possible. As they cheered, my father gingerly poked the rock free. When he dislodged the stone, his nose bled even more profusely.

My father would tell listeners how he tried to pinch the two ragged and slick flaps of split nostril back together as he ran back home. In the waning days of the Great Depression, seeking medical attention would have meant a house call from the neighborhood doctor, who would leave yet another bill on a kitchen table already littered with unpaid bills. A visit to the Emergency Department at the nearby hospital would be even worse. Weighing her limited options, my grandmother did nothing but press an old, stained dishrag to little Nathan's nose until the boy stopped bleeding.

He needed stitches, of course. Maybe even some plastic surgery. But, back then, working people only went to the hospital for broken bones or life-threatening injuries — something pretty serious, I explained. Not for a busted-up nose.

As a cynical teenager already sowing resentment, I could not help but observe that with each retelling, my father's story seemed to grow more lush, like spring grass after a soaking rain.

The volume of spurting blood multiplied until my father seemed to measure it in pints. Soon enough, the stone began to fly with the velocity of a hardball thrown from centerfield by the rifle arm of Willie Mays, and from an exaggerated distance, too. One time, it took flight from 200 feet; the next time, from 250 feet. The boy who hurled the rock took on the persona of a trained Army marksman, his throwing arm more accurate than a sniper shot.

Did it happen as my father claimed it did? Hard to say, I told Lauren. Yet the scales tipped in favor of legitimacy.

The evidence was right there in front of us, I added.

On the face of an active boy, the gashed nostril tore and re-tore. Eventually, it scabbed over but my father's nostril never healed properly. His left nostril was marked by a large, purplish blob of thick, asymmetrical scar tissue for the rest of his life.

Think about it, my father would ask whoever happened to be listening. What are the odds?

He would then pause and cock his head slightly to put his nose on display. He would run a calloused finger up and down the bulbous scar, caressing it like a lucky talisman.

Really, honey, I underscored for Lauren. My father was right. What are the odds that a rock would go straight up his nose?

■ ■ ■ ■ ■

That enjoyable reminiscence brought unexpected relief. A stuck valve had suddenly opened with a squeak. A wellspring of fresh and new memories began to flow. My mood had lightened. Lauren sensed it, too.

Forget the negative stuff — the hurtful times, the times in which he failed you. Just for now, at least, she reminded me. It's going to do you good. Lauren counseled, For the moment, I want you to concentrate on the happier times — the pleasant memories that you want to carry forward to the future. I'm pretty sure that you have them. Everybody does.

It's true. More nice memories than I admit, I acknowledged. It wasn't all terrible. When I was little, I couldn't wait to spend time with him. I didn't see or feel my father's betrayals the way I did when I was older.

Indeed, in my boyhood I would rush home from grade school, sprinting on matchstick-skinny legs to catch my father before he left for his tour at the firehouse

For the next hour, I regaled Lauren with previously buried anecdotes from my youth.

I explained how I would sit with my father while he dressed in his firehouse blues, his silver lieutenant's bars pinned crookedly to his collar. I would excitedly share with him the latest news from school, or review with him an exciting play from the previous night's ballgame.

During Little League season, father would bang ground balls to me in the backyard, imploring me to Stay down! when a grounder caromed off a root and hit me square in the chest, drawing an oomph. Or, he would yell roughly Be tough now! when a bad hop caught me flush in mouth, drawing blood that tasted of iron.

As a boy, I craved my father's attention and he offered it liberally. He knew how to make me feel good on the inside. Of course, this was years before I began to stew in the acidic juices of resentment.

I found myself beginning to concur with Lauren's advice.

This is your chance to remember the good times before you say goodbye, she repeated to me. You should be embracing the special times you shared. I'm not saying you should totally repress those other memories, just that you should acknowledge the good as well.

Let's try it on for size; see how it fits.

■ ■ ■ ■ ■

Another memory surfaced. I was 10, maybe 11. When I shut my eyes, I could picture the two of us sitting together on the wooden deck overlooking our yard.

I recall that my father grew pensive. He hesitated, but appeared gripped by the desire to unburden a weight. When my father began to address me, his tone suggested that what he had to say was not ordinary.

The other night was really black. No moon. No stars. You couldn't see anything, he began.

I had been building a model car from a kit, fitting together and gluing in place pre-cut pieces of plastic. I immediately looked up, curious. My father had never spoken to me like that before.

We responded to an active fire in the projects. The first-due engine. I could see it was going to be bad. A big job, my father said. The sky was already orange. You could smell the smoke from blocks away.

Racing up the stairs, my father had burst inside an apartment seconds after a ladder man used a battering ram to break open the front door. My father quickly led a search of the upper floor rooms. His flashlight illuminated tables, couches and a television already partially melted from the heat. Adrenaline pumping, he and several other men from Engine 43 looked for survivors while pouring water on the blaze.

Search every closet, that's Rule No. 1, he told me that day.

Got it. Search the closets, I said.

My father's flashlight bathed a closet floor, where scared children had been known to hide in fear. Suddenly, my father told me, he heard a thump and sensed something big and heavy toppling towards him. He threw his arms up in defense.

A murder victim shot twice in the head at close range collapsed directly into my father's arms. The two embraced in an awkward slow dance before they both crashed to the ground. The dead man's body landed — limbs splayed out — directly on top of my father and promptly disgorged death's toxic gases.

The guy teetered for a second, then he fell like a tree, my father told me. In that split second, I could see him. Stiff like a monster. One eye was still open, staring. The other one was gone. Completely shot out.

My father actually shivered as he shared that grisly detail.

Whoa. That's awesome and pretty scary, Dad. Weren't you scared?

Yes, Harry, I admit it. I was scared. It shook me up something good.

The unfortunate victim, a small-time dealer, had been propped in the small closet long enough for rigor mortis to set in. The medical examiner would estimate the man had been dead six to eight hours, long enough for the killer to return, spray a few gallons of gasoline on the stairs, and set the whole building ablaze in an attempt to hide the evidence.

My father shared that his screams had alerted the other men. They helped him wriggle out from under the dead body.

Oh my God, Lauren exclaimed, eyes wide in surprise. Lauren was, after all, far more accustomed to shot-dead deer strapped into the beds of pickup trucks than shot-dead drug dealers stuffed into dark, hall closets.

True story, I nodded with vigor.

I can still remember looking at my father and, for the first time, realizing that he was, indeed, mortal. Even super-heroes got frightened sometimes, just like I did.

. . . . .

That memory receded, replaced by a new one stepping up to take its place. Feeling more confident, I inched my marker of trust forward one more space in Lauren's direction.

There's another vivid memory from my childhood. I guess it reveals more about me than about my father. It's something I've never shared with anyone before now. Nobody knows about this, I told Lauren. If I tell you, promise me that you'll never repeat it, for as long as you live.

I instantly felt ashamed. Who would care about something I did nearly 30 years ago?

I'm still learning to trust. To communicate openly. Maybe I can be excused.

I won't tell a soul. I promise. I'll take it to my grave, Lauren vowed, her voice tinged with a sincerity that I found adorable.

Of course, she wouldn't tell anyone.

■ ■ ■ ■ ■

If my father's day off fell on a Friday, he would make a special trip to the South Bronx — and Engine 43 — to collect his city paycheck and see the guys.

I was on the cusp of 12 when he invited me to join him.

Left alone while my father visited with his men over coffee, I would climb the giant chrome steps to the cab of the fire engine, inhaling the intoxicating aroma of charred wood, burnt rubber and smoke. I would imagine myself hammering on the horn of Engine 43, foot pumping the siren, as we raced to a three-alarm blaze or, even better, an all-hands that summoned every available piece of apparatus in the borough.

Next, I would wriggle myself into my father's black rubber turnout coat, struggling not to stumble under its weight. I would clap his fire-scarred helmet, its plexiglass eye shield scratched and opaque, on my head so that I could pretend to be a swaggering action figure, just like him.

I didn't care if anybody saw me. When I visualized myself on the powerful nozzle, imitating my father advancing to knock down walls of smoke and flame, nothing in my little world could top it.

These father-son trips, a highlight of my summer vacation from school, came with one hard-and-fast rule — a strict prohibition my father had set down from the beginning.

Stay out of the basement, son. You don't go down there, no matter what, my father had said firmly. It's off limits. Are you listening? Firemen only. Got it, champ?

I'll stay right here. I promise.

As the summer advanced toward Labor Day, I grew bored playing on the rig. I was done trying on gear stinking of sweat. I felt silly pretending to be a fireman. After all, how many times could I imagine that I was hanging on to Engine 43's back step, free as the wind, in an urgent race to an out-of-control blaze?

Still, I conscientiously obeyed father's stern warning to stay away from the basement until, one day, my father's admonition collided with my own sense of curiosity and adventure.

I convinced myself that, just once, I could sneak down the stairs to the firehouse basement.

Just to check it out. No one would ever find out, I told Lauren.

The stairway was dark. I was too afraid to switch on a light. By squinting, I could see just enough into the abyss. Creeping slowly down, imagining monsters rousing in the rattling pipes overhead, I could make the outline of a large room in the distance — a clubhouse of sorts, lit hazily by late afternoon sunlight filtering in from a grimy sidewalk-level window.

In the dim light, I could make out a round formica table in the center of the room. Gray metal chairs had been strewn about, as if a life-or-death call had interrupted something. Above the table flew a rusted and presumably disarmed World War II-era bomb, one fin broken off. A dart board had been nailed to a wall, with a pitted picture of Mayor David Dinkins — the city's first black mayor — centered at the bulls-eye. A bulletin board of union news and thank you notes scribbled by the burned-out but alive hung nearby. A recycled plaid sofa, its sweat-stained cushions disgorging disintegrating foam the color of vomit, had been pushed haphazardly into a corner. It held a collapsing pile of old magazines and yellowing newspapers.

Next to an old white refrigerator on a far wall, the men of Engine 43 had neatly thumb-tacked a row of *Playboy* and *Penthouse* centerfolds.

I moved quickly, as if in a dream, over to the provocative collection of pin-ups. The arousing kitty of full breasts and triangles of dark pubic hair — pink nipples, too — seduced me, drawing me to the grimy cinder-block wall like it possessed special pheromones. Any trepidation I had felt about my presence in the forbidden basement vanished, as the wondrous mysteries of womanhood spread-eagled before me and my novice private parts tingled.

Miss February! Miss April! Oh, and I will never forget *you* Miss September, clearly a natural blonde!

I remained captivated, nearly breathless, for what seemed like an eternity as I weighed a great moral choice:

Should I take the Playmates home?

But, how could I take just one?

The centerfolds were all, well, *unique*. Each stapled, two-page spread represented a magnificent specimen of female.

It was impossible to choose. I had instantly fallen in love with them all — a sumptuous banquet of flowing hair, luminous eyes and soft curves.

My mind whirred. The flow of blood re-directed from my brain to other body parts. I retained just enough sense for a new revelation: It would be impossible to spirit the centerfolds past my father to my secret hiding place behind the rubber snow boots in my bedroom closet.

Certainly, the beautiful and alluring Miss September would be instantly missed.

I would have to commit the explicit details of my new playmates to memory. I could not wait to share what

I gleaned from this wonderful adventure with all my friends back home.

Ah, I regaled Lauren, I couldn't wait to tell Ferman — or Fudd, as we called him — who was only interested in playing one-on-one basketball in his driveway, and Bradley Allen, a friend who dreamed of one day pitching for the Yankees.

This was way, way better, I planned to tell them.

I explained to Lauren that I knew deep down that, if discovered, I would pay dearly for violating my word to my father. My stomach felt queasy and I tasted bile. The first seeds of guilt had already taken root.

You couldn't take them. Everyone would know who did it. You had to leave them right there on the wall, Lauren correctly surmised.

She erupted in a high-pitched squeal. Look at you, she exclaimed. All these years later and you're still embarrassed. Harry, you're turning bright red.

Don't laugh, I said, laughing myself. It was very traumatic. And I remember suddenly feeling hot and very thirsty.

Indeed, my throat felt as dry and scratchy as sandpaper. My first, vivid lesson in female anatomy had momentarily suspended my ability to swallow.

Fortunately, a Coca Cola vending machine on a far wall beckoned to me: Come hither.

The low whirring of the machine's refrigeration unit promised to quench my physical, if not my carnal, desires. I drew a sticky quarter from my pocket. Allowance money. I firmly inserted the silver coin into the slot, feeling braver and more in control. Next, I quietly pushed the big square button identifying Coke as my choice of soft drink.

The big red vending machine rumbled to life. I heard it convey the 12-ounce aluminum can upwards, before an unseen lever clicked and prodded the can to roll noisily down a long chute to the plastic door at the bottom.

I pushed back the swinging plastic mouth, reached inside and grabbed the soda can solidly, hoping that no one upstairs had heard an unusual bang.

The aluminum can felt sweaty and icy cold. As I drew the can upwards and prepared to pull the tab, a flash of color arrested me.

The can was not red, and its scripted label did not read *Coca-Cola*.

The graphics on the red, white and blue can blared something else.

Budweiser.

The fancy writing below confirmed its contents: *King of Beers.*

I felt dizzy and sick, I admitted to Lauren. I knew I was in big, big trouble.

The men of Engine 43 had rigged the machine in their off-limits clubhouse to vend cans of beer. I understand today, as an adult, that the firefighters may have needed an occasional cold beer to quench their thirsts and augment their courage. They had trained for heavy smoke, back-drafts and flash-overs, not for metal trash cans hurled from parapets by Black Panthers, or plastic bags full of gasoline hung from ceiling fixtures and ignited by arsonists. They hadn't signed on to dodge sniper fire, treat overdoses or to fend off the menacing gangs who encircled their engine company like Apaches around a wagon train.

Let me get this straight. You're not even 12 years old and you just came upon a wall of naked women. You've got this can of beer in your hand and you don't know what to do … Lauren coached me to continue.

You got it, I said. I knew I couldn't drink the beer. I had to find a hiding spot. Quickly. Before anyone found out.

I scouted around the basement. My actions manifested a lingering guilt that, one day, I would pay for violating my sworn oath to my father.

I stuffed the beer can under the cushion of a Lazy Boy chair and ran like hell, I said.

The smiling centerfolds enjoyed my fright. Their comely eyes followed me as I scrambled back up the stairs.

■ ■ ■ ■ ■

I avoided the firehouse for the rest of the summer. In fact, I did not visit Engine 43 again until the annual firehouse Christmas party — months after I befriended the Playmates and they, in turn, had altered my life.

On a sun-splashed Saturday in mid-December, Engine 43 sat gleaming on the concrete apron just outside the big red doors. The ladder truck remained inside, its aerial and bucket at rest along with its heavy axes, roof saws and grappling hooks that hung like medieval armaments.

Folding tables laden with catered meats and home-cooked side dishes lined a far wall, where the men usually stored their gear. Off-duty firefighters and officers stood in genial clumps, talking freely about football, politics and the latest Big Job. They all kept a close eye on Maurizio, the fireman on watch listening to Sinatra on a small transistor radio. Maurizio had been designated by the chief to man the teletype. He would listen for the coded sequence of bells that would interrupt the party and trigger Engine 43 to leap like a mechanized army division into action.

In small, scattered-about groups, dark-haired, fur-wrapped Italian wives mixed easily with fair-skinned Irish-Catholics. The women ate daintily off red and green plastic plates and traded small talk about which Long Island towns had the best schools, which enclaves offered the best real estate values, and which had the lowest property taxes and easier commutes.

Dozens of kids scurried about like sugar-fueled ants invading a backyard picnic. Excited shrieks and screams echoed around the firehouse's cavernous interior, especially when one delinquent boy tied a pre-teen redhead to a Stokes basket with a coil of rope.

Jonathan, Helen and I quickly overcame our self-consciousness to gambol with the other children on top of the ladder truck like she was a jungle gym.

I can still remember the older kids debating with great excitement what early present Santa Claus would bring them that day, I told Lauren, who listened eagerly.

Today? Santa Claus?

Even though Christmas — and my own 13th birthday — neared, I had not entertained the possibility of holiday gifts at the firehouse party. I had believed the day's highlight would be the long dessert table and ice cream sundaes. Besides, I had been too busy remembering to be polite — to say please and thank you; use a fork and knife, and wash up after using the restroom — to notice the pile of wrapped toys stacked near the coatroom. I creased my forehead in thought.

What about those Jewish kids like me who knew little of creches, mangers and the Holy Trinity? Would Santa remember to bring kids like me a gift? Would Santa even know that I'm Jewish?

Before long, the adults shushed the children. Elbowing and pushing, we were corralled into a disorganized semi-circle around the brass fire pole, which rose 25 feet to the second floor before it disappeared into a circular hole in the ceiling.

A booming Ho, Ho, Ho signaled the arrival of Santa Claus. The Bronx-accented voice carried down from high above and echoed around the firehouse floor, arousing an even higher level of pandemonium.

I looked up, craning my neck, to see a fully decked out Santa — a caricature in his red suit, long white beard and rimless spectacles — sliding slowly and one-handed down the brass pole. Both of Santa's legs locked the pole in a death grip while he carefully balanced a bulging white sack of toys over his shoulder.

Ho. Ho. Ho. Merry Christmas, Santa thundered once again to boisterous cheers, as he awkwardly adjusted the throw pillow tucked into the front of his Santa suit as padding. The most admiring applause came from the appreciative firefighters of Engine 43, earnestly saluting Santa for not losing his grip, tumbling from the pole and permanently crippling himself in front of their children.

Someone pulled over a beaten-down Lazy Boy chair that looked as if it had been salvaged, soaking wet, from a bad fire but actually had been dragged upstairs, shedding pieces of yellow foam, from the firehouse basement.

I froze. I was so scared, I told Lauren, who looked at me perplexed.

Don't you remember? That's where I hid my beer, I reminded her. I was terrified someone would find the can stuffed in the cushions.

No way. Couldn't be. Right? Lauren said.

Santa gently lowered himself onto the battered old recliner. A tall, lean fireman with a buzz cut of silver hair organized the children into the semblance of a neat line. He began reading from a list, calling over the Catherine's, Nicky's, Joey's and Anthony's to receive their Christmas presents wrapped in bright, shiny paper.

In minutes, torn sheets of green and red paper flew everywhere. Bows went airborne as if fired from catapults. Excited children tore open boxes of Barbie dolls, electric train sets and yellow Tonka trucks. Less excited children froze with disappointed expressions at games of Chinese Checkers, Battleship, Monopoly and the dreaded Chutes and Ladders. Santa's generous giving and his Ho-Ho-Ho's continued for a long time until the mess of discarded wrapping paper and torn open boxes piled high on the floor. Meanwhile, the line of children waiting before Santa had dwindled to just Jonathan, Helen and I.

Let's see here, what do I have left? Santa said, adding an extra, unnecessary, Ho, Ho, Ho for effect.

Come here, young man, I hear that you've been a good boy, Santa said, gesturing toward me. Let's see what I have for you.

I stepped forward. Santa pulled from his nearly empty cloth sack a neatly wrapped gift. From its weight and shape, I guessed it to be a football — the holiday present that I wished for most of all.

Feeling a little unsure about what to do next, I offered Santa Claus an earnest and heart-felt thank you. To show that I really meant it, I leaned forward to clutch Santa in a little hug of gracious appreciation for being so damn interdenominational.

As my face moved closer to Santa's cheek, the lighting changed and I could see, for the first time, behind the full white beard and mustache glued tightly to Santa's olive skin.

Only then, did I realize that my father had been playing Santa Claus.

His deformed left nostril gave him away.

SIX

'There is no easy way from the earth to the stars.'
— Seneca the Younger

When did my journey to a healthier emotional state begin? I can trace those first, embryonic steps back 20 years when I escaped home to attend Plattsburgh State, one of the few four-year colleges that accepted me — and my C+ average — out of high school.

My years of study offered me a broader view of the world and space to think and breathe. My days at Plattsburgh could be divided simply: Molson's and Coors kept me company in the back rooms of college bars, where I played pool and socialized several nights a week. Homer, Sophocles, Virgil and Plato, among other classical thinkers, dominated my hours spent in class or studying in the school's gothic library. Back then, I wanted so badly to succeed — at something, anything, anything at all — that I did not go anywhere without at least one hefty volume of classical literature as I moved among classmates studying less demanding disciplines.

The volumes of Greek and Roman literature that I devoured like junk food provided me with meaningful insight, deeply reasoned wisdom that hurtled through the centuries to offer new perspectives on life which, from the crouch of my youth, I had never before considered. The great thinkers guided me to a better understanding of my own tortured existence and offered a welcome distraction, too. After all, the classic works contain more politics, violence and sex than the pulpy pages of a New York tabloid or my own Netflix account. The poetry and philosophy I also studied provided me comfort, too. It reminded me that I was not the first or only man to face the arduous tests of life.

In my junior year, I remember writing a lengthy term paper on Virgil's *The Aeneid*. It explored in detail the legendary tale of Aeneas and his wanderings from Troy to ancient Rome. The 12-page paper earned an A+ from the pleasantly surprised professor, a feckless transplant from Southern California who vaguely smelled of stale pot and spoke with an effeminate lisp.

To this day, I can recall Aeneas' parting words to his son Ascanius as he prepared for battle: 'Learn courage from me and true toil; from others the meaning of fortune.'

In late nights and weekends at the campus library, I quickly discovered the meaning of toil. Alas, I never discovered the meaning of fortune. Nor did I learn courage, to be truthful.

These days, my degree and its imprimatur of higher intellect is useful only when the stars align perfectly.

For example, one summer night in North Creek about two years before I met Lauren, I sat in a tavern on

Main Street watching *Jeopardy*. I brightened when Alex Trebek revealed the game board and the categories for Double Jeopardy. As I ate a late dinner, Christian from Nashville selected *Classic Quotables* for $800, stabbed quickly at his game button, then stared blankly as the timer ticked down.

ANSWER:

This epic poem written around
1300 begins with the line:

'Midway upon the journey of our life,
I found myself within a forest dark.'

I slapped the bar with my hand. The sound of flesh smacking wood drew the attention of a three-man DPW crew in lime green t-shirts enjoying a large basket of chicken wings and some cold Saranac drafts after a hot day cleaning up roadkill.

Before Ken, a drowsy-looking urologist from Kentucky, or Eliza, an overweight and bespectacled substitute teacher from Maine, could squeeze their own trigger buttons and answer what Christian could not, I shouted at the television. In the form of a question, of course.

What is Dante's Divine Comedy, Alex?

Look at you, the foreman called out from across the bar. He tipped his half-empty bottle in salute.

My knowledge of classical literature may have impressed a few locals, but nearly everyone else in my world couldn't have squeezed out a narrow, squiggly crap. My own co-workers included. In winter, our crew was too busy with the alchemy of making fresh snow from air and water. My summer team had to contend with toddler-princes smearing chocolate on the seats while commanding the engineer to blow the train whistle until our brains concussed.

I'm a big enough man now to admit the truth. Like most people, my college studies are largely inapplicable to my daily life. Two decades after my formal undergraduate days concluded, my work ethic remains strong. My recollection of what I learned, however, has dimmed to near nothing. Thankfully, I can still pull to the forefront a few passages — wisdom that, even in this writing two decades later, hold visceral meaning for me.

For example: Virgil wrote in Book Six of the Aenid, 'The descent into hell is easy. Night and day, the gates of dark Death stand wide; but to climb back again; to retrace one's steps to the upper air — that's the task.'

Twenty years ago, I re-typed that particular line about perseverance and persistence and affixed it to the door of my bedroom closet above the bent nail where I hang my belts. That verse is engrained in my memory. Still, I frequently read it over and over. It is a talisman of sorts — an inspiration for my hope-starved soul. Especially after all that I have been through.

My therapist Ellen once called this touchstone of mine a prompt. She affirmed my use of this therapeutic device as I worked on my mental health because she understood it is a daily reminder that I have crawled from the abyss, rising like a phoenix from the ashes.

Don't you ever lose sight of that, she once told me. You are a survivor. You've been to hell and back.

Ellen knew that reciting Virgil's verse aloud as I buttoned my shirt each morning transported me back to a place I never again wished to go — a moonless Saturday night in late February of my sophomore year in college when I hit rock bottom.

It was 1992, during the nascent days of the Clinton presidency. Every corner bar seemed to feature Whitney Houston on the juke box and *I Will Always Love You* topped the Billboard charts. My first serious romantic relationship had just exploded. Tears and word-missiles, designed to inflict maximum pain, marked my break-up with Tammy, a junior from the nearby Akwasasne reservation with long, straight black hair and legs so skinny, she resembled a heron from afar.

Today, I can acknowledge that Tammy and I were both too young for a serious, mature relationship. Hell, we were flat broke and stoned on cheap weed for most of the three months or so that we clung to each other like wet sheets. I had no business proposing to her in slurred speech after a night of heavy drinking and she didn't possess the good judgement to say, Slow down hon.

Thus, it was fool-hearty for us to arrive at the County Clerk's office at 9 a.m. one morning still buzzed from a late-night party to fill out a marriage license.

Kevin, an older pal and my regular bartender, and his girlfriend, Barbara, tagged along to serve as official witnesses. Barbara, a sensible woman, tried earnestly to deter us, firmly grabbing Tammy around her slim waist at one point and steering her into the restroom for a stern woman-to-woman talk.

At least you should tell your families, said Barbara, who opposed elopement on principle.

Kevin, just back from a stint in the Peace Corps and a generous pourer of Irish whiskey, had egged us on. In retrospect, his encouragement more suggested a paparazzi at a particularly nasty motor vehicle accident than the selfless dedication of a true friend. Kevin favored marriage, even at our very young age, and pontificated that a morning ceremony before a judge would be the most honorable and appropriate next step in our tumultuous relationship.

Considering how much time you spend screwing, you should at least make an honest woman of her, Kevin said.

While we waited outside the courtroom fighting off hangovers, our rag-tag wedding party focused more on the judge's ill-fitting robe, which barely covered his dungarees and sandals, than any solemn vows we planned to take. I remember Tammy and I both giggling with the giddiness of two kids giving the middle finger to our parents — all the way to the last moment when Barbara put her foot down.

You guys are kidding yourselves, she said. You're like little school kids playing at adults. You're not ready for this. You'll either kill each other or get yourself thrown in jail. 'Till death do you part?' — Ha! You won't last until next Tuesday.

Tammy was just sober enough — and mature enough — to listen.

Harry, you know, maybe it's better if we think on it and come back another time, Tammy said as she backed away from the judge, me and commitment.

We agreed to call it off — before we could be pronounced man and wife. We proved Barbara right, of course. Our relationship lasted about one month more, most of it spent drinking and arguing, before it crumpled and burned like birch bark dropped into a flame.

Tammy's last words to me, fittingly, evoked Whitney's lyrics while making a mockery of the title. This is goodbye, she said into the phone. Harry, I don't want to you to cry. But face it baby. You need help. We both know that I'm not what you need.

The break-up just accelerated my mental crash.

I had felt doomed and trapped during my five weeks at home over the holiday break. The weak light of winter failed to illuminate anyone to my feelings of darkness. No one knew I was unhappy and depressed; that I struggled to make friends and, despite a brave face and hours studying, I staggered under my college workload. The pressure to earn good grades — to justify my parents' investment in tuition — felt suffocating. All I saw in front of me was a sad, hopeless road with no end. I wanted to disappear forever. To cease to exist.

One night, staggering drunk on cheap beer and tequila shots, I surrendered to my torturing demons and formulated a plan for suicide. In taking my own life, I wished to end my pain and spread guilt from the afterlife to everyone around me, especially to my family.

Was I crazy? Well, I wasn't slapping-imaginary-bugs-off-my-shirtsleeves-crazy, but I am sure now, from the safety of therapy and a loving relationship with Lauren, that I suffered from a serious depression when I planned to rush from the trees by an underpass and throw myself into the path of a rumbling freight train. (I had initially planned to self-immolate myself like the Buddhist monk protesting the war in Vietnam, but could not summon the courage.) I was convinced that no one then present in my miserable life would even care or miss me.

I had been taking a final, steaming piss in the woods near downtown when I heard a deep rumble approaching. The railroad gates lowered and warning bells stopped traffic on busy Tremont Street. I never had a chance to see the engineer's face twist into a scream as I threw myself onto the tracks. Thankfully, by the time I pulled up my fly and stumbled slipping and sliding through the deep snowdrifts, the graffiti-scarred box cars and gas-filled tankers were already speeding by in a blur.

Instead of dying, slicking the virgin snow bright red with my insides, I sat on a boulder heaving and crying as the flashing lights of the caboose faded to a pinprick.

In the morning, I checked myself into the college infirmary. An ambulance transported me to a psychiatric hospital where I met with doctors and social workers. I was finally ready to summon the courage to live.

Two decades years later, my life's trajectory continues rising upwards. As Virgil so wisely noted, the challenge of climbing back and retracing my steps up from hell and the forlorn is still a mighty struggle. However, with Ellen and Lauren as my cheering section, I persist, gaining strength every day.

I know who I am, but not yet who I may be.

Thus, I also draw inspiration from another classical source: Roman philosopher Seneca the Younger, who wrote:

Non est as astra millis e terris via.

There is no easy way from the earth to the stars.

To expropriate Virgil's response to that: Upper air awaits.

I must believe that.

SEVEN

'Love conquers all; let us, too, yield to love.'
— VIRGIL

Early evening.
MONDAY, JULY 17, 2013
West Palm Beach, Fla.

Lauren and I unpacked our suitcases. We rested a bit before heading to dinner at an Italian restaurant lit by neon in a strip mall across the parking lot.

That night, the setting sun appeared on the horizon as a hazy orange, like it wished to be brighter and more dazzling but, like us, it was tired from a stressful day of travel and had run out of steam.

Seated at a corner table, I confided anew in Lauren. My fears and anxiety about what awaited me at my father's funeral the next day had not eased, even though I had bared the first layer of my many secrets. Painful yesterdays and an uncertain tomorrow continued to plague me.

Seeing my family face to face after all this time is going to be like cancer treatment, I said to Lauren.

Cancer? Who has cancer? Lauren's tone suggested that she had misheard me.

I cast a sheepish look and swirled some water around in my glass.

I'm sorry, honey, but I have no idea what you're talking about, Lauren said. What cancer? You totally lost me.

I nodded in understanding and sought a new way to explain myself.

Lauren, I want to just come out and admit it. I'm terrified about tomorrow. And just like with cancer, the only certainty is, there's so much uncertainty at how it will turn out.

Indeed, my decision to travel to Florida to pay final respects to my father and to seek closure — and to honor his complicated life and resolve our tangled relationship — added up to just half my worries. What I also feared but had not yet confessed to Lauren was that my attempt at reconciling with my family would explode in my face.

I asked plaintively, Am I ready for this? Is this really a good idea?

The waitress arrived to clear our salad plates and returned to the kitchen to bring out our dinners.

If you didn't come down here, you would always regret it, Lauren answered with reassurance.

Lauren knew what she wanted to say but still spoke haltingly.

Sometimes parents commit acts that appear to be unforgivable but they are not, she said. I believe there is always room for forgiveness. You would always be sorry if you didn't seek closure. If you didn't attend your own father's funeral and at least try to make amends. To try to find forgiveness inside you. I'm pretty certain about that.

No matter how it turns out, you're doing the right thing, Lauren assured me, her hands in a pile in her lap. He is still your father. Still your flesh and blood. It's important for you to be here. For you, above all. Because of all that happened in the past.

(You know what they say, Harry? There's always opportunity in a crisis, Ellen had similarly coached me when I phoned her at her home — my one permitted emergency dial per our agreement. Ellen had added, You are ready to face this. You are strong enough. Go to the funeral. We'll talk about it at your next appointment.)

Without warning, Lauren reached into her purse. She placed a small box wrapped in blue paper on the restaurant table. She reached out tenderly and took my hand into hers.

It's a gift for you, Harry, she said when I looked at her quizzically. I think you're really going to like it.

That's totally unnecessary. You shouldn't have, I said as I slipped my fingernail into a seam and carefully began to open the box.

Inside, I found a silver bracelet adorned with three beautiful garnets. I lifted the piece of jewelry from its case, beaming as I secured it around my wrist and showed it off to Lauren. It fit perfectly.

Lauren had purchased the bracelet back home weeks before and slipped it into her carry-on before we left. She presented it to me that evening in Florida for everything it represented in our relationship.

Lauren told me that garnets — like those quarried at the Barton Company mine near North Creek — symbolized strength and protection. According to legend, King Solomon wore stones of garnet into battle to fend off danger. Saxon and Celtic kings, she said, wore garnets in their belief that the semi-precious gems would protect them from harm.

The bracelet, Lauren insinuated, would be my secret protective armor — a silver shield with three red stones to help fend off whatever I might confront the next day.

I don't know what to say. I love it. I love you, I sputtered.

Garnets also hold a more contemporary meaning, Lauren explained, not yet finished.

Garnets speak to our relationship, Harry. You probably don't know this, but garnets are also considered a symbol of love. For generations, the deep red of the garnet has been associated with the heart. The red in the stone represents blood and inner fire.

I had no idea, I stammered.

Harry, darling, I want you to think of me — and of us — and our commitment to protect each other and love each other whenever you wear it.

I leaned across the table to again take Lauren's hand into mine. In an even voice which reached my ears in a confiding timbre, Lauren began to speak anew and I immediately understood that she wished to tell me a story.

A man is lost on a mountainside enveloped in fog, she began her allegory.

The man wanders in every direction, around downed trees and brush, searching for the trail but he can't find the little round markers and becomes even more lost. He has no cell service. No way to call for help. He begins to lose all hope. As time passes and dusk approaches, the man grows more anxious and fearful. The sun sinks below the horizon; it becomes dark and bitter cold, and he becomes increasingly desperate. Just as this man is surrendering all hope, he stumbles upon a woman walking alone in the same dark woods.

Hey there! Hello! the man cries out, shouting to get the woman's attention. I am lost, cold and very scared. Can you point me to the right trail, the one that will lead me out of the forest to safety?

Lauren paused for effect.

I am sorry but I cannot, the woman answers. I am lost, cold and very scared myself. I don't know the way to safety either.

Lauren's sparkling blue eyes drilled straight into mine. Her red hair glistened in the glow from a candle. Her hands felt warm and soft in mine and she vaguely smelled of lavender.

Harry, you have wandered lost in one part of the woods your whole life, Lauren said. I have been lost for a long time in another. You and I may not individually know the way out of the forest, but we know all about the trails that lead to nowhere.

Let us share with each other what we have learned of the failed paths. Together, maybe we can find the one trail that leads both of us to safety.

I held my breath and I looked at Lauren. The strength of our two hearts beating as one required that nothing more be said. My face froze in awe, as I were a ship captain discovering a new, verdant land after months at sea. I turned my head toward the restaurant wall because I felt my eyes beginning to water.

I shot Lauren a half-smile, hoping my diversionary move would turn back the tears of love that had welled inside me.

Damn, I love you, I whispered because I no clue what else to say. Do you have any idea what the hell you are doing?

Omnia vincit Amor; et nos cedamus Amori.

Also from my beloved Virgil:

Love conquers all; let us, too, yield to love.

EIGHT

'I will never again experience pure love.'

Back at the hotel
LATER MONDAY, JULY 17, 2013
West Palm Beach, Fla.

In a state of perfect happiness and deeper in love than ever before, we completely lost track of time. The restaurant's other patrons paid their checks and rushed off. Only Lauren and I remained in the dining room, lingering, as the waitstaff cleaned up around us.

As I basked in the glow of Lauren's tale and her unmistakable commitment to our future together, Lauren's eyebrows gathered and her expression turned serious. Our eyes met again across the table and I sensed that our consequential evening had a little more left in it.

Something wrong? I asked Lauren. You look like you want to say something.

No, nothing's wrong, she said. It's just that …

There was more about finding the trail that led out of the woods.

Lauren folded her hands and she began to speak to me of her own fragile heart and a past and present inextricably linked.

Harry, I want you to know that I've given up on ever again finding pure love. I say, 'pure love' and not a cliché like 'true love' because the two are not the same in my mind.

I am pretty certain that true love is possible, she elaborated. Hey, you're sitting here right in front of me as proof. Still, I want you to know that until my last breath, hopefully as a very old woman, I will never again experience love in its absolute, purist form.

The distinction puzzled me. Lauren read it on my face. Next, she opened up to me like a delicate flower safe under a shelter of peace.

First, Lauren stated that for the longest time she had not pursued love of any kind. She had grown accustomed to being alone. Unattached. Lauren's Facebook profile defiantly declared that she remained single and the label fit comfortably, like flannel pajamas perfect for sleeping or hiking boots broken in just right.

Lauren looked down at her spoon, which reflected back a kind of melancholy.

All my adult life, the 15 years or so until now, I've just been unlucky in love, I guess, she said finally.

Lauren shrugged, her slender shoulders rising slightly. Lauren confided that she had suffered her share of bad dates and forgettable boyfriends — as well as promising leads that dead-ended at nowhere — as she pursued a lasting, true love and, perhaps, one day, a happy marriage with a life partner.

Once, Lauren briefly dated a repair tech for Frontier Communications, the hopelessly unreliable local internet provider. The tech made multiple visits to her home to troubleshoot an outage, each time spending longer and longer until he finally summoned the courage to ask her out. The repair tech invited her to dinner on the patio of a fancy restaurant in Bolton Landing. Below them, the dark waters of Lake George sparkled in the moonlight. On that beautiful Friday evening, Lauren had allowed herself to glimpse herself celebrating future anniversaries and doting on her grandchildren at that very spot.

When the waitress delivered the main course, however, Lauren's date reached into his mouth with two meaty fingers and pulled out his dentures. He rested them on his bread plate next to a pat of butter without a hint of embarrassment.

They're new. My gums are sore. They really hurt and they're bleeding a little, he complained, before he gummed his way through the rest of the meal.

As that bit of news would make me dizzy with lust, Lauren said sarcastically. I realized the Frontier guy wasn't what I wanted and never saw him again.

Next, Lauren shared with me a little about Andy, a once-serious boyfriend, who had thrilled at making love in between the headstones in the small overgrown cemetery on Route 28 by the traffic light in Wevertown. Afterwards, they would dress, cuddle and listen to the occasional car snake its way down the hill on the way to Warrensburg.

Andy is a good man. I really liked him. We might have had a future together, she confessed, leaning in to whisper. But his kinks petrified me. They iced my own desires. I didn't enjoy being with him in that way. I feared that his cries of passion would wake the dead.

I laughed with her at that until I choked. A young salesman nursing a beer and studying his phone like a Holy Bible turned sideways to stare. When I could breathe again, Lauren giggled, a joyful sound emerging from deep.

Of course, I will never forget this one guy, Lauren said. He was an assistant manager at the bank a few towns over. A friend gave him my number and suggested he take me out — a real blind date. I agreed to go out with him because, well, what the heck?

Lauren recalled, This clown knocked on my door 45 minutes late. He was really buzzed, like he had been drinking a lot. He inspected me head to toe. Looked me up and down like I was a cut of meat. Then, he had the nerve to announce, 'I drove a long way to get out here. Before I lay out a lot of money on dinner, I have a question: Are you going to fuck me tonight?'

Holy shit. What a jerk, I said.

I cussed him and slammed the door on him, Lauren said strongly, sharing how the echo shimmered through the dark woods and the door frame rattled like an earthquake.

I screamed a few more choice words at the asshole as he drove away, she recounted.

Lauren clearly found amusement in sharing her dating misadventures.

I can laugh. I have to laugh, she said. It beats the alternative — being all pissed off at every man in the world. Bad dates and failed relationships are all part of the sorting out process, just like with you and your old girlfriend Tammy.

While she sometimes ached for the soft embrace of a fiancé or husband, or even the attentive touches of a serious boyfriend, Lauren said she always knew she would find a strong and handsome man who would spoon her for warmth on biting Adirondack mornings. Lauren wanted to feel wrapped in safety, a man's body pressed against hers while the winds howled and the balsams and tall pines bent and swayed like dancers.

I was always optimistic that one day I would find the right man — the perfect man for me, Lauren explained. Besides, I figured that if the right guy didn't turn up, it was okay. I was doing just fine without one. I liked being single.

At the restaurant where Lauren worked back home, a younger waitress, curious about why Lauren had remained unattached despite being graced with exceptional looks, had once asked her, Aren't you lonely?

Lauren explained that she had paused to think about the waitress' question. She sighed deeply as she considered it anew.

Harry, I realized that, yes, I was single and, yes, I was often alone, but I was never lonely, she said.

Lauren considered being single like an unexpected gift to be discovered on her doorstep each morning. It offered her boundless freedom to enjoy her life; to do whatever she wished, even as she deep down yearned for a committed life partner.

In summer, this freedom meant Lauren could tend her garden with just soft music as company, pulling weeds and adjusting the fencing around the snap peas, tomatoes, cucumbers and melons which, despite the rocky soil, grew as large as teething babies. In the cool of the evening, she could linger outdoors gazing at the setting sun painting the mountains during the violet hour or decide to camp under a dense spray of stars, watching the night sky later turn the deepest shade of blue.

On Saturday nights in summer, Lauren loved to dance, her body moving like poetry, to the local bands playing the Ski Bowl at the base of the mountain.

Lauren loved autumn, too, when golden foliage lit up the mountains in fiery bursts of yellow and red and she could hike in the cool of the afternoon, drinking in the intoxicating smell of crunching leaves underfoot.

In the winter, Lauren sometimes wandered aimlessly under boughs shouldering freshly fallen snow. And no one judged if she, instead, chose to hibernate under a wool afghan, listening to the groaning of the same trees in the wind while she found escape in a glass of wine and a riveting novel.

So, you see Harry, there is a distinct difference between being alone and suffering from loneliness. Loneliness is a wanting. An ever-present aching in your chest that suffocates you. Loneliness chooses you more than you choose it. Once it grips you in its claws, it's difficult to escape. And that's what I told the other waitress the next shift that we worked together.

Lauren blushed lightly.

Right about then, you had the nerve to show up in my life. After our little breakfast at Rachel's on the day after Christmas — if you can believe that — I said to myself, I'm happy. I'm free. Is he worth it? Should I risk it? Is Harry worth giving up my freedom? My total independence?

I smiled in return and caressed the new garnet bracelet on my wrist. I also recall being unsure where Lauren's monologue was heading.

Lauren observed, No one had ever before aroused feelings in me like you did.

You know, Harry, I didn't see you coming, Lauren added, now with smiling eyes. I was enjoying being alone. I was at peace. Then you rolled into my life and swept me right off my feet.

Lauren confided that my arrival in her life hit like an unexpected gust across the brow of a mountain or a powerful ocean swell built on the winds. I had seduced her with new possibilities just as she had begun to grow tired of her wonderful solitude and again welcomed such a thing as a serious relationship.

In the ensuing minutes, Lauren flattered me with compliments. I truly wished it would never end.

Lauren professed that she respected my perseverance and work ethic, and the way I can be ruggedly strong and softly romantic — sometimes both at once. She knew that I struggled financially, sometimes getting by paycheck to paycheck. Yet, Lauren told me that she respected the resolute way I approached my financial challenges, while —

her words, not mine — being preternaturally gifted with a generosity of spirit that was an everyday companion.

You're a compassionate soul, Harry, although you usually try to hide it. You're always the first to be there for others. I noticed that about you from the beginning.

Lauren reminded me of a time back in February when our relationship was new. I hit the brakes hard, tapped my turn signal and yanked my car (safely and carefully, of course) to the cambered asphalt shoulder. I had pointed back 50 yards or so to an old blue Ford with a flat tire, and a middle-aged woman standing next to it looking dumb-struck and lost.

Lauren gushed, Before the woman even realized what was happening, you had the spare out, the car on the jack and were half-way to getting her back on the road. You wouldn't even accept a tip.

That's my Harry, Lauren had proudly told her father the next day. Harry is always asking, 'How much of myself can I give to others?'

She also thought, but didn't say it aloud:

(Of course, Harry's booming flatulence, as startling as a thunderclap in the wee hours of the night, shakes the walls and his snoring sounds downright bestial. He also swears way too much. If we ever have children together, he'll need to stop the 'Fuck this, Fuck that' which seems to accompany every single one of his frustrations.

On the positive side, Harry can write a sappy love letter; rotate the tires on a car; throw a football spiral with zip and knows what good maple syrup is supposed to taste like. Harry is my best friend, an enthusiastic lover and a good man. He worships me like I'm an altar of pure gold and precious gems. Isn't that enough? Shouldn't that be enough for anyone?)

Lauren had wished to set me at ease. As we approached the stress of my father's funeral, she wanted to reassure me that she was not seeking perfection in me or in any other man.

Harry, absolute perfection in a man is an impossibility. And truly unnecessary, she also said.

I lowered my head, feeling relieved.

Lauren also observed, True love arises from our imperfections, one partner rising to elevate and nurture the one who is faltering. Love means that I will be there when you need me. I unequivocally trust that you will find your way to be there and support me, too.

Lauren paused for a moment. As I recall, she looked almost frightened as she summoned a new energy. And I remember her next spoken sentence exactly.

After Ryan, my disaster of an ex-husband, you are like a godsend, she said.

Lauren's bombshell instantly froze me in place. In retrospect, I am certain that I looked stunned.

I sucked in my breath and held it for an extra few beats. Lauren did not give me time to recover. Over the next 15 minutes, Lauren confided her own past in a rush of emotional honesty. What stayed with me as Lauren unbosomed her own long-held secret, however, was not jealousy or anger but her awe-inspiring strength, cast like bronze in love and loss.

I had a bad experience once, that's all, Lauren started. The first time around, I chose badly. I was young and free-spirited. I didn't spot a bad seed.

Lauren was just 20 when she joined friends at a fire department picnic a few towns over in Newcomb. The heat and humidity of that mid-August day had surrendered to the cool breeze of night-time. The beers and reverie flowed easily when Lauren was introduced to Ryan Burnside, a handsome and mercurial contractor who earned a modest living caretaking and remodeling second homes.

Ryan wore a thick black beard like a bearskin rug. He was tall, lean and muscled. So handsome, his friends goaded him, saying, You oughta just sell your hammer and tape measure and take acting classes. Go to Hollywood. You might actually get somewhere.

That August night, Lauren's kindness and radiant beauty percolated the hard crowd and Ryan noticed her in the way a miner spots a diamond sparkling in a seam. He was immediately smitten.

A bluegrass band played on a small stage. Well, not really a stage. Just some plywood boards set on some cinderblocks. Ryan asked me to dance and I, of course, accepted. I thought he was pretty hot. We held each other and twirled as the music played, and we didn't leave each other's sides for a long time, Lauren remembered.

Captivated and hopeful, Lauren paraded before Ryan her noble spirit, infectious enthusiasm and a commitment to building a romantic love that would last for eternity.

I was just two years or so out of high school. Still a kid. I had a crush and I convinced myself that it was love. You know how it goes?

I didn't answer, still recovering from what Lauren had just revealed.

I was so naive, Lauren said, shrugging her shoulders. Now I know better. Life only plays out that way in movies and fairytales.

Lauren had unfurled all her soft curves and enticing charms, so intent on landing this Ryan Burnside as a husband that she blindly ignored the klaxon bells and flashing red warning lights — the drunken fights; the arrest for possession; then a second one for the starter pistol and gram of dope that the troopers found under the front seat of his truck.

By that time, Lauren had fallen hard. She stubbornly refused to listen to anyone. She disregarded her parents' admonitions and brushed away her friends' forewarnings that she absolutely could not allow this Ryan Burnside to be more than a rebellious minor character in the screenplay of her life.

Defiant, Lauren showed Ryan her love and tried to persuade him in a sweet but firm voice, Put a ring on my finger and marry me.

In return, however, Ryan treated Lauren to more nights alone while he played pool at The Fox's Den in Indian Lake, splashed down too many draft beers and stayed out partying with friends to all hours. When Ryan did eventually return home, his key fumbling and scratching at the lock, he stormed around ill-tempered and he often smelled of sweat, cheap perfume and sex.

Now I know better. I should have thrown his stupid ass out and tossed all his stuff right on the front lawn after him. I should have admitted that I was a fool, taken my lumps and started all over, Lauren sighed at the memory. Would have saved myself a lot of heartbreak. But, I can be pretty darn stubborn. I deluded myself into believing his hell-raising would eventually run its course.

Besides, I loved him — or at least I thought that I did, she added. I naively believed that I could change Ryan. Mold him into a better version of himself. Stupid, I know. Still, I'm not the first woman to fall under the weight of an unfaithful man.

Lauren fidgeted with her hands. She appeared stuck. Unsure of her footing. Lauren knew, however, she could not put a period on the end of her story just yet. She had already navigated too far down the steep and rocky trail towards her truth. So, Lauren inhaled and plunged ahead, disclosing to me the rest of a long-hidden secret that, in the dark of a strip mall restaurant, she knew she must share.

I was 21 and I got pregnant. I'm ashamed to admit it to you now. I should have told you from the very beginning, Lauren said. I'm sorry for keeping it from you. The marriage. The baby. The whole story. All of it. I hope you'll forgive me for hiding it from you.

My anxiety stirred anew. Instead of panicking and retreating into a brooding silence, as surely I once would have done, I, instead, answered, Don't worry, honey. What's done is done. It's okay.

I meant it, too. In our seven months together, I had grown.

Go on. I'm listening, I said next, with compassion and calm.

Lauren looked at me clear-eyed and resolute. Strong.

I purposely stopped taking my birth control, she said. I flushed the pills down the toilet and tossed the little foil package in the trash. I wasn't trying to trap Ryan. Or, at least, I didn't see it like a deliberately set trap, like you would try to snare a rabbit in the woods. But I was wrong in doing that.

She added, I just believed that the baby that we conceived would have magical powers.

Our baby would be the elixir that would stop Ryan's wanderings and destructive behavior, Lauren thought but didn't say.

Lauren had planned to use Ryan's likeness swaddled in a soft cotton blanket instead of non-stop nagging as the crackling whip that would help him mature quicker than he thought he could, or otherwise would. She believed the visage of an infant son or daughter would be so enticing, it would speed Ryan's journey to adulthood. She dreamed, too, that a baby would switch off his anger, alcoholic binges and nocturnal pursuits of a better piece of ass.

My little plan worked. For a little while, she said with resignation in her voice.

We quickly got married. My parents insisted on it. I was beginning to show, she said.

Early on, the two of us sat together night after night, cozy on the couch in our little rental, watching whatever channels we could get on the Dish. I would place Ryan's hand on my growing stomach, so that he could feel his baby — our baby — kick and squirm inside me.

Over the drone of Fox News and re-runs of *Friends*, Lauren told me that Ryan would sometimes put his ear to her rounding stomach. He would listen to the baby's heartbeat transfixed, a big burly man with a volcanic beard in a euphoric trance over the life that the two of them had created.

Lauren's voice brightened. Ryan had begun behaving like an adult in other ways, too.

He stopped playing songs by honking his armpits and started helping out in the kitchen. He emptied the dishwasher and folded the laundry without me even asking him. Once, he took a half-day off from work to drive me to the obstetrician in Glens Falls, where we watched the baby on the ultrasound together.

In the sixth month, they discovered they would be having a daughter. Lauren remembered how they both watched, slack-jawed, at her little hands and feet kicking and waving to them on the monitor's little screen.

Ryan and Lauren decided to name the baby Hannah, meaning 'God's gift,' after Elkanah's wife in the Bible, who finally conceived Samuel after being barren and despondent for many years. Lauren believed that their daughter would be a blessing from God —the gift that would persuade Ryan to spurn all others and bind their new family together in a fresh and joyful new beginning.

Eight months into her pregnancy, Lauren had convinced herself that their nascent marriage was growing stronger and more complete. Ryan drank less, came straight home after work and his cell phone no longer lit up late at night with strange text messages which, before, he had nonchalantly pretended were nothing important but that he nonetheless tried to hide from her.

Just before Lauren's due date, they drove back to Glens Falls in Ryan's blue F-150. The same young ultrasound technician poured cold jelly on the round, hard basketball shape that had grown from Lauren's washboard stomach. Lauren remembered her embarrassment, wondering whether anyone else could have skin as pale and white as hers. Secretly, she wondered, too, whether her new baby girl would leave her with undesirable stretch marks, unable to ever again confidently wear a bikini on the beach.

I don't want to look all tired and haggard like the mothers we see at Applebee's, she had fretted to Ryan, imagining herself wiping food off her toddler's face with the sleeve of her good sweater while her own meal grew soggy and cold.

Lauren, too, vividly recalled for me holding back tears and shaking, instantly feeling very cold and frightened, when the ultrasound machine resounded with silence. Instead of the steady rhythmic beat of a living, beating heart and the faint scent of baby powder, the room suddenly reeked of dread.

Time just stopped. Everything completely stopped, Lauren told me.

She paused to dab her eyes with her napkin.

The young ultrasound technician left the room, her lips quivering. She returned with a white-coated doctor, a youngish man with a scratchy beard who gently re-applied the cold jelly, listened solemnly for several long minutes for the thwoosh, thwoosh, thwoosh of a heart beat, before saying in a voice no louder than a whisper:

I'm sorry, but your daughter is gone.

And, just in case Lauren didn't understand what 'gone' meant.

We can't find a heartbeat.

Hannah was stillborn early the next morning. She emerged perfect in every conceivable way, except for the umbilical cord looped tightly around her neck, which turned her a mottled grey-purple in death.

Lauren held her swaddled, lifeless daughter for hours until a nurse gently urged her to take some photos for a memory book and say her goodbyes. Lauren cursed furiously at God for taking Hannah from her but, inside, was quietly thankful for the brief joy their baby had selflessly gifted the two of them.

In that precious time before the nurses gently lifted Hannah's lifeless form from her, Lauren revealed to me that death and life; hopelessness and hope; dreams and reality, and every other emotion intersected with cosmic force to reveal to her a love that was heavenly, spiritual and pure.

Harry, I take comfort in knowing that I could not possibly have loved Hannah any more perfectly or any more purely, she said, softly touching her own memories. I imagine that people go their entire lives without feeling such a pure, profound love. A perfect love.

Ryan, however, had already begun slipping away. In the small hours before Hannah was physically born but after she was already dead, Ryan surrendered. He gave up.

Lauren had her own interpretation, honed by more than a decade of thought, reflection and tears. It was Ryan's way of blaming her — or himself. Maybe he was sending her a coded message that he was unready for fatherhood and domestication, after all.

He could see the future, but not himself in it, she said.

Ryan was so devastated by their loss, he was afraid to go on. He was scared that Lauren would want to try to have another baby, and that the next pregnancy would haunt him — a daily reminder that life itself is precarious, short-lived and comes with no written guarantees.

After the small graveside service accompanied by family and a few friends in a cold, steady drizzle, Ryan immediately returned to work. He lost himself in construction and drink. He didn't grieve. He communicated in gruff monosyllables and cave man grunts. Worse, he made inappropriate and incredibly hurtful comments — crude jokes when Lauren's breasts engorged and her milk came in despite the drugs meant to stop it. He insensitively remarked that he didn't find her postpartum figure sexy anymore.

Their marriage, frayed and thread-bare almost from the beginning, dissolved into something like the cold, airless space between the planets — a vacuum in which a rewarding life together did not exist. Or maybe never existed at all. They began to fight bitterly, venting frustration and grief.

One day, Lauren came home to find Ryan's drawers and closets emptied, his clothes, tools, work boots and the new 46-inch flat-screen television gone.

Ryan couldn't bring himself to speak to me. He communicated mostly by text or through his stupid friends. Even the divorce papers came in the mail, Lauren said. By that point, I wanted to get rid of him so badly that I signed them right away. Barely even read them.

For several months, every time Lauren passed a building site or saw brawny men wrestling with big yellow machines, she thought of Ryan; her shambles of a marriage, and the unfairness of what God did to them. Her heart-break lingered like a North Country winter. Lauren reflected in disgust, too, once again angry at herself for not vetting her choice of a life partner with forethought and maturity.

I used to wonder what the heck I was thinking. How could I foolishly fall for a man so wrong for me?

It was now my turn to comfort Lauren.

Don't beat yourself up over it. It happened and it's over. You learned from it. It's okay.

And now I'm here. We're together.

Lauren responded as if she didn't hear me, or was still time-traveling to another place in a past decade.

Why was I so desperate to be married? To give up my independence? Why did I have such a low opinion of myself that I stayed with a guy who was so untrustworthy, angry and really, really dumb? Lauren asked. I mean, sometimes I thought Ryan needed two hours just to watch *60 Minutes*.

C'mon, Nobody's that dumb, I said with a smile.

Dumb and always pissed off, Lauren answered. She looked down and scratched at a dry food stain on the tablecloth.

Like he wanted to burn books that were too hard for him to read.

Lauren concluded, Even after he left, I kept analyzing what went wrong. What I could have done. I still wanted to salvage something. I wanted to fill the void in my life.

The one that Hannah had been destined to fill.

That's the problem with me, she explained. I'm no good at giving up.

I'm not sure what that means, I answered.

I'm too patient. Too forgiving and eager to please. Too damn nice sometimes. By the time I figure out that everything's all messed up, I'm fully invested and really vulnerable. I wind up getting hurt really, really bad. Back then, I had always figured, maybe I would be better off if I quit on my relationships sooner.

To which I appeared before Lauren in new light, like a sacred presence.

I responded, Or never quit on them at all.

■ ■ ■ ■ ■

Lauren's emotional account stayed with me for a long time. As I commit my story to paper, Lauren's recounting of Hannah's stillbirth and the nature of pure, perfect love re-enforced my understanding of French novelist Amantine Dupin's writings on the essence of life.

'I am given one mind, one body, one cycle from birth to death to find the one happiness in life — to love and be loved,' Dupin wrote.

Indeed, from that night forward, the simplest of everyday acts — grocery shopping, filling the car with gas, checking the mailbox — brought Lauren and I even greater happiness, because we were together and we were in love. She is the most incredible woman I have ever laid eyes on, and that does not take into account her heart, which is bigger and fuller than all of the continents combined.

Although at the time Lauren and I were just half a year together, I knew then that she would be The One — the special woman I would wed. It filled me with happiness to close my eyes sometimes and repeat, as if in practice, words from the Songs of Solomon that traditionally bound my people in marriage:

Ani L'Dodi, vi L'Dodi, Li

'I am my beloved's and my beloved is mine.'

Lauren's heart is pure. That evening in Florida, I learned that, like me, she had been deeply wounded. Lauren, too, was looking to wash away painful memories and start fresh. To wipe the slate clean, with no secrets between us. Lauren had let me know the scope of her darkness and it re-enforced my desire to meet her honesty with my own.

I would open myself fully to her. I was no longer afraid. I was not afraid of her love.

NINE

*'Becoming deeply loved by someone gives you strength;
loving someone deeply gives you courage.'*

— LAO TZU

Evening.
MONDAY, JULY 17, 2013
West Palm Beach, Fla.

At nightfall, the sky turned indigo and it began to rain. When I re-visit that evening in my memory, I recall that this was no wimpy rain — no delicate mist that tickled the smooth of our skin as we left the restaurant for the hotel.

No, that evening the heavens exploded. A thunderous South Florida rain violently threw down big, heavy drops that bounced and splattered off the pavement like pinballs.

Lauren and I jumped at a crooked flash of lightening and cowered at the boom of thunder that followed. Lit by street lamps casting honey-colored glows, we pulled each other close, hips kissing, and zig-zagged through puddles back to the hotel room. I held my thin windbreaker above us like an umbrella, fighting a gallant but losing battle against the wind. The rain speared our clothing and soaked our hides. The two of us sloshed, giddy in love, through the lobby, past a wave of classic rock streaming from the bar to the bank of elevators. At our floor, I slid the plastic key card in the door of Room 611 by the staircase and vending machines. Its low hum and dim lights invited us over for late night snacks.

Lauren showered, fogging the bathroom like an Adirondack lake on a crisp autumn morning. She changed into her pink satin pajamas, cut to show off her god-gifted curves. She lounged on the king-sized bed like a pin-up. After I, too, cleaned up, an insatiable longing possessed me. I became feral with desire. I kissed Lauren deeply, my tongue dancing in rhythm with hers. I felt a fluttering in my loins, like a bird yearning to take flight.

Lauren would be my late night snack.

We rolled around the hotel bed like break-dancers, passionately latched as one. My penis danced and revved like a tachometer until sparks flew in the dark and charged particles rushed violently, loudly, and Lauren gasped and murmured something that sounded like hmmmmmmmmm. With my lips pressed against her hair, she pulled the blankets over her in modesty and swiftly drifted off to sleep. She purred softly and contently, nestled in my warmth. Not surprisingly, I couldn't sleep. My thoughts gathered and whirled. Unable to make my mind go blank, I lay restlessly listening to the air conditioning unit cycle on and off with a tinny rattle. A vague ache settled below my heart like a pro wrestler had dropped from the ropes to deliver a forearm smash to my solar plexus.

I tossed about in bed, changing positions as quietly as I could, so as not to disturb Lauren's dreams. The minutes marched on endlessly. Tick, tock. Tick, tock. I remained anxious and unnerved, unable to make peace with all the unresolved emotional baggage scattered around me like the damp clothes we had tossed on the floor.

Lauren's secret past had moved me deeply. In the stillness of a night revealing only a cuticle of moon, I understood that I must match her complete honesty with an unconditional, uninhibited honesty of my own.

I silently moved across the room to sit in the nearby desk chair. I slipped on my gym shorts and t-shirt. For some time, I swiveled on the chair. Thinking. Remembering. Remembering some more.

Flashbacks bubbled up as from an angry spring. Long-repressed memories surfaced to the light. They knitted into the deepest held secrets that I now, finally, felt urgently compelled to share with Lauren.

I gently rubbed her shoulder and scalp. She stirred, ever so slightly. I knew it was unfair of me to stroke her hair flaring across the pillow — a corona glowing fiery red.

Lauren awoke with my hand still smoothing her hair.

What? she asked, startled and rubbing her eyes.

She appeared groggy, her mind a hive of confused, crawling bees. In the thin space between sleep and just-barely-awake, I remember that Lauren displayed no irritation or annoyance. She had anticipated that I would need her comfort.

I'm sorry that I woke you. I know that you're tired and it's very late. It's just that there's more I want to tell you about my father and my family, I whispered. Other parts of my life, about my childhood, that I want you to know before the funeral. Things you need to know.

Okay. Give me a minute here.

She should be canonized. A saint, Lauren is.

Once alert and dressed, Lauren absorbed my pained expression and spoke to me calmly.

All yesterday, Harry, I sensed there was something else that you wanted to tell me. You started to share what came between you and your father — and why you feel so conflicted about him. Then you stopped. You backed away. I let it go at the time but I know that there's more. Things that happened when you were little that you left out, Lauren said.

Remember our dinner conversation? When I told you about Ryan and Hannah? Lauren continued. I decided to open up to you — to share some pretty deep and painful memories — for many reasons. Of course, you deserved to know everything about my past. Honestly is a pillar of a loving, lasting relationship. Also, I wanted to show you, Harry, that while it can be incredibly scary to re-live trauma from long ago, you can get through it, especially if you have a strong support system, Lauren said.

Ha! I don't know what you mean, I said half-jokingly, a fish hooked and frantic to wriggle away.

Stop it, Harry. What I mean is that you confided in me that you felt mistreated as a young boy. Victimized. I believe every single word. There's no doubt in my mind that really bad things happened to you and that you buried it deep inside. You repressed all these ugly memories and they ate you up, Lauren said. I don't want to pressure you. Or corner you. But you say you want closure. You say you love me. If that's all true, if you really want things to be better — for us to build a life together — let me help you. Share your life with me.

She lowered her voice into a more soothing tone.

When you decide you want to get it off your chest, I'm right here. I don't care what time it is.

Lauren glanced at the clock radio. It was shortly after 2 a.m. — the dark, empty hour before the birds begin to stir.

This can't be all about your father. You know it and I know it, she said, gesturing for me to begin. There must be more to it. What is it then?

Thank you for this, I said simply.

Lauren sat up straighter on the bed. She fluffed her pillows into a backrest and put her chin in her hands. Her long red hair glowed like a torch by the light of the desk lamp.

Seriously, I'm here for you.

Well, buckle up then, honey. I'm going to pull the ripcord.

■ ■ ■ ■ ■

I entered the dark corner housing my hideously metastasized past. Yet, as Lauren waited expectantly, I stuttered and flailed, searching for the right words. I found them, strangely, in my sudden recall of a quote from Chinese philosopher Lao Tsu. I read it back in my college days but it had vexed me because, back then, I had not yet experienced real love.

'Becoming deeply loved by someone gives you strength; loving someone deeply gives you courage,' Lao had written six centuries before I met Lauren.

In the still of those early morning hours, I finally became one with its meaning.

The strength and courage to finally tell my story would flow from Lauren's love.

Memories spawned feeling. Feelings became ideas. Ideas coalesced into formed thoughts, which soon begot words. Words multiplied into sentences and paragraphs. Together, they gave birth to the history that I would share with Lauren — the unvarnished trauma that I suffered in my childhood and the deep wounds they left on me.

■ ■ ■ ■ ■

Mother was as dangerous as plutonium and as toxic as botulism.

All these years later, I wonder whether she had a sickness and whether it had a name. As a child, however, I didn't enjoy the benefit of a clinical diagnosis, or trained counselors and psychiatrists, or even close relatives to form a protective shield around me. There was no one in my little world to intervene, comfort me or to set a place for me around an oasis of calm.

Mother militarized the English language against me. She loaded her mouth with insults like fodder and fired hateful words which exploded before me like cannons in battle.

Mother told me that I should be ashamed to breath God's clean air.

So, I was.

She labeled me as evil and pronounced me dumb. A stupid fool.

I believed that, too, confessing my shame to Lauren for the first time.

It crushed me, sending me away weeping in a helpless rage, I remembered. Yet, strangely, mother also motivated me to study harder in school, suffering as I did with excruciating anxiety that anything less than straight A's would confirm mother's judgement, that I was a fucking imbecile.

Lauren looked stricken, eyes wide. The room was silent, save for the hum of passing cars from the nearby highway.

Mother told me that she hated me, too. Said she was sorry she didn't abort me.

As a result, I had long believed that I was damaged and unworthy of anyone's love.

Mother regularly warned me that outsiders should never be allowed to know any of it.

It is none of their business, mother would tell me, as if she were sharing the wisdom of a swami. They won't give a damn anyway.

Obediently, I concealed mother's verbal abuse from my friends and anyone else outside our deeply dysfunctional clan. I also learned to hide my own feelings of worthlessness imposed by her scathing put-downs, as I sunk deeper and deeper into a quicksand of despair — like I had been subtracted from the world. A victim of bad math.

What did I know? I was just a child, I said, re-living.

It sounds to me like you were a sensitive little boy who suffered a lot, Lauren consoled.

The air I breathed throughout my childhood bristled with tension, mother's next violent explosion a split second — or a week — away. I never knew which. The high-voltage explosions surely came, however. They came whenever mother's shifting moods dictated they came.

They also came in stinging slaps across the face; beatings with wooden hangers and heavy hard-cover books, or whatever cooking utensil mother held in her hand at the time.

Once, I told Lauren, mother held a knife to my neck and threatened to kill me. Terrified I was about to die, I started to scream like a skater falling through the ice would scream but, as I shook with fear, only a feminine gasp escaped my lips.

Maybe that sounds unbelievable to you. Or melodramatic. But it's true, I said. Every single word is true.

I explained to Lauren that I knew, early on, that my childhood home was not a normal home. The other kids on my block played kickball and running bases, fought proxy wars with GI Joes and, in the embrace of summer, joyfully loped around the adjoining yards catching fireflies in Dixie cups at dusk. They were all carefree and happy — feelings that, for me, alighted with the infrequency of a comet passing in orbit. While other kids exhausted the last light of summer evenings whacking whiffle balls and climbing the gnarled apple tree in a neighbor's back-yard, I existed alone with my fears.

I wish you would die, mother told me again and again, her tone laced with malice.

I can't stand the sight of you, you fucking bastard. I wish I never gave birth to you, she also said.

My entire childhood was like that. Suffocating and terrifying.

In my dreams, I was always untangling the lines of a parachute while I was falling, I said.

It wasn't just me. I got the worst of it, but my mother didn't spare Jonathan and Helen. They were abused and bullied, too, I said.

Nobody will ever love you. Look at yourself. Stand up straight. You look like a monkey, mother frequently scolded Helen, my older sister.

You are a no-good failure. An embarrassment to the family name. You won't amount to anything, mother told Jonathan, her first-born.

You can all go fuck yourselves, she told the three of us repeatedly.

Lauren looked aghast. She thought but did not say, because there was no air left in the room:

Who speaks to their own children with a heart of ice and the tongue of a serpent?

■ ■ ■ ■ ■

Let me tell you about Jonathan's wedding, I said when my voice no longer quivered.

A safe example, I strategized silently. One that did not directly involve me.

Guests mingled joyfully when my older brother married at a private club in Manhattan. Everyone drank champagne from fluted crystal glasses and plucked hors d'oeuvres from polished silver trays while waiting for the band to play and dancing to begin.

Mother, wearing enough gold to bedeck a pharaoh, flashed a phony smile at her future-in-laws who were wealthy enough to pay for the whole wedding weekend. She daintily held my father's hand, presenting an inviting (though misleading) picture of family harmony as they greeted the other guests.

I recalled for Lauren how my mother, as the reception began, pulled aside the beautiful bride, who had just become her daughter-in-law and a full-fledged member of our troubled clan.

Mother placed a firm hand on the happy bride's bare shoulder, an advance guard for the assault she planned to commit. Mother's favorite piece of costume jewelry, a ring set with a stone the size of a grape, dug into the bride's flesh. My new sister-in-law did not recoil or even appear to notice. Instead, she beamed, naively believing that she was about to be warmly and lovingly welcomed into the soft bosom of our family.

Don't you worry, mother said, directing her stare to the bride.

Lauren instinctively recognized the strangeness of mother's comment. Amid the clinking glasses and happy background chatter — on top of the genuine joy and love swelling the room — she recognized that the bride had no cause to be worried.

Because I knew mother's quirks, I remembered, I could sense that her icy tone was foreshadowing an ominous message — one that she was winding up to uncork like a fastball to the ribs.

Soon enough, you'll find out the truth about my Jonathan, mother said.

She lowered her voice and directed a hardened stare towards my stunned and crest-fallen older brother, who had gone to Herculean lengths to avoid sharing with his fiancé our mother's penchant for emotional violence.

As mother lowered her hand to hold Jonathan's new wife at the waist, her smile disappeared like a rain puddle fading in the summer sun. With the heart of a Hezbollah assassin, mother next looked directly at the bride, her eyes burning like anthracite, to line up her kill shot.

Wait until you're married for a few years. When you learn the truth and see what Jonathan is really like. The day will come when you'll understand that he's a big … fucking … loser, mother declared, baring her teeth to reveal her incisors.

I told Lauren, now wide-eyed, that Jonathan had instantly become furious at mother's cruel and entirely unnecessary sucker punch. He did not react, however. Instead, he just stood there, tight-lipped and tense, like he was suppressing an urge to pass gas. Jonathan remained paralyzed by fear and embarrassment, wishing to chivalrously protect his new wife but, at the same, avoid a screaming, profanity-filled fight with his mother at his own wedding reception.

Jonathan should have know that societal norms did not constrain mother.

I know your type, dear. I can see that you're one of those 'my-shit-don't-smell' rich girls, mother added with a sneer. Let me tell you, when you see what a failure your new husband is ... what a loser you just married ... you'll leave him for good. You'll split and go running home. You'll shake your tight little ass as you run straight home to mommy and daddy.

As Jonathan's betrothed recoiled and broke into wracking sobs that quickly produced a flow of mucus and tears that spoiled her professionally applied make-up, I placed my father in the story for Lauren's benefit.

The brave Lieutenant stood no more than four feet away, frozen as a marble statue, convicting himself with silence.

My brother needed his honor and some decency — my father's spine, a reassuring aside, an intervention, anything, I recounted. He got nothing. Silence. My father let it go. Stepped away to get some food and pretended he didn't hear any of it.

My first confessional upended a large stone damming a stream and it released a torrent. There was no going back. Not now. I would, indeed, re-visit my whole boyhood hall of horrors.

Lauren silently wondered how bad it would get — for me and everyone else.

If you want me to stop, I'll stop. I'll leave it at that, I recall telling her, although I had no intention of stopping. You can go back to sleep. We can forget it.

No. Go on. I want to know what I'm facing, Lauren had answered.

Lauren felt warm. She moved to the window and opened it a few inches. We both breathed the humid air smelling of the storm that had passed — and a new one approaching.

■ ■ ■ ■ ■

Quickly, before I lost my nerve, I set the next scene for Lauren — a summertime family outing to the county fair.

The sun had only recently topped the horizon on a Sunday morning, drawing a thin line of pink across the sky. Already, mother was rebellious and acting infantile. She didn't want to attend the county fair. She didn't think we should, either. She insisted that we should be cleaning the house, or organizing closets, or pulling weeds from our little vegetable garden in a back corner of our yard by the willow tree. It was too hot and sticky to spend the day outdoors at a silly old county fair, she complained.

Besides, the humidity will mess up my hair, mother said, scanning around for support.

Mother's hair had been freshly dyed an unnatural hue at the beauty parlor, the yellow of sweet corn straight off the stalk. It was her usual cut and color. Why she feared the heaviness of the damp air was a mystery. She had coated the yellow helmet piled atop her head with enough hairspray to deflect an artillery shell. Even in my youthful innocence, I could sense that mother was being disingenuous. She was trying to ruin our promised day of family fun.

Mother stamped around the house, building tension with each step. She ticked off a new list of alternatives to attending the fair — grocery shopping, sweeping the garage floor, even a shopping trip to Main Street — with the zeal of a lobbyist prowling the hallways of Albany.

I explained to Lauren that although our family was blue-color, middle class — maybe a rung higher, thanks to my father's city job and union card — mother liked to pretend that she hailed from a more admired demographic caste. On that morning in particular, she exuded an especially high level of haughtiness.

We finally climbed into the car and departed with mother still persisting in protest.

What if anyone I know sees me? she pitched in a last-ditch effort to short-circuit the outing. Mother seemed to be insinuating that she was too cultured to possibly enjoy — or even be seen — at such common entertainment as a county fair.

I promised the kids, my father answered, as he accelerated onto the highway. We'll have a good time. You'll see. Give it a chance.

The Lieutenant kept driving, his eyes focused on the speedometer.

After paying the entrance fee and spinning through the turnstiles, I recalled for Lauren the joy and excitement that I experienced at my first county fair.

I gawked in awe at the rumbling wooden roller coaster and the nausea-inducing Tilt-a-Whirl. I rode the miniature steam-engine twice, grinning maniacally. I used up my first handful of orange tickets in minutes throwing baseballs at milk cans. The medley of fair sounds mixed with the calliope on the Midway to paint, amid the flashing lights and smells of fried dough and stale beer, a cliched tableau of Americana.

Indeed, for several hours that morning, I felt happy and care-free. A strange and new sensation. I ignored mother and hoped that a day of light-hearted fun, for once, could be within my reach.

I was having a ball, I told Lauren. I wanted the day to last forever.

Mother, however, simmered — a cheap metal lid rattling in warning.

Once inside the fair's gates, she snobbishly paraded herself as if she existed on a plane high above all the other fair-goers. Mother looked for attention and she preened to find it, as if she was a royal visitor from a more sophisticated planet who deserved nothing less than doting adulation. She waltzed down the Midway, nose held high in a regal posture, as she dodged tossed candy wrappers and unleashed toddlers weaving like daytime drunks.

The other fair-goers — preoccupied with their cups of beer, waffle fries and stuffed animals won by throwing darts at under-inflated balloons — didn't know to show mother the respect she claimed for herself. Nor did anyone move aside in deference to her self-imagined importance.

She was really putting on quite an act, Lauren understated.

I'm not exaggerating. We all knew the game she was playing. We'd seen her behave this way before, I explained. The three of us — Jonathan, Helen and I — we just hoped that she wouldn't boil over.

I described for Lauren's benefit how mother looked down her nose at the sinewy men with their hand-drawn tattoos of skulls and barbed wire peering out from Jethro Tull t-shirts. They held hands with their buxom dates — leather-skinned biker chicks dressed in black and appearing as if they had left the house not fully dressed.

At one point, mother sniffed as if she had stepped in something brown. Mother pursed her lips. Annoyed. She mouthed something incomprehensible but decidedly unpleasant. We braced ourselves, our little spines stiffening.

An instant later, mother perceived a slight. Perhaps she interpreted a tired sigh as a wisp of disrespect. Maybe it was a random bump amid the bustle. Or the ice cream lid that stuck to her shoe that she took as an invitation to fight.

Mother exploded with the earth-shaking percussion of a car bomb.

That's it. I'm done with all this shit, she fanged. The hell with you all.

A few bystanders turned to observe the commotion, like we were fish in an aquarium. Before my father could react, mother rocketed into the women's rest room. There, she locked herself in a fetid stall amid the sewer smells and incomplete flushes.

For two whole hours she refused to come out, I said.

Lauren gasped in disbelief.

Indeed, mother sat on a closed toilet lid, stared at the scrawls of obscene graffiti and fumed. When her back began to hurt, she commandeered a rickety cane chair next to an overflowing sink stuffed with paper towels.

I knew this, I told Lauren, because Jonathan bravely lifted me up several times so I could see mother through the little window.

Mother would not budge, even as my father tried to sweet-talk her into coming out.

The medal-festooned Lieutenant pleaded weakly through the open ladies' room door. He eventually engaged emissaries — sympathetic sorority girls, Pakistani aunties and blue-haired grandmothers rushing inside to pee — in back-and-forth diplomacy.

Still, mother ignored father's persistent coaxing and our wailing cries of frustration and despair.

As memories of that disastrous day spilled out, I recalled Jonathan's bravery.

On the day of the fair, Jonathan was just barely 14. Still a boy with a fine dander on his cheeks. Yet, he had also reached the age where a tingling accompanied new thoughts about womanhood. In my memory, Jonathan tried to project his newly discovered manhood into the chaotic scene.

He acted cool, like he wasn't fazed by my mother's crap, I said.

Still, I could see that he was thoroughly embarrassed and cursing under his breath. He knew that mother had purposely sabotaged our day. Meanwhile, Helen vomited from the stress. She coughed up bits of a half-digested hot dog behind a green wooden bench.

Lauren sat speechless. There was nothing for her to say anyway.

A little later, lashing out in frustration, Jonathan tried to reason with our father but his words come out anguished and harsh.

Screw her. Why don't we just leave her in there? She'll come out when she's good and ready, Jonathan spit.

My father viewed it differently.

What are you trying to do, make this harder than it already is? I have to live with her, you know. I can't leave without her. I'll never hear the end of it. She'll kill me, he reasoned.

After a pause, my father offered a justification, She's in one of her moods. Just shut up and let me handle it.

Handle it?

The Lieutenant turned back to plead through the open restroom door.

C'mon, honey. It's nice outside. Please come out. Please. Let's forget whatever it is that's bugging you so we can all enjoy the rest of this beautiful day, father begged.

He was all Neville Chamberlain and not a single cell of Winston Churchill.

Finally, mother proved her point. Or maybe she simply got bored of being sullen and mad. Mother emerged from the squat concrete building, briskly striding into the now fading afternoon light like a victorious general who had just conquered a small nation. She wore an unforgettable look on her face, like she was constitutionally unable to adopt a contrite air.

I remember her eyes the most, I said, lingering on the image. From behind her horned rim glasses and powerful hairdo, mother burned holes into the three of us, like a welder's torch slicing through steel.

My father, soundly defeated, forced Jonathan, Helen and I to line up and apologize to her in unison.

We're sorry, mother.

Unrepentant and unbowed, mother just stared at us coldly, a brawler triumphant.

Lauren took it all in, but she made no move to change the subject or escape the room. Because I needed Lauren to truly understand the depths of my boyhood trauma, I pulled out another example.

One year, I recalled for her, we proudly fashioned home-made gifts for mother for her birthday.

Jonathan, Helen and I desperately wanted mother to love our gifts and, by extension I suppose, to love us as well.

Helen and I had crafted our birthday presents with our own little hands under the guidance of our school's art teachers. They had praised our creativity and helped us with the modeling clay, popsicle sticks, paint and Elmer's glue. Jonathan made mother's birthday gift in his wood-working class using a pine board and a band saw.

What we lacked in craftsmanship and talent, we compensated for with energy and enthusiasm. We wrapped our birthday presents in the Sunday comics the best we could. We jockeyed to be the first to hug mother and wish her a Happy Birthday in the morning.

Mother reacted as if she had bitten into a piece of rancid meat.

Oh my God, no, you can't be serious, Lauren said.

Mother's face tightened and she tore open the wrapping paper angrily, hemorrhaging cruelty. Without speaking a word, mother ripped apart the wooden napkin holder that Jonathan had painstakingly constructed in shop class. Adolescence was still cracking his voice, so Jonathan protested with a squeakiness that undermined his frustration and fury.

Why? What are you doing? he cried. Don't do that. Why are you doing that?

Mother did not respond, except to shoot him a withering glare.

Next to die was Helen's picture frame crafted from popsicle sticks and colored with crayon. Mother used her knee for leverage to destroy it. She twisted the frame violently until the dried wood snapped like a breaking bone.

Noooo, Helen wailed, her little features grotesque with disappointment and anger.

She burst into tears and ran from the room. Her screams echoed through the house.

And what about yours? Lauren ventured softly, although she had already surmised its fate.

Mother bulldozed her way to the ash tray that I had lovingly molded from clay. She struggled to get a secure grip at first but those extra seconds only delayed the inevitable. Within a minute, it, too, had been pulverized. She stuffed the broken clay pieces in the garbage can, on top of the broken egg shells and decaying vegetable peels.

Mother had wished for something grander and more lavish than homemade crafts to mark her birthday. Something store-bought and, preferably, very expensive. She expected gifts wrapped in shiny paper and tied with elaborate ribbons. Our gifts should have honored her stature as the monarch of our family and recognized the incalculable sacrifices that she had made on our behalf. It was a sign of her insecurity and grandiose sense of entitlement.

She was being ridiculous. We didn't have jobs or money. We were still kids in grade school, I said.

That's just awful. I can't imagine how sad you felt. How much that hurt you, Lauren answered.

There's more, I advised.

Three days later, my father hastily corralled us into the dining room for a ceremony of sorts. A do-over, I ascertained by the way father lined us up according to our age.

Mother acted surprised as she gleefully unwrapped a small square box, which contained a 14-carat gold necklace accented with a neat channel of sparkling diamonds.

It's an extra special birthday gift from all of us. The kids picked it out for you, my father lied.

Actually, he had raided his secret gambling stash, tucked in the rafters above the garage, for a wad of extra cash he kept hidden in an envelope for his forays to the betting parlors. He then lied about an overtime shift so he could visit a jewelry store in Manhattan and, ultimately, restore peace to the household.

Happy Birthday mother, we mumbled to the floor-boards.

Like we were filming a hostage video.

Lauren moved on the bed and began to knead the knot of muscles in my neck and back. I welcomed the warmth of her body and the strength of her hands on my body, relieving tension.

There, there. It's going to be okay, she comforted me.

There's a whole deep well to draw buckets of crazy from, I replied. Every few weeks, it seemed that mother would commit some a new outrage.

Another time, mother pulled a steak knife from a kitchen drawer in a spasm of rage. She waved it like a savage while threatening Helen and I with death.

In her mind, we had committed a felony: We messed up her tidy living room before her wealthy cousin was to arrive for a visit.

If my sister and I had a moment to defend ourselves, we would have sworn that we had not been warned against sitting on the couch. We did not purposely leave shallow indentations on the plastic-covered cushions where our behinds had rested.

Thankfully, mother had an epiphany about the optics of it. How would it look if her cousin rang the doorbell and found the bodies of her two children on the floor?

She rested the knife back on the counter.

Our pardon, however, was not full and complete.

Soon, we cowered as wild slaps and thudding blows began to fall like hailstones.

Lauren stifled a nervous laugh.

Trust me, I know it isn't remotely normal, I said quietly.

To make things worse, mother found additional evidence of our little crime wave.

Helen had sampled the mixed nuts and M&Ms that mother had set out in a crystal bowl, leaving behind a shallow impression of her guilt.

Are you fucking retarded? What the hell is wrong with you lousy fucking kids? mother had roared during Round Two.

Mother smacked us again, each new blow venting little spurts of insecurity and nerves. I recall quaking in fear, secretly hoping that our next-door neighbor — a widowed Ukrainian who we'd been told was a closeted Nazi sympathizer — had overheard the one-sided battle and called the police.

I'm going to kill you this time for sure, mother threatened again. Nobody would blame me. You bastards deserve it.

All this time, my father did not move a muscle. The fearless Lieutenant continued to read the sports section of the *Daily News* in the shade on the deck.

My father did not investigate or intervene. He did not appear to see the need. He did not deem the assault committed on his children as worthy of his heroism, I added bitterly.

I understand now how totally abnormal this was, I also admitted to Lauren.

Back then, as a little boy, I didn't. I suffered a month of nightmares — my cold, lifeless body, dead from stab wounds, bleeding out on a clear plastic tarp so I didn't stain mother's freshly vacuumed carpet.

In my nightmares, too, no one came to my rescue. Certainly not my father.

I suddenly felt like I had talked too much. Like I had violated a loyalty oath and exposed too much of my secret past. I irrationally worried that mother would learn of my indiscretion all these decades later and drag me once more into the abyss.

Lauren shifted her position to make herself more comfortable. Somehow, she knew that I had one last story to share.

Indeed, I did have one more humiliation to confess. It occurred in my senior year of high school when all boundaries of decency shattered like a launched crystal vase.

■ ■ ■ ■ ■

Just mother and I were at home. Just the two of us at opposite ends of the house when my father streamed through the front door, back from an errand to the supermarket. From the kitchen, I heard a commotion. The air in the house moved as if awoken from a slumber.

Mother pulled my father to a seat at the kitchen table and excitedly began speaking. From my bedroom where I had been finishing homework, I thought that she sounded very serious and very upset. At first, I hardly paid her any attention. I mistakenly thought the discussion didn't concern me.

An instant later, I heard my name several times in tandem with mother's rising voice. She began shouting and my ears perked up. I sensed something dangerous. Radioactive. I moved from my desk to my bedroom door, where I could eavesdrop on their conversation.

In a breathless torrent of words, I overhead my mother attack me with a monstrous lie.

She accused me of making a sexual advance on her.

Lauren gasped and instinctively touched her hand to her mouth, like an actress in a B-movie. In the nighttime stillness of the hotel room, only the buzzing hum of insects could be heard over the silence of disbelief. It sounded like all the nearby arthropods were talking it over and they, too, had found the unfolding scene too bizarre for words.

You heard me right, I said. With a straight face, my mother accused me of sexually assaulting her. She told my father that I had pinned her to the sink and cupped her breasts from behind while she was preparing a pot roast for dinner.

My father sat there, arms folded, in his chair at the kitchen table and listened.

He did not challenge the legitimacy of mother's accusation — that his son had, out of nowhere, acted on an erotic Oedipal impulse while he was out buying frozen peas, a loaf of rye bread and a ripe cantaloupe. My father did not attempt to discern whether her preposterous story made sense. Nor did he probe for inconsistencies in my mother's story. He did not sooth her or offer a face-saving alternative version so she could safely back away from her accusation.

I don't think that my father really believed her, I said, but he didn't say so or defend me, either.

The Lieutenant just sat there — the courageous fire-fighter diminished to a flaccid lump.

I let those damning words hang in the air for a few seconds.

Eventually, I was summoned to the kitchen, so shocked and angry that I could barely think.

I tried to control my emotions but I sputtered like a madman, I said.

Anybody would be angry and afraid. If you weren't, you wouldn't be human, Lauren answered in support.

Despite my vehement — and truthful — denials, mother refused to drop it. She didn't want to retract her story. Mother didn't do face-saving. Instead, she delighted in her mockery, watching me squirm in embarrassment and indignation.

Mother grew even more irrational when I finally pulled myself together and challenged her. I told her — so angry that I momentarily forgot my terror — how sick in the head I found her. Mother seemed to believe, however, that if she shrieked louder and more hysterically, she could drown out a complete lack of evidence. To my disbelief, she even added flesh to her trumped up story. New, even more outlandish details emerged on the flecks of spittle that flew from her lips.

In a matter of seconds, my alleged breast-cupping had spiraled into a dangerous attempted rape.

Who knows what was going through his deviant mind? You should be happy he didn't try to use his finger down there, mother said to my father in a sinister under-tone.

Minutes later, mother gained self-control long enough to audibly weigh calling the police. She posed the idea aloud with the demeanor of a restaurant-goer trying to decide between the chicken and the fish. My father responded to the circus playing out before him with his own courageous reasoning:

Let's calm down. Take a minute or two, honey. Consider the consequences. The newspaper story. The neighbors talking. We don't need to involve the cops or any outsiders. It's a family matter and it should stay a family matter.

My father never once said that he believed me.

After a while, my father moved to the den and blankly watched a ballgame on television. I stewed in my bedroom, alone. Jonathan and Helen arrived home and were warned to stay far away from me — their kid brother, the dangerous sex offender.

Mother remained in the kitchen. That night, she sat at the kitchen table, stretching the long telephone cord taut. She dialed her way through her address book to tell her friends her version of what transpired. Again, I secretly listened in from behind my closed bedroom door.

He touched me. I mean, I was wearing a bra, thank goodness, I heard her outright lie at one point. Who knows what would have happened … ?

You have to believe me, Lauren. That's exactly how it went down, I said, still mortified and humiliated all these years later.

I didn't know what to do, I said. I couldn't disprove it. It was my word against hers and I was afraid.

Of course, mother never considered how impossibly far-fetched such a story would appear to others or how devastating the train of gossip would be for both us. She never weighed what her accusation would mean for our family's reputation. Nor did she reflect on the scars her lies would leave on me. Instead, she appeared to glory in the schadenfreude of her son squirming in humiliation.

Back in my room, I replayed the fateful five minutes in question. Perhaps, I thought hopefully, it was a giant misunderstanding. A big mistake. Maybe I had passed through the kitchen and, in my hurry, accidentally brushed up against her.

In reality, mother had successfully gaslighted me — to the point where I had begun to doubt what I knew to be absolute and true.

You know me, I told Lauren in the hotel room. I would never do something like that. No one could be so perverted that they would try to feel up their own mother.

Of course not, honey. Not in a million years, Lauren reassured me.

Later that night, my father knocked softly on the bedroom door. He opened it a few inches and, through a vertical shaft of light, he peered in on me. My father was not capable of offering any high-minded wisdom or salve for my wounded soul. He appeared only to be checking to confirm that I had not hanged myself with a soccer scarf or swallowed a whole bottle of aspirin. He found me red-eyed and curled into a ball.

Your mother is just upset. She has a lot going on at work, my father explained.

My father tried to justify mother's false accusation of attempted rape as a normal response to a bad day at the office.

I shot him a look of disgust.

She doesn't mean it, father said and walked away.

■ ■ ■ ■ ■

Lauren gathered herself and sat quietly. She thought in silence so long, that I worried she might dissolve into the bedsheets. The only sound in the room was a metallic ticking as the air conditioner, between its groans and mighty exhales, rested in the wall.

I think I get it, Lauren said finally. I'm beginning to understand.

Harry, the anger you carry … the way you are so bitter and resentful about your father's place in your life … It's all misplaced, she said. Over the years, you've taken all this pain from your childhood and — plop — dumped it on your father.

Some of it is legitimate, Lauren added. But, Harry, my love, it seems to me that a lot is a cop-out on your part. You've been avoiding the real source of your pain. Just about everything you're feeling was caused by your mother. She's the root of it. The one who hurt you. She's the dangerous spider. She caught you in her web and traumatized you.

I nodded furiously to cut her off.

Lauren, I'm guess that's what I'm trying to help you to see. All these years, yes, I've been really angry at my father. And, yes, a lot of it is justified. He failed me, I said. But I also know that deep down, my mother was the toxic one. She hurt me over and over. She terrorized me. I didn't stand up for myself because I was afraid. Afraid of her. Listen, here's the toughest part: I was scared. But who wants to admit to being scared of their own mother? So, I blamed my father for everything. I vented everything onto him.

Your father was your scapegoat. He bore the brunt of it, Lauren said.

I suppose that's it, I admitted. And now my father's gone. He's dead. I can't tell him that I'm sorry. That I'm an adult now and I understand everything better. I want to forgive him. And tell him that I really loved him and wanted him in my life. It's too late for that.

Tomorrow, I have to face what I did. I have to face all my memories.

And although she didn't need to say it, Lauren added.

And face your mother, too.

TEN

'It is in pardoning that we are pardoned.'
—FRANCIS OF ASSISI

SOMETIME BEFORE, PERHAPS MAY 2013
Glens Falls, N.Y.

My long-time therapist Ellen is a wise soul. She listens deeply, actively and with genuine understanding and compassion.

Bad marriages; bad sex; bad family; bad temperament; bad home-work balance; bad finances; bad DNA? From the leather armchair in her office, Ellen has heard it all. Long ago, she concluded that we humans are not as unique or as special as we think.

Indeed, several months before my father died, Ellen informed me that, to my surprise and annoyance, my perceived childhood trauma was not all that extraordinary in the annals of fucked up families.

The ethics of my field constrain me, Ellen said. But trust me, as a trained social worker with many years of clinical experience, I've heard much worse than your tale of abuse.

Still, in our bi-monthly sessions together, Ellen understood and sympathized with how my childhood preyed on my psyche into adulthood. She also guided me in self-reflective thought and left zero space for my excuses and self-pity.

No more bull shit, Harry. I don't want to hear it, she said when I danced around her probing questions. Stop avoiding what's hard. I want you to work. I'll accept nothing less. We are here to work. You are going to work on you.

Indeed, over time, Ellen led me to understand that the resentment that I had stored up for my father, and which hummed inside me like a machine, was a textbook case of displaced aggression.

You see your father as less powerful, less dangerous. He's a safer target. Probably, because you don't fear him like you fear your mother, right? He didn't terrorize you, at least not directly, Ellen had said. Now you feel tremendous guilt over how it all played out. That guilt is crushing you. In your heart, you know the truth — that your pain and frustration aren't all your father's fault. You put yourself in a box, Harry. You're prideful and stubborn and you don't know how to get out of it.

With Ellen, I also explored why, as a child, I always felt insignificant, like a fly on a tablecloth about to be swatted away from a picnic. We discussed why I frequently felt anxious, like a canine watching as his food bowl is carried away. And together we analyzed the connection between my childhood trauma and my feelings of inadequacy and self-doubt, and why they led to bouts of depression that left me feeling numb and heavy. Like I had been carved from granite.

I explained to Ellen that, when in the grips of a depressive episode, I often felt adrift, like a small raft in the clutches of the wind. Sometimes, I revealed to Ellen, I imagined myself 40 years in the future, a lonesome outcast sitting frail and crumpled on a park bench feeding stale popcorn to pigeons. I would reminisce to strangers about life before the millennium and watch autonomous cars zooming overhead. Then I would head to my small apartment to boil hot dogs for dinner.

My eloquence failed me as I struggled to express to Ellen how sad and lost I felt on those days, which I blamed on the mistreatment I experienced as a child.

When I'm down in the dumps, depressed and sad, I feel like I'm wearing a disguise — a mask, I told Ellen. I hide — moody, distant and detached from the world, especially from Lauren. I don't want it to be that way. I know I can't spend the rest of my days like this, faking my way like a drunk trying to pass for sober.

I know you don't, Ellen had answered in sympathy.

After I had finished unburdening, Ellen offered her own thoughts. She guided me with open-ended questions and challenged me with demands — delivered softly but professionally — for self-reflection, especially when we arced from my fractured family to my budding commitment to Lauren and my hopes for a joyful life alongside her.

I also remember the first time that Ellen called me out. She challenged my unwillingness to accept that it was totally normal to exhibit vulnerability.

Your inability to nourish your relationship with Lauren stems from your desire to protect yourself from honest emotions, especially those that make you feel weak or unsafe, Ellen told me. With Lauren, you're thinking of your mother and erecting this kind of force field against the *anticipated* pain of rejection.

You're saying that I'm looking to purposely vandalize my relationship with Lauren …

Ellen did not have to think long before responding.

Harry, don't you see? As a result of your childhood, you don't trust. As a result, you've deliberately built walls around you to keep Lauren out. They are a defense. You seem to forget, though, that Lauren is not your mother. You seem to think that if you wall yourself off emotionally, you can't be hurt by Lauren and, honestly, Harry, that's kind of silly.

Ultimately, Ellen wanted me to stop considering myself a victim. Instead, she guided me to understand the cause of my inner turmoil; to learn from it and, finally, to consciously work toward change — the only way I could begin to heal.

I want you to think about the future. A future that includes Lauren by your side, Ellen encouraged me.

Like crumbs tossed into a vast sea, Ellen wished me to cast off the most painful moments of my childhood and to exchange them for something better. As an outgrowth of that, Ellen urged me to confidently share my feelings with Lauren, like I was Columbus pronouncing the roundness of the world.

Doing so would narrow the gulf between the man that I am and the man I hope to be.

God squeezes, but he doesn't strangle, Ellen had said. You can do this if you put your mind to it. You can learn to trust and forgive. And love completely.

Looking back, it seems almost as if Ellen had prescient knowledge of my father's looming death — an inkling that I would soon be wrestling with guilt, vulnerability and grief.

Harry, anxiety, fear and anger at one's parents aren't traits passed down from generation to generation, like eye color or dimples or curly hair, Ellen explained. How you manage your memories and emotions are a conscious decision that you make, especially when you are a 40-year-old adult.

Ellen shifted in her chair, wriggling her considerable heft to set herself like a defensive lineman. Then, she looked into my eyes and said firmly,

You're only going to grow emotionally and find the inner peace that you're seeking when you stop blaming your parents for everything wrong with your childhood … when you set aside your pride and hurt feelings and begin to take ownership.

Plenty of happy people didn't have perfect childhoods, Ellen's momentum carried her forward. Yes, your father was present, but invisible when you needed him. Your mother sounds like a real gem. I believe you when you tell me your childhood home was toxic. And, based on what I've heard, it sounds like your mother suffered from deep pain of her own.

I always wondered about that, I responded. My gaze led Ellen to elaborate.

Your mother hurt in some way and so she hurt you. Hurt people hurt people, Ellen answered. Look around. Do you believe you're the only one who grew up like this? That you're the only one with a tough childhood? You've said you might want to have a relationship with your mother someday. Do you believe that she will ever change? Is she even capable of it?

I caught myself reflected in the glass of her coffee table. I could no longer see the face of a child. I saw a man, fully formed, starting to grow into middle age — and emotional adulthood.

Something registered.

Like Maya Angelou once said …

Ellen looked at me, puzzled.

I've read Maya Angelou, Ellen answered warily. I don't see how she's relevant to what *we* are discussing here.

You're right, that was pretty obtuse, I acknowledged. But, when you mentioned my mother's ability or willingness to change, I thought of something that I heard Maya Angelou say on television once — that if someone shows you who they really are, believe them the first time. Or something like that.

Ellen nodded in agreement. She signaled with a wave of her hand for me to continue.

What you're telling me is, I have to accept that my mother — and my father — are who they are. That they're probably never going to change. Mother is never going to grow into the loving mother that I've always wished her to be. She's just not capable. My father is never going to challenge her authority or even stand up to her. And when I accept that and can properly mourn it, I'll be able to finally move on. Or at least figure out a strategy for how to move on.

Exactly, right, Ellen said. You'll come unstuck. That's what I've been trying to help you see.

She raised her arms as if to signal touchdown. Or victory.

Harry, you can choose to carry these grudges around forever. You can wallow in your past and be miserable for the rest of your life. You can dream and pray for the impossible miracle. Or you can choose another path. You can mourn the maternal love that you don't have — and your father's failure to defend and protect you — but then choose the route of acceptance and forgiveness. Of absolution. Then you can begin to move forward with your life.

Ellen paused a few beats to let her message sink in.

There are no perfect families because there are no perfect people, she reasoned. There is a drop of good in even the worst person. And inside all of us, there is darkness. Maybe even a tad bit of evil.

Ellen leaned forward in her chair and slapped her fleshy knees in encouragement.

No one can be toxic all of the time. No one, except maybe Mother Theresa, lives a lifetime generating only love, generosity and compassion. The rest of us? Your parents included … we're just flawed humans doing the best we can in our time on earth.

Ellen pointed toward the windows across the room. She explained that, over her career in counseling, she had learned that children are like perfect panes of glass at the moment they emerge from the womb to take their first breath.

Only for that brief moment.

A parents' touch always leaves fingerprints, Ellen said. Some of those touches are totally benign or, at worst, leave tiny, little smudges. Sometimes, though, parents touch the glass too hard or in the wrong spot or a little too roughly. Sometimes the pane of glass shatters into pieces.

It's a part of life. Get over it, is what you're suggesting, I responded.

Very simply, Harry, yes. When *you* break a glass, do you sweep away the broken pieces and move forward? Or, do you keep stepping on the shards, cutting your feet day after day? Ellen volleyed back. If you want to liberate yourself from all your anger and pain, you have to change how you react. Only forgiveness — unqualified, total forgiveness — will do that. That's how you clean up the pieces of broken glass and sweep them away.

In her small paneled office in front of her diplomas from Bard and Columbia, Ellen could sense my emotions swirling like a November wind. She waited a moment, for the rumbling of a passing truck to rise and fall, before addressing me again. Ellen knew that she had poked a deep nerve, but she also could see the impact of her speech — and the point she had made. Ellen observed me weighing my lifetime of hurt against actually beginning the process of forgiving my mother and father.

Ellen added, I'm not aware of any special potions you can mix to get to the point of forgiveness. You just have to decide you're ready and that you want to forgive.

For the rest of that hour, we explored the meaning of true forgiveness, once as elusive as a leopard stealing through the jungle but now seemingly within my reach.

The more good that you can see in your mother and father, the easier it will be to discard your bitterness and begin to heal, she said.

That doesn't mean what they did was right or acceptable. Forgiveness will not change the past, Ellen reminded me. But absolution has a way of influencing the future. You would be free of your incredible burden. It would create space for you to trust, to share your emotions and, ultimately, to love Lauren fully and completely.

The clock on the wall indicated that a most productive therapy session had neared its end. A morbidly obese man in an ill-fitting suit, with hands the size of snowmobile gloves, had arrived in the waiting room. In the few minutes that remained, Ellen challenged me with an assignment.

A bit of homework, she said with an elfish grin.

Next week, I want you to share with me a warm memory from your childhood, Ellen instructed. She wanted to me to retrieve a memory that hadn't survived the trip from childhood to adulthood.

Prove to me you can do it. Tell me of a time when the laughter and love of your family touched your heart. A time when you were happy, you felt whole, and that you truly felt the pull of family.

ELEVEN

'The comic and the tragic lie inseparably close,
like light and shadow.'
— SOCRATES

About thirty years, it's been, I told Ellen, already grinning as I sat down two weeks later across from her. I made myself comfortable in a rocking chair of lacquered hickory.

I briefly gazed out the office window into the parking lot, where walkers and shoppers weaved and crossed like darting minnows. My eyes momentarily focused on some dancing dark shadows in the foreground — the ground mirroring a waving oak. Ellen sat patiently in her leather armchair, waiting for me to begin to fulfill my assignment and share a joyful family memory.

I closed my eyes softly and set the scene with care. For once, I was eager to begin revisiting an episode from my childhood.

The pleasant memory I had selected began as darkness fell on a blustery Monday in November when I was about 10 — still very much an impressionable boy.

In the fading light, angry winds hit my window like a shove. In my room, I had been reading a comic book, waiting for dinner and looking forward to Monday Night Football. That night, the Giants would take on the Washington Redskins. My father loved the Giants. Thus, I loved them, too, although in that era, they lost more often than they won.

When my father watched football, I recalled for Ellen, he would shout expletives at defensive backs who didn't defend, and plead with whoever was quarterbacking — please, please, Goddammit, stop throwing interceptions. He would coach frenetically while balancing a bowl of chips and a cold beer on his lap. I would slam my hands on my knees and root lustily along with him, bonding with my hero and idol.

Before the opening kickoff, however, our entire family planned to sit down together for a home-cooked dinner — a custom in the Loev household throughout my childhood.

I recalled for Ellen the aroma of roasting chicken and spices in the air. Heat from the oven combined with the hissing radiators to overly warm the entire upstairs. Although it was still 30 minutes until suppertime, I teetered on the edge of sleep. A butterfly's breath would have nudged me to dreamland.

I, too, remembered for Ellen, Jonathan's voice calling out from behind his bedroom door, Hey, Mom. I'm hungry. When's dinner?

And a moment later, as an afterthought, his voice boomed:

When is Dad coming home?

Mother's cheery voice floated back from the kitchen, singing in harmony along with a deep baritone.

That's strange, I thought.

Who's that I hear in the background?

I investigated the source of the music, skipping down the stairs to satisfy my curiosity. In the kitchen, mother sang along to Neil Diamond on the radio. Silently, I watched her at the counter, still in her work clothes in front of a cutting board, rhythmically swinging her hips and singing along as she prepared our dinner.

Mother always seemed to find happiness in the family meal. She loved to prepare home-cooked meals for our family, I said. She even baked these delicious cakes and pies for us. Cooking and baking seemed to provide my mother with a sense of calm. Maybe something like comfort or control. Looking back, I suspect that she tried to redeem herself — to prove that she really loved us and was a good mother — by cooking a wholesome dinner for us just about every night.

In the Loev household, dinner-time was 6:30. Mother would ring a small copper bell to summon us to the table. If my father was off-duty, he would meander in, having spent his day off napping or puttering around the yard. With a joke or a smile, he would take his seat at one end of the table where he could survey the room. And assess whatever mood might be lingering in the air.

Our eyes would go to him for a sign, I said. He was our compass. He would point to how he believed the evening might go.

On rare evenings, too, my father would shed his natural shyness. On those nights, no longer the distant introvert, my father would entertain us like a Borscht Belt comic with corny jokes and bad impressions. My father would spice mother's carefully prepared dinner with stories about fires defeated and the colorful cast of characters who inhabited his world. Mother would smile politely, pleased that he had engaged his children in conversation instead of inhaling his dinner silently. Sometimes, mother even would participate. She would pepper the dinnertime conversation with over-heard gossip from the neighborhood or anecdotes from the firm where she answered phones for a pear-shaped lawyer whose bald head and jowls made him look like Uncle Fester from the Addams Family.

Those nights were like being in heaven, I remembered for Ellen's benefit. We would sit together at the kitchen table for an hour or more, happily enjoying each other's company. It felt like we were just like every other family in our neighborhood. Totally normal. As a kid, I wished that every night could be like that.

I can understand why, Ellen said. Go on, tell me more about that.

I nodded, eager to do so.

When I would head back upstairs to finish my homework or take a bath, I felt renewed. You can even say that I felt hopeful. Even optimistic. Better days seemed possible — and close by. I would think, 'Maybe this is the day when everything will turn around for me.'

In the memory I shared with Ellen, mother continued to exude joy and happiness while waiting for my father to arrive home from an all-day tour at Engine 43. I described for Ellen how she pirouetted around the kitchen, spinning and shaking her hips to the music. I allowed myself to imagine that aliens had landed a spaceship and inhabited her soul.

The kitchen clock had slowly crawled past 7 p.m., however.

My father was late. It was now 30 minutes past when The Lieutenant usually rocketed into the house after a 10-hour shift.

The glass dishes of food had been removed from the oven right on schedule. Mother's fully cooked dinner was quickly growing cold on the formica counter. Still, mother did not appear excessively annoyed or worried when I checked in for the second — and third — time and the kitchen clock edged towards 7:30. She continued to light-heartedly sing along to the radio. A smile and a glow lit her face and her hair spangled in the lights from the kitchen chandelier.

The pieces did not add up. Something truly weird was about to happen, I sensed.

Suddenly, I recounted, my father's Plymouth bucked to a halt in the driveway. The headlights went dark. The car door slammed. Forty-five seconds after the engine coughed and shuddered to a stop, my father breezed through the front door. He shouted a string of hearty hellos and grabbed mother around the waist. He dipped her like a dancer and leaned in for a kiss, like a soldier cele-brating the end of a war.

Hey, kiddo, he called to me with a toothy smile. Ready for the game?

He tossed me an imaginary football. I pulled it in, us-ing two hands like he taught me, and faked a spike in the end zone.

Hi Jonathan. Hello, Helen, my beautiful girl. Honey, I missed you, he said to mother. He bent at the waist, lean-ing in close for a second kiss.

I love you so much, he said.

Mother quickly pulled herself away. She extended her arms in a push. Mother's smile evaporated with a poof and a look of aggravation crossed her face.

My father reeked of body odor.

Nathan, can't you smell yourself? mother asked him. You really stink. You're gross. Don't you come near me until you've cleaned up.

She scowled. Her look said she meant business.

Nathan, now go and wash up. And hurry. Dinner's already getting cold. Put on some clean clothes while you're at it, she barked.

She wasn't wrong. My father stunk like a septic tank, I observed. The offensive smell of sweat and smoke carried all the way into the hallway. I thought I was going to gag.

As mother began reheating the chicken and a tray of baked potatoes, her expression registered disappoint-ment. She bit her lip. She no longer sang and swayed. It would be another 20 minutes until the family would sit down to eat dinner. Before she could utter anything else harsh and disapproving, my father disappeared into the master bedroom, presumably to take a quick shower.

The house had become so quiet, I recalled for Ellen, that I remembered the sound of him whizzing, his stream bubbling loudly through the open bathroom door. Moments later, I heard the bathroom faucet turn on and almost instantly squeak off.

On this night, my father would not be showering before dinner. Nor would he be changing his clothes.

Instead, my father stripped off his blue work shirt and dropped it onto the bedroom carpet in a lump, where it began to ferment like a middle school science experiment.

In no time, he returned to the kitchen table and wordlessly lowered himself into his chair.

Father wore only his work pants and a dingy t-shirt, stained and stinking of something approaching animal decomposition. Sprigs of long black and gray chest chairs protruded at his neck like wild dandelions on a lawn. A trail of his belly hair aired in the open. Below, I could see the outline of his manliness because his dirty work pants lay sprayed out, unbuttoned and wide open at the crotch, exposing a little more than just the thin white elastic band of his underwear.

I could sense the make-up of the air changing. Atoms charged and circled with buzzing electrons up to no good.

Mother's buoyant mood had completely evaporated. She stared menacingly at my father. In an instant, her tongue mutated into a blowtorch.

How many times do I have to fucking tell you? Don't you dare come to my dinner table stinking of the firehouse. Go get yourself into the shower right this second. Don't you even try to come back here until you're washed up and wearing clean clothes.

My father didn't twitch. He didn't move. He remained seated in his chair.

You know the deal, Natan, mother said, using my father's given name for emphasis. Go get yourself washed up so we can sit down and eat.

She shot him a withering look that said, Right this instant.

Father was indifferent to her directive. He speared a slab of butter and slathered it across his potato.

Not tonight, my dear, he might as well have declared. So sorry to disappoint you.

I recalled looking to Helen, who stifled a nervous giggle by touching her napkin to her lip. Jonathan stared at his hands, which formed a steeple on his lap.

Mother set down her silverware a little harder than necessary. The water in our glasses rocked.

Show me some respect, Natan. You're not the only one who had a tough day. I worked all day, too. And I busted my ass over a hot stove to make this dinner for the family and you don't even have the common courtesy to call me to say you'd be late.

Father didn't apologize. Again, he didn't move. He chewed contently, still immobile.

Mother erupted with the suddenness of a brain aneurism and the life-shattering force of a nuclear missile.

You selfish cock-sucking bastard, she screamed. Who do you think the fuck I am? Your whore? Some kind of fucking servant?

(Socrates once wrote: The comic and the tragic lie inseparably close, like light and shadow.)

My father tilted his head at a strange angle, as if mother had adopted the argot vocabulary of a remote tribe. Yet, her profane outburst failed to register in father's brain. It seemed like mother was trying to reason with a painted rock or a fat old hamster.

My father remained unfazed by mother's burst of hurricane-strength temper. He simply dropped his head and resumed eating, ignoring her. Once, he grunted oaf-like, a sound more fitting a ravenous steer than a suburban father of three. That night, it appeared to me, my father would not allow mother to minimize him, or shame him, or bully him into showering and changing into clean clothes. He appeared tired, hungry and, truthfully, braver than he had ever been before.

I explained to Ellen that, in my eyes, my father tried to re-assert his manhood with an uncommon fortitude, the way a majestic oak holds its leaves against winds threatening to strip its branches bare.

The room suddenly darkened, like a storm cloud had moved in to blot out the moon. Mother's face cinched into a tight grimace and her eyebrows raced in opposite directions, giving her the air of a comic book villain.

Jonathan's face registered fear.

Oh shit. This is going to be really bad, he muttered under his breath.

Mother did not pay attention to my brother, anyway. She, instead, angrily banged the bowl of vegetables on the table. The sudden collision of earthenware and table-top set knives and forks bouncing. This time, our drinks sloshed on to the clean tablecloth, soaking it.

I braced myself for more screaming profanities, thrown projectiles, hand-to-hand combat or worse — all three simultaneously.

To my surprise, vicious war-fare did not erupt at the dinner table that night. Mother swerved at the last moment, veering and braking like she had spotted an innocent fawn grazing on the roadside.

It's fine. Really, it's totally fine, she said as she bit her lip. Mother's tone was even and not at all convincing.

Nothing about what had just transpired — and certainly not my mother's track record — registered as all fine to me, I suggested to Ellen. Mother's face was still red and she remained agitated, like an angry bull lanced in the ring.

I'm not going to get upset. I'm going to breath deeply and calm myself down, she said in a low voice. Nathan, I don't want to start a fight with you. I know you're tired. You worked hard. You can come to my dinner table any way you wish.

She threw up her hands in capitulation.

Tonight, Nathan, you win. Really, you win. I surrender.

I thought to myself, That was way too easy.

I don't believe her for a second, I thought, too.

Mother drew a deep breath and gathered herself like a general prepping an army for a second offensive. She directly addressed my father once more.

I get it. You're hungry. You've had a long, tiring day. But, Nathan, if you think that it's acceptable to sit down at my table in your dirty, disgusting t-shirt, stinking to high heaven … if you think you can disrespect me like that in front of the children … I'm not going to ruin *their* evening by fighting with you, she said.

Mother's sarcasm signaled that she had another point to make.

I guess, Nathan, you've decided that the rules have changed, mother said in a surprisingly agreeable tone. If it's now acceptable to sit down for dinner dressed in your underwear — and smelling like a pile of you-know-what — I can only conclude that it's polite and respectful for me to act like that, too.

Before anyone could fully comprehend what mother meant by her declaration, she rose from the table and stood defiantly next to her chair.

Directly opposite my father, mother flexed her fingers and quickly began to unbutton her blouse. She quickly, expertly — even theatrically — worked her fingers in and out of the button holes, starting from her neck.

At the fifth button, mother's blouse flopped open to expose her ample cleavage, her breasts covered by a white, metal-girded brassiere.

My father's eyes grew very wide. He stopped all chewing. A tiny floret of broccoli observed the surreal scene — and mother's pale décolletage — from the tight corner of his lower lip.

No one dared breathe. We all stared straight ahead, trying not to see. My heart seized in mid-beat. A cold bead of sweat tickled my armpit and slalomed down my side to my waist.

Ellen, too, sat spellbound in her own chair, I noticed. My therapist had frozen in place, with her yellow legal pad listing precariously on her lap, waiting for my happy family memory to emerge as I had promised.

I sat there, wide-eyed, not knowing what to do, I recalled for Ellen.

Ellen laughed quickly.

I don't blame you, she said diplomatically. That's a very normal reaction to what sounds like a very unusual family dinner.

Unusual? It was more like an episode of *The Jerry Springer Show,* I said.

Mother's demand remained unmet. My father did not rise from his chair and move in the direction of the shower. Or to put on clean clothes. Or to do anything else mother had asked.

Just going to just sit there? mother challenged him again.

When my father did not flinch, mother shrugged her shoulders and began to slowly peel off her blouse.

With an exaggerated flair, mother jiggled her pillowy breasts. She wiggled her hips sensually and dramatically flicked her blouse over her left shoulder like a burlesque queen.

I turned my head in time to see mother's blouse hit the wall, barely missing a shelf full of knick-knacks. The blouse fluttered to the floor, as if bowing to an appreciative audience.

Mother posed victorious before my father in her brassiere, its steel underwires holding aloft her breasts.

Again, I dared not look. In his nine circles of hell, Dante had prophesied the consequences if I had dared turn my head.

Hope not to see Heaven.
I have come to lead you to the other shore;
into eternal darkness; into fire and into ice.

Mother walked around the table to loom over father. She shot lightening bolts from her eyes, as if to say, Don't you ever dare mess with me.

She walked back to her chair and promptly sat down in her bra to resume dinner — all adrenaline, nerve and feminine power.

Head lowered, with his elbows resting on the dinner table, my father, in his dirty undershirt, remained inert. The Lieutenant stared into space. For what seemed like an eternity, he remained perfectly still. He did not sway an inch. Inside, however, he surely shuddered — fearful that, with one miscalculation, my mother would choose to peal off her bra as well.

My mother would have been topless. Totally exposed. I was afraid to breath for every moment of their stand-off, I told Ellen.

Out of nowhere, my father croaked. His voice made

an unnatural sound — one that suggested his mouth was unable to form intelligible words. A few more suspenseful seconds passed, an inhale and an exhale, before he finally broke the tense silence with something literate and human sounding.

Would you please pass the chicken? he asked politely, in a voice two octaves higher than normal.

Mother laughed at the incongruity of his question. Instantly, she snapped out of her fury, no doubt amused by what she had engineered.

In response, my father released from his gut a deep laugh of his own. It sounded a lot like relief.

Like a fast-moving storm, the danger quickly passed. Peace had been restored to the family dinner table.

Mother adjusted her bra and continued to grin broadly. Unbridled laughter swept around the dinner table. We recounted what we had just witnessed like play-by-play announcers reviewing a slow-motion replay. Before long, the evening evolved into an uncommonly normal family meal, if you overlooked my mother daintily lifting her fork to her mouth wearing only her bra and slacks.

At dinner's conclusion, we carried our dishes to the sink and I returned to the safety of my bedroom. As I climbed the stairs to my room, I looked back one more time.

Mother in her sturdy bra, and father in his sweat-stained t-shirt and unbuckled pants, worked at the sink as one. They loaded the dishwasher together as the radio played a soft ballad about enduring love.

TWELVE

'You never know. The gun might be loaded.'
— MICHAEL 'YELLOW MICKEY' O'CONNOR

Lt. Natan Loev's Funeral
TUESDAY, JULY 18, 2013.
West Palm Beach, Florida

On the morning of my father's funeral, a casual breeze carried the sweet smell of fresh-cut grass. Its scent was pleasant enough, but too light and fleeting to negate the aroma of baking asphalt which exhaled heat like an oven door flung open.

Arriving at the funeral home, I remember glancing at the digital clock on the dashboard — 9:49 a.m. and 86 degrees already. I hurriedly scanned the quickly filling parking lot for an empty space.

A sudden flash of movement caught my eye. A gecko, brown and confused, darted down a rainspout. I swiveled my head in time to watch the tiny lizard skitter nervously across an island of wood chips and disappear into the shade under a late-model Lincoln.

Two hundred million years of evolution fucking wasted, I grumbled into space. Even the dumbest of lizards should know to stay off the hot pavement.

A split-second later, my attention was drawn to a bent octogenarian leaning on a cane, his pallor a presage of death. Momentarily distracted, I breezed the car past the first available parking space — a barely forgivable error. As I circled the parking lot a second time, the clock inching towards 10, I grunted impatiently.

Fuck. Shit.

Followed instantly by a more emphatic, Shit. Fuck.

Really, Harry? Lauren glared at me. She thought, You can recite Socrates and Virgil from memory, but you swear like an ignoramus at the slightest provocation.

I grimaced but did not respond as the chill streaming from the air conditioning vents birthed another wildly disconnected thought. I bobbed my head in acknowledgement: The weather girl on *Sunrise Florida* had called it correctly.

Indeed, the morning had quickly turned into a scorcher. The sun had risen rapidly, red from exertion. It threw down its fire like a thunderbolt, swiftly erasing the morning mist from the freshly barbered grass. Now, the sun's rays magnified in intensity through the windshield and baked the two of us like casseroles.

What little shade existed at that hour of the morning threw its cooling shadow towards the sand-colored Star of David Memorial Chapel. At its stuccoed entryway, bright flowers planted in mulched beds — rectangular, like cemetery plots — bloomed under the spread fingers of mature palms. The funeral home spread out imposingly beyond the parking lot, whose entire first row consisted of handicapped parking signs. The signs' little blue wheelchairs stood sentry atop their metal posts, sparkling like glitter in the brightness.

I finally steered the car into an empty parking space adjacent to a shiny blue Lexus. I parked the $29.95-a-day Hertz rental car perfectly between two painted yellow arms spread parallel in welcome.

I scanned the scene again, this time in the rear mirror.

Here's what else I recall from that morning:

A silver hearse with a Landau top idled under the portico, its business end wide open and ready to receive its cargo. My eyes zeroed in on the hearse's middle-aged driver, a paunchy Cuban in a straw hat and white guayaberas shirt. The man's ample belly hung four inches over his belt, imitation brown leather deployed as a defense against sartorial disaster.

My mind wandered again. Clearly, I was stalling. I wondered what the driver could be doing as he casually leaned against the hearse's front fender, checking text messages on his cell phone. For sport — a game I play sometimes — I ventured a little side bet.

He's probably got a hot date … a little lady waiting for him to finish up here.

I talked more nonsense. No, that isn't it, I proposed aloud. He's on the phone with his bookie. Probably has 10 bucks on the third race at Saratoga.

This time, Lauren shook her head in exasperation. She deduced — correctly, of course — that I had lost myself again. No doubt she was annoyed, but she suppressed any dismay. In her own bubble, Lauren remained silent rather than adding an unwelcome lecture — or fresh oxygen to my antics.

Lauren, of course, wrestled with her own case of nerves. In minutes, she would be meeting my entire family for the very first time, having just learned that my family's serial dysfunction exceeded even her worst fears. Indeed, Lauren had heard enough over the last two days to place her own inner-wager. She anxiously wondered, What are the odds of making it through the day unscathed?

About the same as Dale Earnhardt Jr. pitting at a liquor store during the Daytona 500.

The Star of David's long-time owner had the architect design his building with two graceful wings — one for the comfort of the bereaved; the other for the profitable commerce of death. The chapel wing for mourners featured a room of sturdy but stylish couches; carefully arranged wing chairs and cherry end tables with strategically placed Kleenex boxes. It adjoined through the curve of a gently arched doorway a carpeted 200-seat sanctuary featuring a high-tech sound system.

Inside, the chapel's interior presented itself in consoling tones of mauve and beige. The walls were accented by faux silver sconces and reproduction Chagalls hanging on the walls. The funeral home's chapel wing smelled of flowers and calm, with a whisper of sentimentality. Its profusion of bright directional signage — big block lettering with bright red arrows pointing this way and that — shouted loudly to myopia and senility.

This was South Florida, after all.

In an office of the Star of David Memorial Chapel, a semi-retired rabbi hired the night before for $300— Cash would be preferable, he had whispered — shuffled nervously one last time through his hastily written index cards.

Twenty feet away, alone in the sanctuary, a roughly hewn pine box, its joints held together tightly with wooden pegs, rested atop a maroon velvet cover. A part-time funeral home worker had arrived earlier than usual to drape the regal looking cover over a bier of flame oak with elaborately carved feet resembling the claws of a lion — a lion of Judah. He had brushed the soft material and centered it exactly, double-checking so that the metallic gold thread of the Jewish star faced the seats. Then, the simple pine coffin — The Daniel, Model 264, draped in an American flag — had been briskly rolled in from the refrigerated storage room, lifted evenly by several burly men off the stainless steel gurney and lowered gently atop the wooden platform. Buffed to a shine to remove any fingerprints, the hand-stained casket now absorbed the warming rays of yellow, blue and red light that filtered through the chapel's stained glass windows.

Inside the casket, wrapped simply in white muslin in keeping with the tradition of our people, lay the remains of my father, Lt. Natan 'Nathan' Loev, who was resting finally, permanently and, presumably, in peace.

I checked my watch again: 9:53 a.m.

I climbed from the car and circled to the passenger side to assist Lauren. I closed the car door firmly and kissed her lightly, seeking to make amends. Our lips brushed in a reassuring way. I have the distinct memory of tasting tart cherry and the wax of her Chapstick. I hand-pressed the wrinkles from my button-down shirt and khakis; straightened my tie; adjusted the knot one last time, and remarked with some energy: Right on time. Let's go.

The two of us locked arms and walked in silence through the thick, humid air. We joined the other late-arriving mourners making their way across the searing hot parking lot.

On the inside, I remained rattled. Anxious. Nerve-wracked. My mind sifted through the many possible paths pointing to reconciliation, resolution, forgiveness and love. I also considered the pot-holed road to the cold-shoulder, resentment, hurt feelings and shouting.

Really, what are the odds of making it through the morning unscathed?

Since man's earliest days, he has imagined the impossible and then dreamed it to be so.

Electricity, antibiotics and spaceflight. The world's finest minds had once dreamed all of them and had their visions of the future rejected as foolish, futile quests. Yet, today we read by the light of lamps; are cured by Penicillin and still marvel at Neil Armstrong's one giant leap for mankind.

Everything and anything is possible, I considered.

Even forgiveness, reconciliation and love. A new start with my family.

Besides, my conscience lectured to me:

Go inside, Harry. Bask in the fond memories of your father's good and eventful life. Mourn with your mother and siblings as one family. Be gracious. Be open-minded. Find the path to reconciliation and forgiveness in your heart.

■ ■ ■ ■ ■

As Lauren and I walked arm in arm towards the imposing cedar doors, I nodded in greeting to a much older couple. In a lifetime as a married couple, it appeared that the elderly man and his wife had begun to melt into one. They dressed alike, each wearing bold patterns and summer pastels as if Hunter Thompson had designed fashions for JC Penney. They looked alike, too. The couple's stooped posture and curved spines mirrored parentheses — or that, together, they were simultaneously searching the hot asphalt for a lost button.

I re-set and re-considered. Instead of chuckling, I surrendered to a more satisfying thought: God willing, someday Lauren and I will look — and possibly even dress — just like this adorable man and his wife.

As I turned my head, I noted a second elderly couple crossing the parking lot. As they neared, I gazed in appreciation at the old gentleman, for he was stylishly dressed in a dark blue suit and yellow tie. His fashionable clothes complemented a striking white mustache that meandered like a country road across his wrinkled cheeks.

The man looked achingly familiar and I worked furiously to make the connection.

How do I know this distinguished looking man?

It took a few seconds but the answer arrived. He had lived nearby throughout my childhood. The man walking towards me was a former New York City cop who, 30 years ago, played in a regular poker game with my father and other men.

I offered the man a warm greeting wrapped in a guess.

Mr. O'Connor, is that you?

The man looked up and touched his mustache in startle. His wife, too, appeared trapped in that uncomfortable moment between blank forgetfulness and partial recognition.

Do I know you? The man's question boomeranged back to me. He hesitated and coughed, like an unloved automobile trying to crank to a start.

Then, surprise! His memory returned like it had discovered a latent jolt of juice.

Harry, it's you. I almost didn't recognize you. It's been a long time. How are you? How have you been?

He extended a firm handshake.

I'm sorry about your Dad. He was a tremendous firefighter and a great guy. I want you to know that, most importantly, he was a good man. An incredibly decent man. We're all going to miss him terribly.

Thank you, I answered, as a I stole a glance toward his waist. Just as I remembered, the man in the bespoke suit and the stylish mustache possessed just four fingers on his right hand. A purplish nub and a jagged but faded scar marked the empty space where his index finger had once been attached to the rest of 'Yellow Mickey' O'Connor, now standing before me in the sunset of his life.

I set aside father's approaching funeral and my own nervous misgivings to again transcend time. I returned to an unforgettable afternoon with my father about 25 years earlier when I was a teenager and things between us were still okay.

■　■　■　■　■

My father and I had stopped by a local pizza joint for late afternoon slices. In the parking lot, we crossed paths with Mickey O'Connor, who had just dropped off his wife's dry cleaning a few stores away.

Back then, O'Connor regularly dyed his hair the same shade of yellow worn by Marilyn Monroe. In addition, every eight weeks or so, O'Connor visited a salon and paid a beautician to apply chemicals and curl his hair into a tight perm. During these sessions at the beauty parlor, O'Connor loved to flirt. He held court among the suburban housewives thumbing through their *Ladies' Home Journals* while they waited for a stylist to cut, color and chemically alter their hair.

As the two men exchanged conversation, I recall questioning O'Connor's fashion choices. On that day, he wore white patent leather shoes, white pants, a white belt and a colorful silk shirt decorated with a riot of paisleys. O'Connor left three buttons on his shirt open, revealing a large gold cross and a weedy patch of chest hair. My teen-aged self didn't know what to make of it.

Minutes later, we sat down in a booth and waited for our cheese slices to emerge from the oven. My father had observed me staring at Mr. O'Connor.

Hey, my father said with a knowing smile. If a guy wants to walk around town wearing a bright yellow mop on his head, dressed like some dippy hippy with every-one whispering and mocking behind his back, it's not my business. Or my problem.

He pulled some napkins from the aluminum holder and handed me one.

It's the other stuff that O'Connor did … the other crap that he pulled that I find repulsive.

All these years later, I still recall my surprise. My tight-lipped father apparently wished to open an adult conver-sation with me. He appeared eager to make a meaningful connection by telling me a secret about Mickey O'Con-nor. I leaned in to engage him.

What's with Mr. O'Connor? Yeah, he dresses weird but what did he do to you? I asked.

Did you get a look at the guy's hand? my father be-gan. O'Connor has a stump. You had to notice that he's missing a finger on his right hand, didn't you?

Looking around the pizza parlor to ensure we were alone, my father shared a colorful story.

Years earlier, Mr. O'Connor had been a beat cop in the South Bronx. He had once fought crime in the same tough neighborhoods as Engine 43 fought fires — a blood brother with my father in combatting the anarchy that ruled that borough in the late 1970s.

While O'Connor's uniformed brothers in blue battled crime and protected the public — and my father led Engine 43's men into fiery danger — 'Yellow Mickey' O'Connor spent his days relaxing in a chaise by his backyard pool, usually with a cocktail in hand.

'Yellow Mickey' had quit on them.

O'Connor shot his index finger off while cleaning his service weapon.

Not by accident, either.

As the South Bronx boiled, a cauldron of crime, decay and racial tension, I learned from my father that Mickey O'Connor had become increasingly paralyzed by the not-so-irrational fear that each radio call could be his last. The danger to anyone wearing a blue uniform had grown more real. No one had any respect for the police any more. Recently, an addict had pegged a few random shots at O'Connor and his partner from the roof of an abandoned apartment building, like they were tin cans sitting atop a fence post.

O'Connor couldn't take the stress, my father said. He was tired of being fearful. He also realized he didn't fit in with the other guys at the precinct, which made matters worse. O'Connor wanted out of the police department and he concocted a plan — a way out.

Hey, a cop without a trigger finger is like a porn star without a dick — completely fucking worthless, my father said in explanation.

Before I could mentally process that visual, my father thankfully pushed ahead. I remember basking in my father's undivided attention, leaning in closely as he shared that O'Connor had an epiphany one Friday afternoon after a few Jack Daniels' while his wife was out on a shopping expedition.

He had schemed a way to retire with a disability pension and full medical benefits.

A buddy in Internal Affairs would conclude that O'Connor's service weapon had discharged — careless, perhaps, but definitely an accident. He would be docked vacation days for the accident; be placed on light duty for several months, then — with the strength of the PBA at his back— O'Connor would be allowed to retire with a disability pension. They would even throw him a rowdy retirement bash.

O'Connor weighed the pain of a .38 caliber bullet blowing off a finger against a lifetime of tax-free payments from the city treasury.

It was no contest, really.

As proof of premeditation, Mickey O'Connor had set a bowl of ice on a table. From the kitchen, he retrieved several dish towels which he lay next to him on the couch and over the carpet. O'Connor squinted to aim carefully. He looked at his intact hand one final time, pulled the trigger and, apparently, never suffered any lasting regrets.

He planned it. No two ways about it. He moved the goddamn phone right next to him. He protected the furniture for God's sake. O'Connor knew what he was doing the whole time, my father said in disgust.

The lead slug embedded itself in the wall behind the walnut-colored paneling. O'Connor's finger, all tendon and pale bone, bounced twice and landed softly on a towel, just as planned, next to the sofa. When Mrs. O'Connor returned home, she found an ambulance, lights swirling, in the driveway and paramedics attending to her husband, who winked at her from the gurney and waved with his good hand as if to say, My little plan worked.

For years, the bullet hole remained in the wall, the denouement to a story that always began with Mickey O'Connor's somber caution to be extra careful while cleaning a service weapon.

You never know. The gun might be loaded, he would say.

Although they remained friends, and O'Connor continued to join the regular poker game, my father shared that he could never fully forgive his pal's disgraceful act. My father saw life as a ball field with clear lines marking fair and foul territory. O'Connor's little scheme kicked up chalk on the foul side. The Lieutenant felt strongly that one of New York's men in blue had dishonored his uniform and cowardly abandoned his brothers still on the battlefield.

Thus, my father's judicious verdict was that, while he would remain on friendly terms, Michael J. O'Connor would forever be known to him as 'Yellow Mickey.'

Not for the dyed color of his hair, but for the cowardice he displayed in abandoning the city's Finest and Bravest.

My father, swearing like a mobster, put it this way:

He may be a good guy but the chickenshit chose the chickenshit way out.

■ ■ ■ ■ ■

I pressed forward into the present. I carried no such grudge. I patted Mr. O'Connor on the shoulder and bent to give his frail wife a gentle hug.

Thank you for your kind words and for being here, I said with grace.

I noted more cars turning into the parking lot, filling it to over-flowing. I allowed myself a breath of satisfaction and smiled wryly. I had to admit. My father was something else.

Time to head inside.

THIRTEEN

'Whoever saves a life, it is considered
as if he saved an entire world.'
— The Talmud.

The rabbi-for-hire had never met my father. The chapel director selected him from a list he maintained for the unaffiliated, disconnected and non-believers.

I pray that your husband's memory will always be for a blessing, the rabbi had said when he dialed mother at home.

The rabbi had expressed his deepest sympathies, drawing on his years of pastoral experience to provide comfort while moving the conversation along. In his 25 minutes on the phone with mother, he collected anecdotes and biographical detail about my father's life, taking care to get everyone's names straight. He gently inquired about what kind of service would be most comforting.

Upon meeting in the hallway about 30 minutes before the official 10 a.m. start to the funeral, the rabbi hugged mother with sincerity and again offered his condolences before clasping my brother and sister in a similarly warm embrace.

Amid all that love, I wonder whether anyone noticed that I had not yet arrived.

Lauren and I had been busy parking the car and speaking with Mickey O'Connor. We arrived at our seats at 10:05, rushing in just as the rabbi ascended the carpeted steps and approached the lectern. I sat down at the moment he placed his note cards alongside a worn prayer book opened to the page for funerals. He breathed deeply as he gazed upon the mourners gathered before him, waiting in expectation.

Suddenly, the nervous chattering stopped. The chapel fell silent, as if a maestro had snapped his baton to the ready. The air conditioning flipped on abruptly and cold air whisked in. The scent of flowers, talcum powder and moth balls gently alighted among the mourners. An elderly woman shuddered.

Lauren and I had found aisle seats in the third row — near enough, but not directly among the immediate family. I did not wish to be trapped without a viable route to escape.

From my seat, I could see Jonathan and Helen, and their children —my nieces and nephews now all grown up. They sat expressionless in the front row not far from mother, who occupied a seat of honor in the center.

I coughed gently to raise their attention, nodded in their direction and stage-whispered a sincere hello. They brightened in return, like they had witnessed sediment rising from a forgotten jar. They appeared truly pleased that I had traveled to be there to join the family. Helen pointed to Lauren and mouthed what I interpreted as an enthusiastic, Wow. She gave me a thumbs-up from the fold of her lap. It warmed my heart, I have to admit.

I pulled Lauren close to me, to smell her perfume and feel the comforting heat of her skin. I looked around at the sea of unfamiliar faces.

Narrowing my field of vision, I brightened at the welcome presence of my Aunt Gertie, my father's sister. She sat next to mother, their shoulders touching. I grinned broadly as I took in the extravagant splendor that is Gertie — a chain-smoking compulsive gambler and one of my all-time favorite members of our wacky family.

In contrast to her frail bones and wrinkled bags of skin that swung loosely from beneath the sleeves of her dress, Aunt Gertie still dyed her hair the bright color of a rebellious university co-ed — a shade of red popular with punk rockers, circus clowns and comic book villains.

Somehow, now past her 80th birthday, Aunt Gertie's bosoms still defied gravity to protrude like the prow of a Viking ship. She wore large dice as earrings and a beauty mark dotted her right cheek. In fact, Aunt Gertie had drawn in the beauty mark that morning with eyebrow pencil, just as she had every morning for as long as I had known her. That the artistically drawn beauty mark resided on slightly different parcels of Gertie's wrinkled cheek from day to day was a mere technicality. It did not seem to bother her a bit.

Ah, Gertie, I thought to myself, squinting into the sunlight streaming into the chapel. You've outdone yourself. It's good to see you haven't changed. You are still a wonderful character. Thank God that you are free to be you.

. . . . .

I found it unnerving to observe the coffin containing the remains of my father. I was grateful for any distraction and swiftly found it.

I directed my stare to two towering men dressed in blue — a pair of New York City Fire Department honor guards who had assumed sentry posts and now stood ram-rod straight, at attention, at the head and feet of my father's flag-covered casket.

The two men looked noble and stately in their ceremonial dress uniforms. They stood shoulders back and with a stiff military bearing. Ribbons and medals adorned their chests, each representing a flaming, smoking battlefield in The Bronx or a life saved miles away and years ago.

The two firemen had buffed their shoes to reflect rays of light like stars and ironed their trouser legs to crisp, knife-edges. On their hands, they wore cotton gloves the white of freshly fallen snow. Their arms rested straight against their legs as they bookended my father's body exactly eight feet apart. Appearing like the sculpted statues found in the temples of Rome, this final tribute to The Lieutenant's eventful life added dignity and majesty to the most final of goodbyes.

I felt proud. Emotionally moved, even.

My father would have loved it, I thought.

Mother, I'm pretty sure, did not notice my arrival. I observed her gazing sadly at the casket. She sat close enough to touch it lovingly, if she had chosen to do so. She wore a black designer suit and enough gold jewelry to deplete a South African mine. Beyond the sparkle, however, mother appeared frail and sunken. Her hair, once dyed bright like the sun, was now white, like ice. The passing years had raked deep lines into her face, as if they had been scored with a chisel. Mother's back was no longer stiff, strong and straight. Rather, she appeared small and bent, like a nail half-hammered and felled by a crooked blow. She folded inward, crumpling as if conceding to age and the heavy burdens of her dwindling years. She appeared so different from the last days we spent together, when we were both so angry that we threw hurtful words like spears and the space between us seemed insurmountable.

Mother's hands trembled. She briefly rested her head on Aunt Gertie's shoulder for comfort. It was a sign of grief and love — and, perhaps, even weakness— that I never would have imagined from her in my trauma-filled youth.

Bathed in the warm light streaming from the chapel windows, mother suddenly looked less imposing and dangerous than I remembered. Like all her poisons had been bleached away by time. It dawned on me that mother's appearance had changed; that I had changed, too, and that while I now had Lauren by my side, mother would now be alone. Forever.

My sentiments towards mother began to shift anew, changing shape like a sand dune morphing in the wind.

I lingered on that vision — my anger and resentment at mother captured by the winds, tiny grains taking flight, blowing away — and I squeezed Lauren's hand lovingly so she could feel the renewed sense of hope in my fingertips.

Looking around the room and absorbing this revelation with a filling heart, I noted that some of my parents' elderly neighbors and friends appeared relaxed and reasonably healthy. Others appeared uncomfortable. On edge. Several breathed from oxygen, tethered to blue bottles with knobs and dials that rested on small wheeled carts. Three or four clutched wooden canes between their knees, or rested their arms wearily across aluminum walkers. One frail woman had already fallen asleep in her wheelchair to the consternation of her bony Haitian aide, who looked out of place and uncomfortable as psalms in ancient Hebrew filled the air.

I wondered if their approaching mortality frightened them.

What must it be like for them?

This Greatest Generation — my father and mother among them — had defeated the Germans in Europe and Japan in the Pacific. They saved the world from Hitler and Hirohito, communism and nuclear annihilation. They and their contemporaries bore witness to the Holocaust; defeated polio; marched for civil rights; dispatched flights of Apollo to leave footprints on the moon; invented amazing technology that bent the trajectory of our lives, and built the greatest nation in the history of all mankind.

Now, they gathered with unsettling regularity to say goodbye to their contemporaries. In the American rituals of death, surely they must visual the end of their own years growing closer and closer.

I contemplated the fullness of their lives; their romantic loves; career ladders climbed; glass ceilings smashed; historical moments witnessed, and their own children, grandchildren and even great-grandchildren raised and set free, in the words of the great poet Khalil Gibran, to dwell in the house of tomorrow.

When I reached their age, my days on earth dwindling, I silently wished that I would cheerfully and bravely greet death as a dear old friend, in peace and with Lauren at my side — with no hate or bitterness toward my family rending my heart.

This way, the finality of death would not unnerve me in the same way that the setting sun does not unnerve me.

■　■　■　■　■

As I scanned the wrinkled faces around the chapel, my focus again returned to the Fire Department honor guard, as I badly wished to permanently etch the whole poignant scene into my memory.

The indelible picture before me: The honor guards were not fragile old men, nearing death. They appeared to be recently retired. They maintained mostly youthful faces with just a few creases of age, and the thick necks, broad shoulders and the bulging chests of powerlifters. The silver buttons on their dress blue jackets seemed to strain under the press of impressive muscles manufactured at Gold's or other gyms.

The firefighter stationed at the foot of my father's casket appeared to be within reach of 60, not yet even eligible to collect Social Security. In any other occupation, too young to be retired. His wavy hair remained lustrous and black, with just a few sprinkles of gray propagating at his temples. He appeared imposing and rough, like he could still play linebacker at a small Division III college, or bull his way into a blazing apartment at the spear-tip of a nozzle.

On closer inspection, the firefighter's features spun into focus, like I had adjusted a camera lens with precision. Decades had come and gone, but I could now, unbelievably, identify one of the retired firefighters now paying final tribute to my father.

Standing at attention beside The Lieutenant's casket was Fireman Anthony James Spinelli III.

For many years, I remembered, a young A.J. Spinelli drove Engine 43 under my father's command. In addition to his driving duties, which required knowing every street and hydrant in Engine 43's sector, Spinelli had total responsibility for hooking the three-inch hose lines to the hydrant and running the pumps and valves that charged the lines and sent hundreds of gallons of water per minute racing to the nozzle, where The Lieutenant's Engine 43 always attacked and never retreated.

My father trusted Spinelli completely and cared for him like a brother for all those years they worked together.

Spinelli, I remembered, too, rose to legend for his daring behind the wheel but also for being one of the company's better cooks and the house's off-color jokester, always cracking wise about the length of his hose. In return, the men of Engine 43 ascertained that the NYFD already possessed a surplus of Anthonys and AJs. Thus, from his first days as a probie — probationary firefighter — to the day he signed his retirement papers downtown, Anthony James Spinelli III would be known throughout the battalion as Three Sticks.

I chuckled to myself. Yes, that was 'Three Sticks' Spinelli standing at attention — knees locked, heels together — honoring my father's eventful life.

The second firefighter paying tribute beside my father's casket looked younger — closer to 55 and maybe not even that. He stood 6-foot-4 and well over 225 pounds. A specimen of man still in his athletic prime. This firefighter, standing stiffly by the head of my father's casket, wore his sandy brown hair stylishly long and parted in the middle. He set if off with a sparkling diamond stud earring. The silver-plated pins on his uniform collar confirmed what what I wished to know: This firefighter — still unknown to me — had, too, had once served in Engine 43 under my father's command.

Who was he? What did my father mean to him?

I wondered, curious, as I sat and stared, practically awestruck.

Look at the two of them. It's giving me the chills, I whispered to Lauren. My father would be so, so happy and so proud if he could see this.

He loved being a fireman. He loved The Job. He reveled in the excitement and camaraderie, and being called one of New York's bravest. I'm sure he's looking down, thrilled that he's being remembered all these years later, I added.

A voice broke through to grab my attention. The rabbi looked to the congregation of mourners, down to our family and, finally, back to the rows of mourners again. In a baritone richer than I imagined, the rabbi began his eulogy by quoting the Mishna, the second-century book that interpreted Jewish law.

In the hour of a man's departure from this earth, neither silver nor gold nor precious stones shall accompany him, only Torah and good works, the rabbi said. He recognized my father's hero status — lives saved, medals won — and read from a Talmudic tract about the holiness of life.

The sanctity of human life is above all. Whoever saves a life, it is considered as if he saved an entire world, the rabbi quoted. By that measure, today we can say with gratitude that Lt. Natan 'Nathan' Loev saved the world many times over. He may not have been a particularly observant Jew and no regular at Shabbat services …

At this, gentle laughs and nods of agreement circled the room.

Yet in saving lives — in selflessly protecting the citizens of The Bronx from harm, day after day — he worshipped the God of Israel, the king of kings, in his own unique way.

Ah, the irony of that, I also chuckled to myself.

My father had abandoned organized religion long before he reached adulthood. He never cared much for Judaism's unbending dogma, hidebound rituals and voodoo customs — and once remarked that he wasn't meant to be one of God's chosen people. After all, a God who had selected him as a member of a holy tribe surely would have provided him a much richer lot in life, he told me once.

The rabbi's words, however, did unlock new memories. My mind whipped back to recall father's many acts of heroism, for which he was richly celebrated by a grateful city in the days when such exploits seemed bigger than they are today.

Father earned his third medal for extraordinary valor when he nearly sacrificed his own life rescuing an elderly couple from a burning home.

While my recall all these years later is hazy — I was a young boy, after all — an album of newspaper clippings now in my possession provides a clearer record of his bravery.

When Engine 43 arrived as first-due engine, a double-parked car blocked access to the nearest fire hydrant. 'Three Sticks' Spinelli could not pull the engine close enough to hook up a hose and begin the flow of water needed to drown the blaze. With the two-family home fully engulfed in flames, Spinelli had no choice but to drive Engine 43 down the street to frantically look for a working source of water, and then stretch a hose line back to the burning home.

My father had jumped out of the engine. While Engine 43 and its men worked to get water, he urgently called in a second alarm on his radio.

On the street, The Lieutenant heard neighbors screaming hysterically. An elderly couple was unaccounted for. They had not made it out. They remained trapped upstairs and needed rescue. They could not wait, the bystanders shouted.

My father bounded up the four steps into the home and, locating the banister in the dark, climbed the stairs to begin a search. In a back bedroom, he discovered the frightened couple huddling together in the dark, not a minute from death. The elderly man was already semi-consciousness and his wife initially would not release her grasp on him. Demanding every muscle in his body to work at super-human strength, my father pulled the elderly man down the stairs through the thick smoke and flames while shielding the man's frail wife with his coat.

With the couple safe on the porch, my father instinctively ran back into the burning structure to begin a secondary search for additional victims. Within seconds, he became a victim himself — overcome by the poisonous smoke. When the rest of Engine 43 rushed in minutes later, their air packs hissing, they found my father in the foyer by the stairs, lying crumpled on the floor like a discarded coat.

After he was pulled to safety, administered oxygen and treated at the hospital, my father was released in the morning. He suffered from smoke inhalation but otherwise checked out fine, considering how close he had been to death when found.

The tabloids and local television stations celebrated my father as a hero once again. The courageous Lieutenant won front page treatment in the *Daily News* and *Post* and merited a small story in the metro section of the New York *Times*. The next day, the local television station and our hometown newspaper also sent reporters to our home. My mother put out coffee and store-bought danish. I read the papers' accounts over and over, committing the inky words to my memory.

My father — with the entire family in tow — was summoned to City Hall a few days later for a press conference about the dangers of double-parking. A reporter for the *Daily News* cornered my father after he posed for pictures with the mayor and fire commissioner. Working on a follow-up, the reporter uncapped his pen with his mouth and flipped open his notebook.

In a few words, why did you do it? the reporter asked.

The Lieutenant thought about it a moment. A man of few words provided exactly three.

People needed help, he answered.

As the funeral service droned on, I flashed back to how often my father shoveled neighbors' driveways unbidden after snowstorms; visited the sick and injured in the hospital; changed flat tires for stranded motorists, and never turned his back on the homeless — charitable acts that would accompany my father's memory forever.

Again, Ellen's wisdom tapped me on the shoulder.

It's not too late to absolve my father. And forgive myself, too.

I wrestled with my pride. Where had I been for the last 20 years?

Why did I stubbornly ignore my father's plaintive invitations to sit down and talk it out. To reconcile our differences while there was still time?

To set aside my rancor and, instead, listen and seek to understand.

Perhaps, if we had sat down man-to-man and done the difficult work of excavating our differences — and communicating them honestly to each other — we might have picked from the rubble a few stones to lay the foundation for a lasting peace. Or, even better. We could have nestled into a loving and respectful father-son relationship. We could have enjoyed each other's presence in this life.

Listen to my side, father spoke to me over the phone several weeks after that final argument had scattered me to the winds. His voice was full of ache as he searched for the right words. It must have been a hard phone call for him to make.

You mean the world to me, Harry, You're my son, he had said. I don't want to fight with you like this. I don't want to lose you. It's not worth it.

My father wished for me to see the landscape as he did.

He explained, Your mother has a good heart. She really does. I know she can be difficult. A pain in the ass. But she's my wife. I love her. You haven't been married. You haven't had to try to keep the peace, so I can't expect you to understand or see the situation the way I do. But I'd like you to at least try.

I scoffed. Excuses.

Bullshit, I thought to myself.

In hindsight, I should have asked my father the questions which gnawed at me. I should have vented my anger. Or at least heard him out, like he had asked.

Would I have understood why he didn't intervene? Protect me from being devoured? Why he allowed mother to carve a river between us, separating the family into a left bank and a right bank?

Maybe I would have forgiven him. Maybe I would have told him to fuck off.

Instead, I dodged the difficult conversation entirely.

Truthfully, I thought I had plenty of time.

Turns out, time had me.

Like a cat toys with a mouse, time held me, taunted me and misled me.

Dad, I can't talk now. I don't have time. I have to get to work.

I sidestepped the difficult conversation with an excuse. A lie of my own.

Stupidly, I rebuffed my father's earnest plea for reconciliation. He never broached the subject again. Neither did I, as time and opportunity slipped away.

Over the months that faded into years, genuine regret consumed me. There was so much between us that needed to be said that had been left unsaid.

I had curled my fingers and squeezed my open hand into a fist. Peace between father and son had slipped upwards to the heavens and dissipated like wisps of smoke.

In the chapel, the rabbi's words blended together into a rubbery mush. I entered a dark tunnel and emerged in the spirit world. My eyes closed briefly and father's ghost spoke to me. His voice and spiritual presence did not scare me because he was not a stranger. Rather, our supernatural communion had the feel of familiarity. His weathered face was framed by a leather helmet — the face of a man just past 40, about my age, roaming the firehouse as a hero, a warrior ready to knock down an advancing wall of flame. A hero who would do anything in his power for me.

My imagined conversation in the midst of his funeral placed the two of us, father and son, at an equal station so we could accomplish what I stubbornly did not allow during his time on earth.

You have matured and grown, Harry, my father's spirit said. Like a towering oak, you have not always grown straight, tall and direct to the sun's rays. Still, I cannot deny that you have grown strong. You are a man with your own will and it breathes stronger in you than you know. You will win the fight within you and find the comfort you seek.

I squeezed my eyes tighter to concentrate, not wishing his voice to fade.

Take advantage of your new strength. Try to see me — and your mother — in a new light, Harry. I know my own faults and weaknesses. I am profoundly sorry. Understand that I love you. I have always loved you and will love you forever and ever.

I found father's vision to be pleasant and hopeful. I remembered the gates of reconciliation remained open.

Anyone may enter.

The answers I sought lay in building new bridges to the love of family. Reconciliation now would not be like hiking the same mountaintop twice. It was not the same mountaintop and I was not the same man. I knew that I must permanently release my anger like toxic balloons to be untethered and allowed to rise and float away on a breeze.

I was more sure of it than ever before.

■ ■ ■ ■ ■

I snapped back to attention and looked up from the floor. A sudden, dry cough — trouble-sounding, like a pebble lodged in a throat — radiated from the front of the chapel, interrupting the communal act of mourning.

A poignant tableau unfolding at my father's casket commanded my breathing to a halt.

At one end, 'Three Sticks' Spinelli stood impossibly erect, tight-lipped, solemn and proud like a Marine from a recruiting brochure. He stared unflinching, his jaw set, with intensity into the pews and the neat rows of mourners fanned out in the chapel seats before him.

His younger partner — stationed on the opposite end of the bier holding the earthly remains of my father — appeared gaunt and haunted. He worked his mouth back and forth nervously. The muscles in his face tightened and he squeezed his eyes shut. He appeared to me distraught, and close to losing a battle for composure.

Spellbound now, I watched the younger firefighter at the casket struggle to maintain the last dregs of his poise.

Observing the second firefighter, it seemed as if my father's death was not a death easily forgotten, dust to dust. This firefighter's unexpected display of raw emotion and grief moved me, even more so when his eyes glistened and tears began to well in the corners.

What could trigger this deep expression of mourning?

This imposing firefighter, unknown to me, sniffled once, and again.

He slowly lifted his white gloved-hand to his nose to rub away the wetness, his tears now held in check by willpower alone. I briefly looked away from this intensely personal moment of grief, hoping my gesture of kindness and respect would somehow bestow upon this firefighter the privacy he deserved in his sorrow.

I remembered, too, that reverence for the dead is the one entirely selfless and pure act of love that one can perform. In it, there is no expectation that such a generous and thoughtful deed can ever be repaid.

The last minutes of father's funeral service passed in a blur. The rabbi offered the traditional words of comfort to the grieving. He led the congregation in the Mourner's Kaddish, the haunting ritual prayer for the dead that expresses a yearning for the establishment of God's kingdom on earth. For the first time in decades, I prayed in Hebrew along with them:

Yitgadal v'yitkadash sh'mei raba

Glorified and sanctified be God's great name throughout the world …

When the prayer concluded, silence hung in air.

Cries of mourning were not heard. Instead, the entire funeral gathering was moved to stillness by what they witnessed — a saluting firefighter crumpling in grief for his fallen hero.

FOURTEEN

'What you leave behind is not what is engraved in stone monuments but what is woven into the lives of others.'
— PERICLES

The brief service drew to a close. As the mourners rose from their seats out of respect for The Lieutenant, my eyes met mother's as she rose and turned to me. In my unguarded state — my emotional armor penetrated by memory and the solace-seeking ritual of prayer and community — mother's lengthy gaze took me by surprise. She looked at me warmly; so warmly that I initially wondered about the sincerity of the act.

In return, I froze, surprised and also delighted. My expression, as Lauren described it later, was that of a man first glimpsing the magnificence of stars lighting the night sky.

My eyes followed mother as she gently caressed my father's casket one last time. Her wrinkled, arthritic hand rubbed at the pine where the flag did not touch. She then slowly turned her diminutive frame toward me, her face open and sincere in welcome.

I found myself trembling as I self-consciously advanced slowly to the center aisle, where I planned to join my siblings for the solemn obligation of bearing my father to the hearse that would carry him to his final resting place. Mother stepped forward to meet me and spoke first.

Harry, my son. Look at you, all handsome and grown. You're even getting a little gray, aren't you? she said. I heard her voice now brittle and tinny with age as she asked, How are you?

Before I could formulate an answer, she added, You don't know how much I've missed you.

Mother dabbed a tissue to her eyes and crossed the remaining distance between us. She reached out and embraced me tightly. I allowed it, bending my body into hers with a tenderness for her that I did not know I possessed.

How little and frail she is, like a sparrow, I thought. I could feel her thin, tired bones beneath her clothes and I wondered silently:

Am I finally ready to forgive her?

I missed you more than you'll ever know, mother said again.

Rather than curdling ill feelings, her words touched me. I found myself emotional, concentrating so I did not myself shed tears. I remain uncertain whether mother's words scraped away buried feelings or merely opened a valve to relieve the decades of stress and anxiety that had been trapped in the crucible of a familial war. Either way, the moment moved me in a way that no one had warned me to expect.

Thank you for coming, for being here with us, mother continued, looking up at me as if to re-commit my features to her memory. Your father would be so happy that you're here. I'm so happy, too. It means a lot to me at my age to have my whole family together again, especially for this.

She lowered her voice so I had to strain to hear her over the bustle. She said, You know, Harry, your father loved you very, very much. And so do I. I've been doing a lot of thinking. I don't want to fight any more. We can't dwell on the past. We have to let the past be the past.

I could sense her sincerity and even, I believe, maternal love in her voice. I squeezed her tightly in return and I admitted to myself that, yes, it felt good to do so again.

It all happened so quickly. I had been so disarmed by mother's words that I had barely spoken.

Before I could formally introduce Lauren, the funeral director gestured for the immediate family to come forward and to take our positions. Behind the Fire Department honor guards leading the processional, my siblings, nieces and nephews slowly wheeled my father's casket down the aisle, past the other mourners, to the waiting hearse.

We lifted my father gently and slid him inside, stopping only when the gurney's legs folded underneath and clicked into place with a final thunk.

We waited together in the parking lot as one united family. A line of cars with magnetic decals and white carnations affixed to their hoods began to form behind the hearse and limousine. While we waited for the procession to organize, Jonathan and Helen rushed over. As mother accepted condolences from neighbors and friends, my siblings greeted Lauren and I, and re-introduced me to my nieces and nephews. Jonathan repeated his invitation that we join everyone at a nearby restaurant following the brief interment service. He slipped me directions printed on a small piece of white paper and told me how great it would be to be together.

We've got a lot to catch up on. Right, stranger? he said, smiling widely to Lauren. It's all going to be all right. Don't you worry.

■ ■ ■ ■ ■

Within moments, I spotted Fireman Spinelli moving with authority across the parking lot to his car, jangling a set of keys in his hand. He had shed his uniform coat and seemed more comfortable in his white shirtsleeves. I swiftly moved in Spinelli's direction, taking advantage of my younger legs to eat up the space between us. I intercepted him and jabbed my hand forward in introduction.

Yo. Sir. Mr. Spinelli, I called out into the summer sun.

He rotated his body toward me.

A.J. Spinelli? Fireman Spinelli? Am I right? I asked.

The older firefighter in his Class A dress blues looked to me. His eyes brightened, and he appeared pleased that I had remembered him.

Captain Spinelli. I made it up the ladder. I retired as a captain, he said, pointing to the insignia pinned to his collar.

I'm so…

Before I could apologize, he interrupted me with a gentle jab to my shoulder.

Don't sweat it, brother. I'm just breaking your balls.

Let me introduce myself. I'm Harry Loev … Nathan's youngest son, I answered in response. It's been a very long time, but I remembered you — I recognized you up there from my dad's days at Engine 43, when I was a little kid coming to the firehouse with my father and you were, well, a fireman and his driver.

Spinelli answered with another cheerful laugh. He extended his own hand in greeting. I noted a tattoo on the inside of his bicep.

You're making me feel really old, Harry. Great to see you again. I wish it were under better circumstances.

He appeared to be at a momentary loss for words.

Call me A.J. or, even better, what everybody in the Engine called me — Three Sticks, he said.

He added, That was a crazy time. The whole Bronx — shit, the whole city — seemed to be burning all at once. We never stopped. We did something like 8,000 runs a year, getting our asses kicked night after night. Your father … he was our leader. The Lieutenant. He was an incredible guy and one of the bravest son-of-a-bitches I worked with in all my years on The Job.

He glanced down at the pavement and back at me.

I'm so sorry for your loss. I should have said that first.

As he uttered those words, the throaty roar of a sports car engine interrupted, assaulting our ears like the first shuddering chords of a guitar solo. In tandem, we turned to see Spinelli's partner — the second member of the honor guard — drive past the gathering of mourners and merge into traffic. I recall watching him run a hand through his parted hair, absentmindedly touch his diamond earring, upshift into third and speed off into traffic like a ghost.

Spinelli gave a brief wave and resumed his personal tribute to my father.

Your Dad was something else. I worked with him for 15 years and maybe longer than that, he said. I probably knew him better than anyone. Your father was like a brother to me. And a father figure to the younger guys, too. The way he watched over them and guided them. He taught them everything. How to think in a fire and stay alive, he added, tapping his forehead. You should be very proud of him. They don't make firemen like him any more.

I caught myself beaming. This time, Spinelli's glowing recollection of my father's legacy as a hero filled me with pride. Instead of resentment, I felt honored to have his blood in mine.

Well, that's great of you to say that, I told Spinelli, adding, On behalf of everyone, I want to thank you for coming today. For what you and the other fireman did for my father. You know how much he loved you guys — his men. How much he loved being on The Job. It would have meant so much to him to have you here.

No problem at all. Really, our pleasure, Spinelli answered. Hey, I'm thrilled that after a few years living down here, I can still fit into my dress uniform.

Spinelli stopped in thought, like he had left something essential behind. He remembered one more point he wished to make.

Your father sacrificed so much of himself. He put our welfare above his own. And he knew what he was doing. Hell, for chrissakes, sometimes he would charge into a fire screaming and yelling commands, and we wondered whether he was trying to get us all killed. But, it always turned out right. Today was nothing, really. What I'm trying to say is that Fireman McGuirk and I were honored to be here. It was our little way of paying The Lieutenant back. And saying thank you.

Spinelli rubbed his thick brow with his forearm, erasing the tiny beads of sweat that had pooled in the furrows.

When Robbie — that's Fireman McGuirk — saw your father's obituary in the paper, he called me right up. He said, 'Captain, I have to go and say goodbye. Pay my respects to The Lieutenant. I need you to come with me. I don't think I can go alone.'

Spinelli continued, It was all Robbie's idea to be an honor guard and salute your Dad one final time. McGuirk loved your Dad. For as long as he's alive, McGuirk won't forget what your Dad did for him.

Well, thank you again, I replied. Honestly, I'm ashamed to admit that I don't remember this McGuirk guy at all.

And, then I said:

But, after today, I don't think I can ever forget him. I watched him at the end of the funeral. He was very emotional. He must have cared very deeply for my father.

Captain Spinelli bit his lower lip gently and paused, uncertain whether to continue.

I think you should know this, he said. When I said that McGuirk won't ever forget what your father did, I wasn't BS-ing you. I really meant it.

As his words hung in the air, Spinelli appeared to regret them. Like he had gone too far.

I lost you, he heard me answer in response.

Spinelli hesitated.

Ah, what the hell … Your father saved McGuirk's life.

I remember feeling momentarily unattached, floating. I quickly composed myself and gently pressed my father's old driver for more.

Look, Captain. My father and I weren't especially close. He's gone now. I'm only left with my memories. To hear that my father rescued McGuirk from a burning building or saved his life after a collapse or an explosion … well, that's a story his grandchildren and great-grandchildren should know and be able to pass on.

(To quote Cicero, The life of the dead is placed in the memory of the living.)

Spinelli scanned the parking lot, distracted by two motorcycles slicing through traffic. He hesitated once more, cornered by his own well-meaning words. With a sigh, Spinelli set another one of my father's secrets free.

It wasn't a fire. Or a collapse. Or anything like that.

It was drugs.

Back then, Fireman McGuirk was a drug addict.

My mind went blank. My expression, however, re-

vealed something resembling astonishment. As if someone had died and been miraculously resuscitated before
my eyes.

I know it's hard to believe, Spinelli said. McGuirk
owes everything to your father. He'd be in prison or dead
if it weren't for your father. No doubt about it, Harry,
your father saved McGuirk's life.

FIFTEEN

'Where there is no tie that binds men,
men are not united but merely lined up.'

– ANTOINE DE SAINT-EXUPERY

Spinelli clasped his hands behind his back, drew a deep breath and held it an extra second or two. He stared straight ahead, at nothing. The unrelenting sun, now directly overhead, continued to beat down on him. The dots of sweat that trembled on Spinelli's forehead now had their origins in another era and in a far-off place — the South Bronx in the early 1980s.

It was so many years ago. So much has happened, it's hard to know where to begin, Spinelli said.

The retired firefighter explained that McGuirk, upon graduation from the Fire Training Academy on Randall's Island, had been assigned to a quiet house in Brooklyn — a probationary firefighter with much to learn about The Job. Although chances to shine were few in that sleepy corner of the borough, McGuirk quickly earned a reputation for aggressiveness, brute physical strength and quick-thinking under pressure. In other words, Spinelli said, McGuirk needed a little more experience but had all the makings of a good fireman.

At the same time, Manhattan's bright lights beckoned McGuirk, a single guy with dashing looks and a wad of fresh bills always stuffed in his wallet. Not surprisingly, it wasn't long before McGuirk began hitting the clubs and discos of Manhattan with distressing regularity.

McGuirk knew all the after-hours places, too. Joints where he could meet girls from NYU out clubbing or wealthy older women —today they're called cougars — looking for a thrill. When the bars closed at 4, McGuirk knew the secret places where he could grab a few more drinks or score some blow. Anything to keep the party going, Spinelli said.

Too often, the sun was already reflecting on the glass skyscrapers of Midtown when he finally arrived home and climbed into bed. As one year stretched into two, the other men in the Brooklyn firehouse grew tired of Mc-Guirk's antics. They resented covering for him when he was late, hungover — or both. In their eyes, McGuirk's personal failures had piled too high to tolerate any longer. McGuirk's irresponsible behavior added to the acute danger they already faced on every shift.

McGuirk's reputation for non-stop partying also drew the attention — and condemnation — of the higher-ups. The battalion brass, rather than forcing the young firefighter to seek help or initiating disciplinary charges, opted to transfer McGuirk to Engine 43, which, at the time, was the busiest house in the South Bronx.

They called it 'pass the trash' back then, Spinelli said. It was easier than doing all the paperwork and fighting the union to get rid of him. Back then, the commanding officers also believed that by transferring McGuirk to 43 Engine, he would be so exhausted from fighting fires and running to stabbings, shootings and all the other box alarms, he wouldn't have the time or energy to stay out all night. Or, Spinelli suggested, one chief or another thought that McGuirk would be so scared by what he witnessed on the streets, he'd knock off his carousing.

Spinelli grimaced at the memory and resumed his narrative.

So, McGuirk arrives at Engine 43 one day. For some reason, I remember, it was quieter than usual. He strolls through the open doors of his new house carrying his gear over his shoulder. Everyone stops what they're doing to give him the once-over. On top of everything else, McGuirk's hair is too fucking long. Against department regulations. He's got this diamond stud earring and this goofy, open-mouthed smile. Some of the older guys — men who had been around a long time — wanted to smack this cocky kid at first sight, just on principle.

Before McGuirk had an opportunity to prove himself in his new house — to bond, make friends and become fully acclimated at Engine 43 — he enjoyed another wild night on the town.

McGuirk got so drunk at a bar near Times Square, he could barely hold himself upright, much less find the men's room, Spinelli said.

McGuirk drops his fly, whips it out and takes a piss on the side of a bar at some joint on 41st Street. He splashes a suit having drinks with a beautiful girl after seeing a show. Words are exchanged. Somebody shoves McGuirk. He shoves back. It triggers a brawl with punches flying and tables getting knocked over. The beef ended only after some precinct guys had everyone cuffed face down on the sidewalk, Spinelli added.

That's crazy. I guess that was the last straw. What did they do to him? I asked.

McGuirk's sprawled out and bleeding from a cut above his eye, Spinelli answered. He gets the cop to reach into his back pocket and pull out his wallet. The cop sees McGuirk's badge, realizes that he's on The Job and, to make a long story short, they cut him loose. Sent him home in a cab.

Unfortunately, that night wasn't just a one-time thing, Spinelli reminded me when he resumed his story.

Just like in Brooklyn, McGuirk regularly smelled of booze in the mornings. His glassy eyes and wobbly step suggested he reported for duty still drunk or high on drugs. Word filtered up the Engine 43's officers: The men were concerned and worried but also angry. They didn't want a junky in their house.

Spinelli pointed to the idling hearse and continued, Your father took the other side. He thought McGuirk was, at heart, a big kid — and a good kid — who needed to grow up. To mature a little.

And apparently worth saving, I noted.

Your father put the word out. The Lieutenant would take personal responsibility. He would get McGuirk straight. Your father stuck his neck out for a guy he barely knew and who had certainly not earned it. Your father put his own reputation on the line. It made quite an impression on the guys, Spinelli said.

I put my right hand to my forehead to block the glare. It must have looked like a salute.

Respectfully, sir. You still haven't told me how my father saved McGuirk's life.

Spinelli answered, Your father understood that McGuirk needed something else besides a hard kick in the ass. He needed a father figure. Someone to mentor him and give him a little direction. He needed a friend. Maybe some tough love from someone he respected. That's how their relationship began.

Your father began sitting with McGuirk at meals and during down time in the firehouse. They watched TV together. He was building trust. Even a friendship, Spinelli explained. Your father made a deliberate effort to listen to the younger man. He gently offered McGuirk tips — on firefighting strategy, but also on how to handle his finances, stress and life's challenges. Your father passed down to this young firefighter what his experiences had taught him about responsibility, leadership and The Job.

The whole time he was guiding McGuirk on how to be a man.

Your father's message could not be any more direct. His investment was personal. He cared, Spinelli said. The

Lieutenant jeopardized his own reputation to vouch for a troubled firefighter with two strikes on him, and who had already begun to swing at an un-hittable pitch for strike three. But only if the guy did his part. Your father expected McGuirk to use this last chance to finally get his act together, Spinelli said.

Over several months, my father's approach seemed to be working. McGuirk cut his hair neatly above the collar, drawing good-natured ribbing from the other men. He pared back his partying and arrived for his shifts on-time and sober. Most importantly, McGuirk seemed to grasp that he owed Engine 43 something more than he had been giving. He finally understood that all their lives depended on selflessness, professionalism and teamwork.

One day, your father goes downstairs to the basement, Spinelli continued. The men had a little clubhouse down there with couches and a table for the men to relax and hang out. They would watch television on slow nights. They even had a vending machine with soft drinks.

Yeah, I know about the vending machine, I answered, biting off a smile.

Your father ... he goes down there and finds McGuirk passed out on the couch. His head is tipped back and he's really out of it, barely conscious. There's a folded piece of paper on the table with white lines of powder — obviously cocaine — and a credit card for cutting it.

Holy shit, I said.

Yeah, holy shit is right, Spinelli said. Your father flew in a rage. Furious. He kicked over the table and started hitting the guy, really belting him around.

Guys came running down the stairs from the main floor. They see your father smacking McGuirk over and over, cursing him with every word in the book. Throwing punches, too. McGuirk is doubled over and crying, trying to defend himself and apologize at the same time. He knew deep down that he had blown it. He had disappointed your father.

Spinelli recalled that my father's eyes blazed. His uneven nostrils flared like an angry bull.

I'm done wasting my time with you, The Lieutenant roared in front of all the men. Look at you. You're no better than the pieces of shit we see in the projects with needles in their arms and puke down their shirts. Do you have any self-respect? You want to end up in the gutter? Or dead? 'Cause that's where you're heading right now.

Now, Harry, Captain Spinelli said to me, You saw McGuirk today. Your father gave up about eight inches and maybe 50 pounds to this guy. About 30 years, too. Your father didn't fear anything. Your father was so disappointed — so fucking angry that McGuirk let him down — that he beat the crap out of him. Right there in the basement in front of all the guys.

The other men separated the two and steered The Lieutenant upstairs.

McGuirk lay crumpled on the couch, sobbing uncontrollably.

McGuirk had hit bottom. Later that day, he visited my father in the officers' bunk room. He apologized over and over, and begged for one more chance. He wanted to earn back the respect of those he had hurt and prove my father wrong. McGuirk wanted to show that he could really turn his life around, Spinelli said.

You know what? Your father listened. He gave McGuirk that one last chance. I wouldn't have done it. None of the other guys would have, either. But your father did, Spinelli said. I guess that says something about the man.

The next day, my father wrote out formal disciplinary charges. He made McGuirk read the written allegations and eyewitness testimony. He warned McGuirk that, with one more slip-up, the old charges as well as new ones would be filed downtown. The evidence and testimony from his brother firefighters would end McGuirk's career dishonorably. He might even face arrest and a criminal indictment.

My father put the charging documents in a folder. He slid the whole incident into a desk drawer.

Your father continued to mentor McGuirk, Spinelli said. He stayed on him — or, more to the point, he stayed *with* him. Your Dad checked in with McGuirk every day, even when they were both off duty. He told him over and over that he still believed in him. Urged him to seek help and make the most of his last chance.

Spinelli gave McGuirk credit, too.

The man changed. This time, he quit the drugs totally. Cold turkey. He pretty much stopped drinking. He got himself clean. No one could believe it. Over time, McGuirk became an exemplary firefighter. The men forgot his past. By the time your father retired, McGuirk was well-liked. He had earned the respect of everyone in the firehouse, Spinelli said.

McGuirk loved your father, too.

Your father saved his life.

What you witnessed at the funeral just now was a man saying goodbye to his hero.

SIXTEEN

'History is a cyclic poem written by time
upon the memories of man.'
— PERCY BYSSHE SHELLEY

TUESDAY, JULY 18, 2013
After my father's burial.

After the brief interment service at a nearby cemetery, Lauren and I drove to the restaurant in silence. The day, not even half gone, had already torn my emotions asunder. Vivid scenes from the morning rewound and replayed on a loop, leaving me exhausted and spent.

Sure, genuine relief bloomed inside me. My entire family, including my mother, had demonstrated good will. Even affection. Kindness, too. The seeds of reconciliation appeared fertile before me, ready to grow in the sunlight of a new beginning.

Still, I fretted nervously. How exactly would I find the path forward? How would I scrub away the rest of the bad blood? Had I set my expectations too high, greed imposing its will?

As we neared the restaurant, the GPS cooing directions, I wondered, Glass empty or glass half full?

Neither, it turned out.

My glass had no bottom at all. Every emotion poured into me that morning suddenly rushed out, draining me empty. I felt hollow. I needed to cry for real, like I did not cry at my father's grave.

Ever intuitive, Lauren noted the change. She asked me, You all good?

As good as I can be, I answered, feigning cheeriness and bravado.

Everyone has been great so far. Really, they have, I recounted. I have to admit, it was nice seeing my brother and sister again. And the kids. I didn't realize how much I missed them. Mom said hello and gave me a warm hug, which surprised me. And I still haven't fully processed the whole honor guard — and the incredible story that Three Sticks shared about my Dad and Fireman McGuirk.

You're doing great, honey, Lauren reminded me. As I said before, take the day for what it is — an opportunity to start fresh. To find peace. When it's all over and we're back home, you'll be glad that you did this.

I think you're probably right, I said, still very anxious. I'll tell you for sure after lunch.

■ ■ ■ ■ ■

The family luncheon was one last opportunity for family and friends to share their fond memories of my father.

A last farewell and salute to a great man's life.

Yet, still time for trouble to find me.

Please God, I recall pleading softly at the restaurant's threshold, beseeching him (or her) for the strength to cope with whatever lay ahead. A young Latina hostess heard my prayer and turned with a hand on her hip, posing. I caught her staring at me quizzically, like I was a lost supplicant and she was a deity.

I beelined it to the men's room to wash the cemetery's dust from my hands and gather myself.

Jonathan sidled up behind me at the sink. He leaned over my shoulder to speak.

You may not want to hear it, but let me give you some brotherly advice, he said. Your mother is past 80 and now with Dad gone, she's all alone for the first time in her adult life. Almost 60 years. Mom knows that her time is short and, I guess, when you get nearer to the end, you become wiser and more reflective. She's more self-aware now. She sees how her words hurt people and I think she's trying to change. For the better, thank God. Please, Harry, give her a chance. Let bygones be bygones.

I nodded to show him that I understood. Although our interaction was brief, I had sensed a shift in mother's attitude. I wanted badly for my brother to be right.

He counseled me again, layering on more wisdom.

Show Mom some patience. Some understanding. She's not going to accept any blame. You know that. She might say something to piss you off. She can't help herself. But, Harry, every comment doesn't have to be answered. Give her the opportunity to make things right.

Promise me that you will, Harry.

I took his words to heart. I would seek grace. I told him that I looked for reconciliation as well.

I will, I said, repeating the words to myself. I will.

■ ■ ■ ■ ■

Mickey O'Connor shuffled to a place behind me on the buffet line. I thanked him once again for attending the service and for his expressions of sympathy. For paying his respects and being part of my father's life.

We waited, exchanging small-talk about the Mets' pitching staff and the weather while the waitstaff replenished the lasagne, gently lowering a steaming metal tray into place. The odor of burning Sterno filled the air and lingered on our tongues.

Ah, the smell of a chemical fire. Must be a sign from above, he quipped.

O'Connor looked to me and turned serious. He had a point he wished to make. Some air he wished to clear.

It was a long time ago, so I don't know how much you remember, Harry. I played in a regular poker game with your father. There were six, seven, eight of us, rotating in and out, O'Connor began. We drank a few beers, told stories and played a few hands of cards. Guy stuff.

O'Connor laid his cane at an angle and balanced it against the back of a chair.

I know your father didn't approve of what happened — my little accident with my service revolver — and how I handled myself back then. I give him a lot of credit.

He kept quiet about it. A lot of the men shunned me — or they had their fun at my expense — but he wasn't like that. Your Dad and I stayed friends. Nathan didn't hold a grudge, O'Connor said. I want you to know that I appreciated that, coming from someone like him.

O'Connor stroked his mustache with what remained of his right hand. The old man would say no more of the circumstances behind his sudden retirement and I didn't correct his recall of my father's reaction. Instead, I leaned in and listened as O'Connor launched into a story — and another memory of my father.

When we played poker, The Lieutenant was dead serious. Your father didn't say much. Mainly, he just took it all in quietly. Every once in a while, he would let loose. He'd get wound up like a toy and decide to tell a story. When he'd get rolling, he could be very funny. We would laugh our asses off at some of the stuff your father did. He was quite a character.

To tell you the truth, I interrupted O'Connor, my father didn't say much about The Job at home. A few anecdotes here and there, sure, but he didn't talk much about what he did. Remember, I was a kid most of his time at 43 Engine. I was born when he was in his 40s. That's pretty late in life. Later on, we had a falling out. We didn't have much contact. So, honestly, there are big chunks of my father's life that are a mystery to me.

I heard about that. Sorry, he said.

I responded hopefully: Mr. O'Connor, listen, if you can remember any of these stories and if you don't mind sharing, I'd love to hear them. It would fill in some blanks and give me more to remember my father by.

O'Connor broke into a broad grin. Like he had been expecting me to invite a story or two.

Well, since you asked, the black limousine behind the hearse before reminded me of something. Funny how the mind works, O'Connor said. The stretch limo brought it all back — one of the craziest tales I heard in all my time as a cop. Of course, it involved your Dad.

I couldn't wait to hear what O'Connor had remembered.

Harry, you know that your father moonlighted as a chauffeur to earn some extra money?

Vaguely, I answered. To earn extra money, my father chauffeured a few star athletes, movie stars and wealthy socialites around Manhattan on his off days. He would be hired to drive them to dinners, society galas and Broadway shows. Sometimes to the airport. He got paid by the shift but made most of his money in tips.

That's right, O'Connor said. There is one night in particular that stands out. A night when your father chauffeured one of the richest women in Europe. A member of a very famous family. A royal family. What happened that night is legendary. Your father was in the middle of it.

Go on, I said eagerly. This I want to hear.

O'Connor straightened and began to reminisce about that long-ago evening.

In O'Connor's version, my father answered the phone at home late in the afternoon. The limo company's dispatcher came on the line. He urgently needed my father to chauffeur this high-profile client to a dinner and, afterwards, to a swanky fund-raising ball. It would be a long night but a lucrative one. The dispatcher had warned my father to be careful. This older woman, an heiress and princess in line to the throne of a minor European monarchy, had reputation for being difficult and demanding.

I'm going to trust you with this one, Nathan, the dispatcher had said. Don't screw it up.

My father had worked an overnight tour at the firehouse. Engine 43 had answered several middle-of-the-night alarms that robbed him of all but a few hours of sleep. Still, my father eagerly accepted the opportunity to chauffeur a member of a storied royal household. And to earn a big tip.

My father had been due at the Waldorf-Astoria at precisely 6 p.m. Unfortunately, lost paperwork delayed his departure from the garage. In addition, the previous driver had left the gas tank nearly empty, meaning my father had to make an additional, unplanned stop for a fill-up. A cold rain and heavy mid-town traffic that Saturday night set my father back even further. He was running late and getting increasingly stressed by it, O'Connor recollected.

My father did not arrive at the hotel until well past 6:30. In the days before cellular phones, that meant the princess, unaccustomed to waiting, had been stewing in the lobby bar for at least 30 minutes before her limousine — chauffeured by an over-tired and disheveled Bronx fireman — finally pulled to the curb.

Enough time for her to gulp a few cocktails if you know what I mean, O'Connor said.

My father climbed from the shiny black car with barely a nod to the uniformed doorman.

He had missed several patches of whiskers while hastily shaving and had failed to brush his teeth. His uniform was badly wrinkled, like it had been tossed on the floor after his last assignment. He had dribbled coffee on his tie while getting gas and neglected to put on his navy blue chauffeur's hat. It lay on the front seat on top of a folded copy of the *Daily News* while his wet, matted hair dripped streams on his jacket and pants.

Rushing around and shouting, my father roughly pulled open the rear door and tried to quickly hustle the old princess inside. He stepped hard into a cold puddle, splashing icy rainwater onto the hem of the woman's dress.

The princess glared at my father. She looked upon him condescendingly and vocalized her disapproval.

She shot a few sarcastic remarks at him before they reached the first traffic light, O'Connor said.

The way I remember your father telling it, O'Connor said, is that this Princess So-and-So wouldn't shut up the entire ride to dinner. She complained about the weather, about being late for the dinner, and mostly about how, well, *commonly* your father had treated her. The princess had this very thick European accent, too. Your father would have been smart to ignore her. To act like he was deaf. Instead, he mimicked her accent loud enough for her to hear.

Meanwhile, the cold, steady rain had turned to an icy sleet that slicked the roads and slowed traffic almost to a stop.

Your father could barely see out the windshield. The defroster wasn't working right. Plus, traffic was terrible. Stop-and-go. He hit every red light, too. They inched along, with the princess haranguing him the whole way.

And he didn't have a ton of patience behind the wheel, I noted.

Exactly, O'Connor said. The princess continued attacking him and commenting on his driving. She criticized him, 'You're going too fast. Be careful.' Then she scolded him again about the stains on his tie. She called him a slob. Your father was quickly losing it. To his credit, he tried to keep his mouth shut. For most of the night anyway.

Instead, my father aggressively cut off a few cabs, weaving in and out of his lane. The cabbies leaned on their horns and shot the middle finger. My father saluted back, which didn't help to calm things.

On the return trip to the hotel, the princess, who had become even more intoxicated throughout the evening, astonishingly continued to bully my father with foul language.

She called him a stupid ass. A big dumb ox. A low class slob, O'Connor said. Your father told us later that he felt trapped. Like he was under siege with no way to defend himself.

Here, Mr. O'Connor began to laugh. He wound up to deliver the punch line.

Finally, your father had enough. He reached the end of his rope. He slammed on the brakes and pulled the limo to the curb on a dark stretch of street. Steam was coming out of his ears, O'Connor said. Your father lifted himself up and turned in his seat. He twisted his body so he could get as close as he could to the lady's face.

My father lost control completely. He unleashed a torrent of expletives at the princess.

That's it, you bitch. I don't need this, he yelled. I've had enough of your fuckin' crap. Get your fat ass out of my car right this second.

He threw a princess out of his limo onto a dark Manhattan street.

My father's outburst was so outside his usual character — and the man that I knew as my father — I grinned in amazement.

Could it possibly be true?

O'Connor laughed boisterously at my reaction. Around the room, heads swiveled.

You bet, he said. Your father tossed the princess out of the car. He fired her. Made her get out in the pouring rain. Then he drove off. He left her drunk and screaming and cursing on the sidewalk.

Captain Spinelli heard us laughing above the din. My father's Engine 43 comrade returned to the buffet line. He joined us in time to catch the end of O'Connor's memory. If I had doubts about O'Connor's re-telling, Spinelli dispelled them immediately. He remembered hearing about the princess, too.

Back at Engine 43 a few days later, my father shared his version of the evening with the rest of the company.

My father naively questioned why he had been terminated — ordered to immediately turn in his chauffeur's uniform and cap.

I don't know what they're so mad about, he wondered to the others at 43 Engine.

She started it.

■　■　■　■　■

We laughed until our sides hurt and the veteran fire captain turned serious.

Spinelli said, You know, Harry, your father was a straight shooter. Fearless and bold. As strong and tough as he was, though, your father never bullied anyone. He never showed off, either. He was always modest and unassuming. And he had principles, which he showed through his leadership.

It wasn't just his handling of Fireman McGuirk, Spinelli added. It was the way your father approached life. Character and integrity meant everything to him. Let me tell you, your father influenced the way I look at the world and I'm not the only one who feels that way. You should be very proud of him, Harry.

Spinelli divulged one more illuminating anecdote: That my father was one of the more progressive officers in the Fire Department in the 1970s. Spinelli recalled that, amid a push to integrate the uniformed services following the racial unrest of the late 1960s, there was considerable distrust and unease among the men about what it would mean for The Job.

Your father reacted as if he could see the future. He always seemed to be two or three steps in front of everyone, just as a leader should be, Spinelli reminisced.

Your father knew it was just a matter of time before Engine 43 would get a few black guys. Some of the men had their backs up about it. They grumbled and protested. For whatever reason, they didn't want to work and bunk with black firefighters, Spinelli said.

O'Connor affirmed Spinelli's recollection with a nod. Race relations and integration in the police department were — and still are — difficult and complicated subjects, he said.

As the two older men discussed the city's long-ago efforts to crack generations of patronage and nepotism to open the police and fire departments to all, I again slid down the chute of memory. This time, I emerged on the basement stairs of our home, during one of father's regular Thursday night poker games.

■　■　■　■　■

I had positioned myself just out of sight. I wanted to listen in. To put myself in the middle of the action.

If a truck company had been slow to break windows to vent toxic black smoke or an engine man had cowered in the face of flames licking the ceiling overhead and retreated from the nozzle, the cops and firemen at the card table would shake their heads and whisper in sad voices as if in mourning.

Once, my father regaled the group about a night

when Engine 43 had been ordered to wait for a second engine company to set up before entering a vacant warehouse that had exploded in flames. Insulted and eager to show their mettle, The Lieutenant and his men ignored the chief's orders and boldly attacked anyway, racing to drown the fire from the inside in order to save its contents. When daylight broke and the fire had died to embers, Engine 43's men discovered they had rescued from danger a few pallets of Made in China air conditioners and a rusted fork lift.

The men around the table laughed uproariously at that one.

The cops, too, had their stories. In between hands, O'Connor and the other men in blue shared their own accounts of street-tough thugs, tear-inducing tragedies involving children and uncommon bravery, like the patrol officer from across town who had chased down, then single-handedly disarmed and arrested a drug dealer who had already killed three. Nods of respect circled the table after that re-telling.

These stories — told by the men around the table — enthralled me.

On the night of my memory, the discussion around the poker table centered on the sticky realm of social justice and civil rights, specifically the political battle to appoint more minority cops and firefighters. From my perch just out of sight, I recall flinching on hearing raised voices of disagreement. Some revealed their bigotry with the casual use of racial slurs.

On this night, I heard my father retort, I don't give a damn if a guy is black, white — or green with bright polka dots on his chest.

His voice rose with conviction.

The only thing I care about is, 'Can he do the fuckin' job?' my father said. Is he strong enough? Does he know what the hell he's doing? I don't give a fuck what color his balls are. I just want to know that he has 'em. If I'm trapped or hurt or running out of air, I want to know the guy will be there for me.

We have white guys who can't do the job — guys who are cowards, my father added. The only question you should be asking is, 'Can I trust a guy with my life?' If the answer is yes, that's the only answer that matters. If he can do the job, he's an equal. He's welcome in my house anytime.

I recall a smattering of murmurs. Dissent evaporated like a drip of water on a hot stove.

Today, I understand that my father had disregarded his own popularity and stood up to his friends to reject vulgar racist language and take what was then a liberal position on race relations. The Lieutenant had once again led other men. My father demonstrated over a game of five-card draw that courage takes many forms. Lesson imparted, he quickly moved on.

Who's turn is it? Who's got the next deal?

SEVENTEEN

*'If you press me to say why I loved him, I can say
no more than because he was he, and I was I.'*
—Michel de Montaigne

As the luncheon in celebration of my father's life continued, mother seemed to rally, buoyed by the love and support of friends and family. At one point, I recall that she
called out to Lauren and I in a lively tone.

Harry and Lauren, have you met your father's friend
Danny?

We turned in unison like perfect shadows. Mother
explained the man sitting nearby had grown up with and
attended grade school with my father. They had known
each other their entire lives.

Danny is one of your Dad's oldest and best friends.
They're like brothers, mother said.

Mother's use of the present tense unnerved me. I
opened my mouth but swallowed my first thought. There
was no advantage in correcting mother, so recently had
something precious been stolen from her. Instead, I

turned to Danny, whose name I had heard in conversation but had never met. I shook his hand in greeting.

Mother immediately pivoted to Lauren. She appeared captivated by my girlfriend's presence at the post-funeral meal.

Light-hearted conversation pinwheeled around the table as if this first meeting between Lauren and my family was an amiability contest, with prizes for congeniality to be awarded after coffee and dessert.

While Jonathan and Helen conversed with other guests, mother and Aunt Gertie tag-teamed to engage Lauren in pastel tones. They asked about her flight to Florida; her job back at home and her family's deep roots in the Central Adirondacks. They quizzed Lauren about where she had attended school and marveled about the uniqueness of graduating in a high school class of six.

What's it like to live so high up in the mountains? Gertie wondered in awe, as if reaching the front door after a winter day in the Adirondacks was a feat of endurance, like summiting Everest.

I remember when we lived in New York, mother added. We suffered through some incredibly tough winters. Sometimes we would get storms of six or eight inches — just terrible. Lauren, how much snow do you get where you live?

About six to eight feet. Sometimes more, depending on the year, Lauren answered. Usually it's not all at once.

I tensed up. Mother didn't countenance jokes at her expense. This time, however, she enjoyed Lauren's little joke and I felt relief.

Lauren, her face aglow, did not allow the staccato stream of questions to ruffle her — even when Gertie pressed her interrogation by pointedly asking if we planned on marrying anytime soon.

I don't want you to think that I'm being nosy, she said, before nosily inquiring whether she could look forward to an engagement ring and an Adirondack wedding.

My aunt also touched her beauty mark and good-naturedly commented on Lauren's freckles, which cover her face like tiny pink islands dotting the sea.

Mother overpraised her shoes and handbag.

They match your blue dress perfectly. The color looks just gorgeous on you. And the way it flatters your figure …

Thank you. They were on sale. I got them at the outlets in Lake George.

You know who you look like? I heard mother say. You look just like Nicole Kidman with that lovely red hair. She's a little taller than you are, but I think you're more beautiful than she is.

I don't know about that, Lauren said, smiling in the way one smiles at over-the-top flattery. I appreciate you saying so anyway.

Such enthusiasm! It's like an invasion of aliens! I thought, disbelieving my own ears. I rejected a fleeting thought — that Lauren must believe I invented my tales of family dysfunction and emotional abuse.

More than likely, mother had mellowed over the years. Maybe upon reflection, she had consciously worked to be less toxic. Less mean. More understanding.

Maybe my therapist Ellen — and Maya Angelou — had been wrong in their conclusion.

Maybe, mother could change after all.

I relaxed my fortifications. I decided to engage with Danny, my father's oldest friend, who was deliberately chewing his food in the chair next to me.

The advancing years had not been especially kind to Danny. He wore a hang-dog expression and sagged in his chair like a marionette hanging from broken strings. Purple stains mottled the papery flesh of his hands and his earlobes hung oversized and clownish. A food stain — roughly the shape of Italy — blotted his shirt. His jacket appeared two sizes too large and two decades out of style like he had concluded that, at his advanced age, purchasing a new sports coat would be fiscally irresponsible.

Yet, Danny's mind remained mostly clear although, like many in their sunset years, he recalled the long-ago with crispness and acuity but had absolutely no memory of driving himself to the restaurant.

Danny initiated our conversation like he had vigorously spun a wheel of conversation starters and the dial had clacked to a stop on that random memory.

Your father broke both his arms three times in one year. I was with him all three times, he said.

You don't say. Three times in one year? I replied. What did you do, push him?

Danny instantly looked alarmed. His brows furrowed his eyes to a thin squint. He loudly insisted it had all been an accident. Danny had been too slow to catch my winking joke. I had playfully teased the old man and it had backfired.

I'm so, so sorry, I said. I was just kidding with you. Forgive me. I'll start over. Tell me, how did my father break his arms?

Playing tackle football on the street in front of the house. There were no parks or grass fields nearby back in those days. Only concrete. The road was the only place we had to play, he said, now crossing the threshold from the 1930s to today in one confident leap. I remember one of the times. Nathan was running with the ball. I tackled him and he landed on the curb. I could hear the bone snap.

I grimaced. Before Danny could continue, Aunt Gertie interrupted him.

Harry, your father was quite the athlete. Very wiry. A really fast runner, too. He played all those games — baseball, football and stickball. He loved stoop ball, too. Like Danny just said, he was one of the best athletes in the neighborhood but he was always getting hurt, she said.

One memory displaced another. Gertie added, Your father's arm was in a big white cast when he watched the Hindenburg fly over. Your Dad was on the front steps looking up, waiting for it.

My father saw the Hindenburg go overhead? I said, with a tone of incredulity.

Yes he did. A matter of minutes before it exploded and all those people died.

Aunt Gertie explained that the newspapers and radio had trumpeted the expected arrival of the German airship's first transatlantic flight of the season and its planned arrival in Lakehurst, N.J. later that spring afternoon. I pulled out my phone, entered a few words in a search engine and did the math. My father would have been about nine in May 1937 when the giant dirigible crashed and burned in one of the worst air disasters of the era.

It was big news back then, Gertie said. Your father was mesmerized. He waved at the Hindenburg as it went overhead. He was all excited because he believed the passengers were waving back down at him.

I could imagine my father sitting outside in the fading sun, his arm in a sling, patiently waiting for the giant shadow cast by the German airship to pass overhead.

The effects of the Hindenburg disaster did not remain with Nathan for long, Gertie continued.

That was the same year as all the trouble with the police. When your father got sent away to live with relatives … she told me.

Gertie instantly noticed my eyebrows arch in question. What? she said.

I never heard any of this, I answered hurriedly.

Aunt Gertie looked to me quizzically. Danny's face remained flaccid and inert, which I understood to be a default expression.

When I did not smile or give myself away by throwing back my head knowingly, Gertie sat up straight in her chair. She set her knife and fork on the table. I recall her nervously tapping at her beauty mark from which, for the first time, I noticed a white whisker sprouting. She busily ran her hand through her bright red hair, like she worried it might be consumed by flames.

Gertie grasped that I had no knowledge of the circumstances that had befallen my own father — and a generation of my nuclear family — when he was a young boy.

Gertie weighed her next words carefully.

You really don't know, do you? Gertie asked me in a low tone.

Gertie looked to mother, who had turned away from Lauren and had been listening in. Mother bowed her head twice in agreement, blessing disclosure of this life-altering but closely held event from my own father's childhood.

Gertie took a sip of water and began her recollection. She explained that, as the school year wound down to its final, lazy days, the Loev household faced an excruciating set of choices — all set in motion by my paternal grandfather, Israel 'Izzy' Loev.

Gertie closed her eyes and traveled back in time to excavate her own memories.

My parents — your grandparents — sat me down after dinnertime for a serious talk. They explained that I would be spending the summer living with my best friend across the hall. Her family was going to take me in as a boarder ... like I was being invited for a really long sleepover, Gertie explained.

Makes sense. Go on, I replied.

There was no one to watch over your father for two months over the summer. He was an active young boy.

Prone to getting into mischief. He couldn't stay home, unsupervised, all by himself, she said.

Instead, Gertie explained, my father would be sent on a bus alone, with his ticket pinned to his sweater, six hours north to New Hampshire, where he would spend the summer with distant relatives — a childless couple who owned a junkyard in Laconia.

That was the only way they could manage it. My mother had to work to pay the bills. Our father — your Papa Izzy — was away doing time, paying his debt to society.

I'm not sure that I'm following, I said.

What are you, dense? Gertie said, a little too sharply.

Mother quickly jumped to my defense.

By 'doing time' Gertie means 'going to jail.' Prison. Your Papa Izzy committed a crime. Well, it was considered a crime back then. He had to serve time behind bars. The whole thing just crushed your father. He was devastated when your papa was sent away. It changed your father forever.

■ ■ ■ ■ ■

Israel 'Izzy' Loev was the grandfather I never knew. A phantasmal figure in my life.

Growing up, he appeared before me only in whispers and coded words. From a young age, I understood that the man's mark on our family, whatever it was, would best be forgotten.

In the restaurant after the funeral, my paternal grandfather — 'Izzy' Loev — fluttered to life on the fading breeze of his elderly daughter's memory. With her remaining years now a flickering ember, Gertie seemed to deduce that this might be the last opportunity to document her own father's rise and fall — to put a spin on that nearly lost chapter of family lore for me and for the generations that followed.

'Izzy' Loev sailed to America on a third-class ticket from what is now Poland. He arrived on a passenger ship, the *Zeeland,* in the wave of immigrants escaping The Great War in Europe. He met my grandmother, Frances, at a Friday night dance sponsored by the Jewish Resettlement League, my aunt recounted.

As a young woman, your Grandma Frances paraded herself around very elegantly. She smoked like a chimney. Always puffing away. Izzy saw her across the room and came over and lit her cigarette. He told Frances on that very first night that he loved her and would marry her as soon as he found a good job, Gertie said.

It took a full year, but Izzy energetically threw his shoulder into that promise until it became true.

They married very quickly. They had to, Gertie told me, because after courting just a few months Frances learned that she was pregnant. The baby was your father.

In those days, your grandmother couldn't parade herself around single and pregnant, wearing the stink of cigarettes and indecency. Everyone would be talking about her, Gertie told me.

Gertie again touched her hand-applied beauty mark, perhaps to ensure that it had not melted off in the heat.

I barely had time to register these new facts — that my hero father was the bastard son of a jailed criminal — before my aunt continued.

With his heavily accented English, no formal education and your father, Baby Natan, to feed, Izzy Loev struggled to hold his grip on the American dream, bouncing from menial job to menial job, she explained.

Your grandparents were very poor. They weren't educated. Life was difficult for everyone in those days, but especially for them, Gertie said. I can remember being cold in the winter because they couldn't afford to buy coal for the furnace, and opening the kitchen cupboard in the morning to find it mostly empty.

It took years, but Izzy eventually found a decent job in a factory that produced men's hats. His job was to stand at a large vat for an entire shift, often in sweltering heat, and continually stir the mercury nitrate — a chemical used to process animal pelts before they were cured into the felt that, later in the process, was cut and made into hats.

The long hours breathing in dangerous chemical fumes ravaged Izzy's health. He suffered balance problems and acted strangely, which worried the family. Before long, he was slurring his already difficult-to-understand English and complaining of severe headaches.

Word spread in the neighborhood that our father was a drunk, Aunt Gertie said. It wasn't fair and it certainly wasn't true. Your grandpapa drank very little, actually. But, as his behavior grew more erratic, the talk behind his back got louder and louder — and harder for us to deny.

Izzy Loev developed uncontrollable muscle tremors and twitching limbs from prolonged exposure to the mercury vapors. He began hallucinating. Once, he stripped naked at the Sunday market, complaining that his insides were burning. My Grandma Frances was summoned to come get him and bring him home, wrapped in a coarse blanket, Gertie remembered.

Your Papa Izzy was very ill but they didn't know exactly why, she explained.

Danny emerged from his own little world to pipe up.

The neighborhood kids teased your father constantly. They would mimic your grandfather stumbling around and blabbering nonsense in a thick accent. When your father couldn't take it anymore, he would challenge the other boys to fight. Your Dad would fight anyone to defend his family's honor. I recall him getting into some pretty big scrapes over it, Danny told me.

Worried sick, the family convened a meeting. Ten or 15 people crowded into their little fourth-floor walk-up in the Bronx to discuss how to save Papa Izzy's health and still enable him to earn a living.

A roomful of cousins and neighbors insisted that Izzy quit the hat factory job before it killed him.

Of course, your grandfather refused, Gertie explained. He was a stubborn, stubborn man. You have to remember, it was during the Depression. He worried — legitimately — how he would be able to find a job to support our family.

A thick-chested neighbor — rough looking, like a villain in a James Bond movie — stepped forward. The neighbor said that he knew some people who had a job for Izzy. He asked for a few days. He believed that something could be worked out.

And, Harry, that's how your Papa Izzy began running numbers and doing odd jobs for the mob, Gertie revealed.

In those years, Murder Incorporated and one of its leaders, Louis 'Lepke' Buchalter, controlled the Garment District and the city's heroin trade. Buchalter wished to add bookmaking operations to the gang's highly profitable heroin and racketeering gigs.

Izzy Loev's new job would be a runner for a neighborhood bookie. The assignment took him on daily rounds to visit butchers and barbers, shopkeepers and trolley drivers in their mostly Jewish, working class neighborhood. On his route, Izzy would collect cash bets from his clients and pay off the winners the next day. The winning numbers, Gertie remembered, were the last three digits of the daily handle at the racetrack.

Izzy's health improved and he enjoyed the work. Made enough money to get by, Gertie recalled. He was a sociable man once he got away from the mercury and it did him good to be out in the air.

Eventually, Papa Izzy's string of good fortune ran out. A beat cop picked him up with a thick wad of cash and a brown paper bag stuffed with betting slips. He was arrested and indicted for conspiracy to promote illegal gambling and weapons possession — the gun charge tacked on when the cop found the small pistol he regularly packed in a holster under his coat.

Your Papa Izzy wasn't a violent thug like the others. He was more of an imitator, a wannabe. He carried the gun to puff himself up. To show off, Gertie insisted.

Izzy stubbornly refused to cooperate. He played dumb when detectives and, later, the district attorney pressed him to give up information about the wider bookmaking operation. They interrogated him for hours, demanding to know where Izzy delivered his betting slips at the end of the day, and where he got the wad of cash they found wrapped in a handkerchief stuffed in his front pocket. Scared that divulging any information about mob operations could cost him a beating — and maybe his life — Izzy Loev spurned their offers of leniency and suffered in silence.

A judge slammed down his gavel and gave Papa Izzy three years in Sing Sing to think about his life choices.

With no income coming in and abandoned by their mob friends, Grandma Frances was forced to find a job and work, Gertie explained.

And that's why your father was put on a bus, all alone, to spend the summer away in New Hampshire, fostering with distant relatives he had never met, Gertie added.

This was all hush, hush. Nobody talked about it, Gertie explained. It was only long after my father passed away that I heard the whole the story myself.

Whoa, I exclaimed when my aunt finished her story. You've got to be pulling my leg. Mother, when did you find out about all this?

Only after we were married, mother answered. I

doubt that I would have gone out with your father if I had known about it. My parents were very strict. Seeing your father would have been forbidden. By the time I did find out the family secret, it was too late. I was in love with Nathan and your father was in love with me.

Indeed, Papa Izzy had died just after that.

Your grandfather had heart attack while watching the Friday night fights on television, mother said. He died on the couch with your father holding him, waiting for the doctor to arrive.

Dumbfounded, I could not will myself to speak. As I tried to make sense of this chapter of my father's life and the impact it had on him, Aunt Gertie piped up again. She wished to share one more footnote to her story.

Izzy served about 9 months in prison before being released on parole, she said.

Once your grandfather got out, he wasn't home free — even though he kept his mouth shut, she said. Papa Izzy never let go of the fear that Murder Incorporated would find him and kill him.

As a parolee, Izzy could not legally carry a gun, Gertie reminded me.

So, your Grandma Frances carried the gun for him, stuffed between her cleavage in the padding of her bra.

■ ■ ■ ■ ■

These new pieces of my father's puzzling life came at me like a thing with legs.

How badly did these traumatic events scar my father? How much did his harsh childhood contribute to his aloofness as an adult?

Or, perhaps, I wondered, did my father learn independence, self-reliance and toughness from those life experiences? Did he see an advantage in raising me to experience — and grow — from the same kind of rugged adversity he had experienced when he was a young boy?

∎ ∎ ∎ ∎ ∎

Wordlessly, Captain Spinelli rose from his seat to occupy the vacant chair next to me.

The rabbi's eulogy and our conversation in the parking lot had fired his own memory, which circled back to him like a comet in orbit.

Remember that rescue I told you about? When I couldn't find a working hydrant because of the double-parked car? Spinelli asked me. The night your father pulled the old man and his wife from the burning house and almost died?

I was thinking about that while the rabbi spoke, I answered truthfully.

Your father was unconscious at the base of the stairs when we rushed in. God knows how much time he had left, but it wasn't much. Who do you think got to him first?

Before I could answer …

McGuirk found him. Fireman McGuirk found your father on the floor in the dark. He didn't think. He ripped off his own mask and gave your father his oxygen. Brought him back to the world of the living.

Even today, I still marvel.

My father saved McGuirk from the ravages of alcohol abuse and cocaine.

McGuirk saved my father from smoke and fire.

Even now, a year later, the day's events strike me as implausible, like a poorly conceived scene from a late-night movie. Yet, it happened. Life stranger than fiction. Spinelli's recollection quickly begot another family secret — this one also wildly inconceivable but, everyone insisted, absolutely true.

The divulging of this final hidden secret would free me like the spores of a dandelion are freed by the wind.

■ ■ ■ ■ ■

A tabloid reporter reached my father at home after he had been released from the hospital following his daring rescue and own near-death experience.

Mother recalled that the reporter asked a few cursory questions. He inquired about my father's health and asked how often double-parking interfered with firefighting efforts. The real purpose of the reporter's call, mother explained, was to ask follow-up questions based on a folder of frayed, yellowed clippings discovered in the newspaper's morgue.

A 19-year-old Natan Loev of The Bronx had been pardoned by President Harry Truman for an offense committed on the USS Missouri as the presidential party cruised home from Brazil in 1947, two years after the conclusion of hostilities with Japan, the reporter read aloud.

Yes, that was me, my father confirmed.

It was my lucky day, he added.

Inexperienced with the press and spare with his words, my father did not elaborate or explain. He said goodbye, climbed back into bed and went to sleep, exhausted from his ordeal.

The next morning brought a ringing telephone, great shock, and 72 hours of renewed headlines, beginning with:

SMOKIN' HOT
Hero Firefighter Once Jailed for Leering at Truman's Daughter

The front page led with a dramatic photo of my father receiving oxygen in an ambulance. The photo was placed side-by-side with one of my father as a young sailor on the battleship *Missouri,* shaking hands and smiling alongside President Truman. The exposé jumped to page 9, where the article continued next to a photo of a buxom actress lounging poolside.

Mother again cast herself as narrator. Pointing to me with a finger resembling a splintered twig, she escorted another long-buried event from my father's past to the surface.

Mother anticipated (correctly) that I knew little about the Truman family in the late 1940s. She explained that, as part of a post-war tour in September 1947, President Truman cruised home from Brazil to Norfolk, Virginia on the *Missouri*, an 887-foot battleship nicknamed

'Big Mo' — the same ship where the Japanese surrendered to the Allied forces two years earlier.

President Truman, a proud Missourian, was accompanied by his wife Bess and daughter Mary Margaret — a 23-year-old aspiring singer and flame-haired beauty who loved the spotlight.

Young Nathan Loev was aboard as well as an electrician's mate. My father had enlisted in the Navy just after his high school graduation, eager to escape turmoil at home and see the world. At basic training in the South, his bunkmates — who had never before met a Jew — had rubbed his head looking for horns, my mother recalled. Later, he boarded the Missouri and was assigned to work on the storied battleship's 16-inch guns, which could fire artillery shells weighing 2,400 pounds up to 24 miles.

Nathan and the other enlisted men had been ordered to stay out of sight in the mornings, when President Truman and his daughter would stroll the *Missouri's* decks to get fresh air and a little exercise.

In mother's retelling, Nathan — technically, still a teenager — wanted to catch a glimpse of the president in person. Of course, he really wished to cast his eyes on the president's attractive and shapely young daughter when he decided one morning to sneak up to the top deck.

He was just naive and excited. Still a boy. He really didn't mean any harm, Aunt Gertie interjected.

Nathan busied himself by a railing, pretending to inspect one of the battleship's 40mm anti-aircraft guns. A rear admiral spotted him — easy, because Sailor Nathan

Loev wore dirty blue overalls and not the crisp service whites required while the president and his family were on deck.

Hey you! Sailor! You're not supposed to be up here. Get yourself down below deck right now, the stern officer barked.

My father snapped to attention and saluted the officer.

Yes, sir. Sorry, sir, he responded.

My father turned quickly and broke into a run, hell-bent on returning to his post and avoiding discipline.

Unfortunately, when my father rounded the corner, he crashed directly into the President and Mary Margaret Truman. The collision knocked the president's daughter to the ground, scraping her knee.

My father quickly extricated himself from the tangle of her legs. He apologized profusely and unsuccessfully. The president's daughter, startled, did not speak and my father apparently had no time for an introduction.

Very quickly, two military police grabbed my father. They escorted the young sailor to the brig in the bowels of the *Missouri,* where the clanging of the steel doors were followed quickly by a long, echoing silence.

For two days, my father ate, slept and stewed with no company but a cold steel bench and a small sink and commode. The Naval adjutant officer who visited told him that he would likely be court-martialed and dishonorably discharged for disobeying direct orders — a stain that, just two years after the war concluded, would destroy his life.

Fortunately for Nathan, mother now explained, the USS *Missouri* would be crossing the equator in a few days — on September 11, 1947. As a Navy tradition, those seaman who had not previously crossed the equator, known on the ship as pollywogs, would be initiated in a boisterous ceremony led by 'King Neptune,' with singing, dancing and even a fair bit of unofficially sanctioned drinking. The pollywogs would officially graduate into 'shellbacks' after they ran a gauntlet of men swinging stuffed pillowcases like billy clubs.

President Truman and his family joined in the fun.

It was featured in all the papers at the time, mother said, enjoying the reminiscence. There was no other news about the president to write about.

The president's 23-year-old daughter, wearing a gold crown, took a seat next to King Neptune under a banner marked with a black skull and cross bones and the words, 'Expect No Justice.' A 'prosecutor' even charged the Missouri's 'virgin' crew with made-up offenses as part of the equator-crossing ceremony.

President Truman became so caught up in the fun, he issued a general pardon to 'anyone and everyone who may have found some mischief aboard this ship.' He looked over at his daughter and her bandaged knee as he said it, and both President Truman and Margaret Truman laughed.

Mother recounted, One minute, your father was below decks alone in a prison cell, fearing he would be sent home in disgrace. Then, with just a few words from

President Truman, he was saved. Reborn a free man. All was forgotten.

Of course, mother said, the press aboard the ship learned of the pardon and the reason for it. They recognized a good story and ran with it, especially when young Nathan was summoned to meet the president and Mary Margaret, so she could accept his apology in person.

The New York papers went wild, Gertie added. The New York *Herald-American* carried a headline, 'Pardoned by the President' with a nice picture of your father. All the stories portrayed your father as an innocent young man just out for a peek at a nice-looking girl, who happened to be the daughter of the president of the United States. It was all in good fun.

As Gertie completed the story, mother looked to me with a triumphant grin.

I finally connected the dots as a new question rushed towards me.

Mother didn't allow me to ask it.

Yes, Harry, she pre-empted. That's why your father insisted that you were named after Harry Truman, mother said.

Your father told me that it could not be a coincidence that you were born on the very night that President Truman died, she said.

There was no arguing with your father, mother said. It was the only time in our marriage that he ever stood up to me.

EIGHTEEN

'In our sleep, pain which cannot forget
falls drop by drop upon the heart until, in our
own despair, against our will, comes wisdom
through the awful grace of God.'
— AESCHYLUS

On the flight home to New York the next day, my heart beat a little lighter.

Over the span of a few days, the tightness in my chest vanished like a weighted vest had been lifted and set down away from me. I had shed darkness and despair for something else — a feeling more inviting than the heaping of bitterness that I had lugged around like an overstuffed sack for most of my adult life. What I had discovered with Lauren at my side was a fresh beginning. For the first time in years, I felt at peace.

As lovingly told stories about my father boomeranged around the table that afternoon in the restaurant — and the celebratory laughter of family and friends filled a back room — I realized that I wanted to be a part of it.

I wanted it to be a part of me.

It was then that I knew I would be all right.

My worst fears leading up to those days in Florida? Unrealized, I had to concede.

How easily, I recall thinking on the flight home, that pleasant memories and new perspectives can float on the currents of emotion to alight wherever and whenever they are ready to be embraced.

Gratitude and admiration nudged aside my harsher judgements of my father. A new portrait of Natan 'Nathan' Loev — The Lieutenant — began to form in me. It was embryonic but very real. Compassion and respect flowed slowly but most assuredly to fill hollow spaces, slowly easing aside all those years of my carefully curated resentment.

I could now visualize my father as a hero, a mentor and a leader among a circle of men who looked up to him.

I, too, caught glimpses of him as a father and husband who cared deeply about his family, and who persevered against adversity and overcame his own, tumultuous upbringing.

I pictured a young man at the precipice, thrust into the spotlight by a savvy and good-humored president.

Had I misjudged him all along?

A year later from a perch above, surveying, I acknowledge that I did.

There must always be room for reassessment.

What settled in me could not be full dispensation, however. To absolve my father of all blame — to release him from all fault — would be too much, even in death.

Rather, I reconciled that I had become tired of being dried up by disappointment and blighted by bitterness.

In the sunlight cast by my memories and the memories of others, I ultimately chose to see my father as an imperfect man in an imperfect life who loved me as perfectly as he could — the only way he knew how.

Indeed, there had always been a place for me under his golden glow.

It had been there all along.

All this would have been unfathomable before Lauren entered my life. Of all the things my hands have ever touched, Lauren is, by far, the best.

Lauren listened openly and compassionately. No scowls of judgement ever creased her face. She would be my partner as I completed my journey to emotional healing. She would remain beside me as a loving partner to the end.

I cursed myself for ever doubting her.

Back at work this past year, grooming ski trails and punching railroad tickets, I resolved to work harder at building a relationship of enduring strength and beauty. I would communicate openly and honestly. I would trust Lauren from this day forward as I had trusted her that weekend, for I planned to ask for her hand in marriage.

Lauren had it wrong on that rainy night at the restaurant, when we spoke to each other from the heart and our intimacy bloomed in full. Lauren's singular devotion to me was not merely love. Not even true love. It was — it *is* — something far more magnificent.

Lauren's love for me is the pure love that she believed she could never offer to anyone else.

I am sure of its power and infinite life. She will be my partner for eternity.

And, of my mother?

After the luncheon concluded, as waitresses busily cleared the tables, I slipped away to stand alone in thought, struggling to bring order to all that I had learned that day.

Mother approached me from behind. She slipped her hand into mine as if I were, once again, her child — her little boy. She looked upward at me and drank in the features of my face, possibly for the last time, and nakedly asked,

What do you think of me now?

An unusual way of putting it, I thought.

With mother, too, I recognized that there was no point in regurgitating all my bitterness. It would do no good to re-live every anguished moment from my childhood, as if I were counting the rings on a long-dead oak. Every monstrous act that I endured did not need to rise up like a zombie from the underworld to be re-recorded and studied over and over.

There is nothing more dispiriting or corrosive than looping back over the same worn-down tracks, hoping to discover a new ending.

I knew that in my heart.

Even if it were, indeed, possible to banish every ugly memory of my childhood years, it would not be to my favor.

What would I make of all my pleasant childhood memories?

Of Little League practice, home-cooked meals, a surprise from Santa Claus, toppling dead bodies and sultry Playboy centerfolds pinned to the walls of Engine 43's basement?

Of flying brassieres performing acrobatics at the supper table?

It would be cheating — unethical — to disregard those happier memories, I considered.

Seconds flew by.

I found mother's question to be too direct to dodge. The future squared off against the past. I could see the merits of forgiveness. An opportunity for grace lay before me — one that had been gestating for a long time and was now ready to be born. It would be cruel to stall any longer. I did not wish to assault mother's dignity by making her squirm.

What *did* I think of mother now?

I thought, I am a different person today. What harm can come to me by listening to her, by building a bridge?

I recognized what Ellen had predicted when she sagely guided me to this moment.

Mother may be incapable of change, Ellen had said.

I am not. I hold the power to shed my bitterness and anger. To forgive. To choose love

I, too, recall, one final thought: Breathing new life into our relationship would require a death — the permanent letting go of my lasting anger and resentment.

I paused at the headwaters before starting my journey. Blinding jolts from my childhood flashed before me, vivid like a fever dream, pulling me backward, backward, backward.

Yet, I discovered in that same breath that all my remaining anger had already receded. No longer did mother intimidate me. Nor did I fear being ambushed by her anymore. I could joyfully toss back my head and risk exposing my neck to her.

The old had died away to allow the new to be born.

I quickly negotiated the terms of a truce — one that honored my accumulated, burdensome memories but allowed for a future in which we could both abide.

Who am I now? Who do I want to be?

First, I said to mother that I did not need or want her apology.

An 'I'm sorry' at this late hour wouldn't count for much, even if mother's words could be delivered straight from the heart, I thought to myself. What I wanted was a simple acknowledgement. For mother to admit that she had hurt me, and that she had looked inward and had learned from it, and that she didn't wish to hurt me ever again.

The end to my own personal war would arrive too quickly for some, I considered. Unrealistic, they would protest, to tie up a lifetime of torturous memories in a neat box and resolve all my animus with a few saccharine words. Don't let her off the hook, those voices would scream. She doesn't deserve it.

Yet, somehow, at that moment, mother's acknowledgment would be enough for me. It's all it would take.

I looked down at mother and formulated an answer to her question, selecting each word with care.

Mom, I began, using words of a happier child.

I understand that you loved me the best way you could, I said. Now, with Dad gone, it's up to you to make peace with what you did, just as it's up to me to change how I react — now and in the future. I would like to try. I really would.

It was her turn to speak. The voice of my mother, now an old, frail woman with milky eyes, fell to an unearthly whisper. I struggled to hear her skinny voice over the din. My own lids fluttered and I suddenly felt tired, like I could sleep for weeks.

Mother's own anguish and pain at our estrangement formed into words.

In my trance-like state, I heard — or, maybe, I dreamed that I heard — what I had yearned to hear mother say all my adult life.

I know that I said and did terrible things. I used words and did things that I shouldn't have done. That no mother should ever do to a child, she said. I can see it now. I treated you badly. My time on this earth is short so you must believe me. I am filled with regret and sorrow.

This, too, I think I remember.

Harry, my son, my baby. Please come back to me.

I had been told that salvation, should it come, would reveal itself with uncertainty. Ambiguity did, in fact, remain. The future could not be told. Yet, it is also true — because I remember it clearly — that the two of us, mother and son, hugged tightly. Our tears mingled as our cheeks touched and we began a new chapter of reconciliation and repair.

In that moment, flesh to flesh and bone to bone, I also learned that even when blinded by bitterness and strife, and held together by frayed scraps of string, a family's love is more enduring and lustrous than I ever imagined.

ABOUT THE AUTHOR

From the day in 1972 when his father, a decorated firefighter in one of the busiest engine companies in the
South Bronx, performed a heroic rescue and made the
front pages of the New York City tabloids, Carl Korn
dreamed of becoming a journalist. He fulfilled his ambition by working as a reporter and editor for the Associated Press, United Press International and the Albany
Times Union. In his second act, Carl served as press sec-
retary for one of New York's — and the nation's — largest
labor unions. Now retired, Carl lives with his wife, Cara,
in Saratoga Springs, N.Y. and Indian Lake, N.Y. This is his
first novel.